A LIFE WITH YOU

OUTBACK HEARTS

SUZANNE GILCHRIST

MALLEE STAR ENTERPRISES

A LIFE
WITH YOU

Suzanne Gilchrist

OUTBACK HEARTS
Big Hearts, Small Towns

When Stars Collide

Bargain with the Enemy

Touring the Stars

The Slave Trap

Apocalyptic/Dystopian:

Paying the Forfeit (Search for Home)

Storm of Fire (Search for Home)

Quest for Earth (Search for Home)

Don't Look Back (Warders of Earth)

CONTEMPORARY ROMANTIC SUSPENSE

Scent of the Jaguar (Deadly Forces series)

FANTASY/ANCIENT WORLDS EROTIC ROMANCE

Bound by Love

Bound by Lies

*For my close friend, historical romance writer, Sandie James
– this book is for you.*

Living a double life had some perks and this was one of them—the peace and solitude of pre-dawn.

With sunrise a good forty minutes away, this section of Mindalby was deserted, the inhabitants still sleeping, but Sasha Bernstein didn't mind. She pumped hard on the pedals of her bicycle, enjoying the burn in her thighs and the pull on her calves. The swish of her tyres and her own breathing was all she could hear. *Perfect.*

Night still lingered, cloaking the small town in shroud-like darkness. Pale pools of yellow light spilled from the streetlights making the black asphalt gleam. Overhead, the stars clustered in their inky bed glittered in crystal glory.

With an extra spurt of speed, she rode past the boundary fence of the local freight company on her right and the SES grounds on her left. A lone security light glowed near the transport company's front office.

Past the speed hump she slowed on the tarred road dividing the Mindalby Cotton Company compound from the employees' carpark.

Both properties were well lit, signifying the start-up crew and the foreman had already arrived to make ready for the first shift. Her gaze skimmed over the ten-foot high cyclone fence on her right where the huge cylindrical packs of cotton waited to be processed in the module yard.

The silhouette of two double-storey buildings housing the administration section and the cotton-ginning mill came into view.

Of their own volition, her eyes zeroed in on the narrow, shadowed alleyway that lay between. It brought back the unwanted nightmare of another alleyway, another country and the terror of being trapped as war raged around her.

The familiar cold slick of sweat clung to her spine. Her pace faltered at the exact moment her heartbeat galloped out of control, threatening to leap from her chest. For five long seconds, her vision blackened.

Horrific memories hammered her—brilliant white light, the stench of burning rubber and flesh, the screams that still rang in her ears, the agonising pain of flames melting her skin.

They're gone. I can't help them. Friends and colleagues she'd worked beside for nearly twelve months and who'd paid the ultimate price. The young boy she'd wanted so desperately to save. Lives destroyed forever with nothing left but nightmares to haunt the survivors.

She shook her head, blinked rapidly and attempted to claw herself back into the present. Her clasp on the handlebars tightened, the brittle plastic biting into her palms through her thick woollen gloves.

And just like that, she beat back the monster prowling inside her head.

Her shoulders slumped; weariness from waging this constant battle dragged at her soul.

She swallowed hard on her nausea. If only these panic attacks would cease, then she could get back to her passion of helping others, going wherever she was needed most. But before she could think about applying for a mental health assessment, she had a job to do.

One that involved working outside her field of expertise. One that saw her masquerading as an account's clerk far from all that was familiar. One that was her family's last hope of freeing her uncle from jail, found guilty of a crime he hadn't committed.

With a start, she realised she'd stopped pedalling. The bike wobbled and she quickly planted her boots on the ground to prevent an embarrassing fall.

"You okay, love?"

The deep, gravelly male voice broke through the last whispers of her nightmare. She realised she was surrounded by workers who, at this time of the day, should have been inside the gates already.

The security light on a pole outside the front gate blazed down, illuminating the faces of people she'd grown familiar with in the four months she'd been living in Mindalby. Her fellow employees, bundled up in beanies, with heavy parkas and jackets over their uniforms, were milling about chatting with each other. She turned towards the guy who'd spoken to her and her heart slammed against her ribs.

Snakes alive! What a honey!

A few wisps of jet-black hair protruded from the edge of his navy-blue beanie but it was the crystal clearness of his blue eyes that held her transfixed. They reminded her of her favourite gemstone, Swiss blue topaz. Her eyes locked on the sensual curve of a sinful mouth. Going by the crinkle of laughter lines beside his eyes and his easy air of self-assurance, she thought he might be in his mid-thirties, around her own age. With his firm, square chin, razor-sharp cheekbones and heavy-lidded bedroom eyes, he should have been adorning the front cover of 'Country Living' as an enticement to draw women to the region.

Not rugged up against the icy-cold morning in a small, rural town on the edge of the outback. A place where there was nothing but cotton fields and dry plains dotted with sheep and, everywhere you looked, reddish-brown dirt.

She drew in a deep, slow breath hoping to quell the

unexpected fluttering low in her belly. The hit of frosty air surging down her windpipe and filling her lungs made her grateful for the thick parka and heavy cotton-drill pants she wore over her Lycra bike gear. 'I'm fine, thank you. What's going on?'

"That's what we'd like to know. Whatever it is, it doesn't look good." The man jerked his chin in the direction of the yard. His grim, thousand-yard stare travelled over the five hundred metres separating those outside the gate and the small huddle of people standing near the office entrance.

Sasha frowned. In the glare from the spotlight outside the reception office stood the CEO of Mindalby Cotton Company, Don Carter, muffled up in a camel-coloured sheepskin coat that reached his knees. Next to him were two local coppers and Warren Leadbeater, the mill's foreman and union rep, wind-milling his arms about in an agitated fashion.

Four firies, clad in their yellow protective gear, stood a little away from the group. Three were busy rolling up a hose onto the back of the rural fire-brigade truck and stashing gear into the side storage compart-ment. The other firie spoke into his mobile. Don Carter's silver BMW sedan was parked nearby, and judging by the cloud of steam emitted by its exhaust pipe, his driver had the engine running.

Ready for a quick getaway?

As she watched, Don shoved a placard at Warren, turned sharply and strode to his car. He yanked open the door then slid inside. Everyone fell silent while the vehicle disappeared around the far corner of the building, no doubt heading for the exit gates.

One of the firies retrieved a thermos and cups from inside the cabin and passed them around. Another set up several camp chairs. It looked like they weren't going anywhere soon. The police and the foreman trudged towards the front gate where Sasha stood with the others. She squinted trying to make out the writing on the placard the foreman carried but with the light behind them, she couldn't decipher the words.

"All right, you lot. Move along. There's nothing to see here," ordered Sergeant Johnson. His young constable stood by his side, with her hands hooked over her utility belt, her plain face composed, looking ready for any unwelcome actions.

Grumbling under his breath, Warren took some wire ties out of the toolbag slung over his shoulder then proceeded to attach the placard to the gate.

Sasha exhaled loudly and, muttering an apology, thrust her bike towards the hot hunk who, to his credit, took it without a murmur of protest. She pushed her way to the front of the group.

"Excuse me. I work in the office. I need to get through or I'll be late clocking on." Even as she spoke, she was reading the notice on the sign: *Due to unsafe work conditions, mill closed until further notice.* What was that all about?

The sergeant, a man in his forties with red-rimmed

eyes and deep lines of bitterness chiselled into his face, shook his head. "No one is allowed on the premises. Mind my words, you lot. It'll be criminal trespass if anyone tries to enter."

"Can you tell us what happened?" she asked the union rep.

His face thunderous, Warren's gaze swept over the small crowd. "It's a bloody outrage. Carter can't do this to us, the tosser. We've got rights," he bawled, raising one fist to the sky.

"Oi, what's up, Wazza?" called one of the module truck drivers, a short, skinny guy with dirty blond hair poking out from a grubby-looking beanie.

Warren growled, "It's a major safety hazard, Cody. That's what it is! We could have all been blown to smithereens!"

"Stone the crows!" another voice cried.

"That's enough, Leadbeater. You and I both heard Mr Carter explain the situation," the sergeant snapped, his voice ringing with authority and effectively shutting off the rising mutterings. "There's no need to start unnecessary rumours."

Cody Nossiter, the blond truckie, hopped from foot to foot and raised his mobile phone in the air. Probably streaming the situation onto Facebook and every other social media site.

"Turn that bloody phone off, Nossiter," demanded Sergeant Johnson. His lips thinned even further when the truckie continued to film then addressed the crowd. "Leadbeater discovered a leaking gas cylinder when he was doing his rounds this morning. But there's no need to be concerned. The situation has been stabilised, and there's a gasfitter testing the other cylinders for tampering."

Sasha gasped. "Tampering?"

Warren snapped. "Tosser reckons someone left a valve open on one of the cylinders outside the ginning plant. What a load of crock. We've got checks in place to ensure nothin' like that happens."

"Come on, Leadbeater. Tone it down, mate," Johnson said.

"If the situation is under control, why are the firies still here?" Sasha leaned to the side to take another look at the fire truck.

"Standard procedure. Rosco knows his job and we don't want anyone getting hurt," growled Warren, referring to the local rural fire brigade's well-seasoned captain, Leon Rossini.

"I get that. Any idea when we can get back to work, Warren?"

"Not a clue at this stage, Sasha." Warren's jaw worked as he glanced back towards the office. "The boss sent me over here to tell everyone what's what. Until the gasfitter's checked every blasted valve on the site to ensure nothing else has been sabotaged and reported the incident to SafeWork, we're stood down. I don't like it."

"Wazza, for pity's sake, mate." Johnson shook his head.

Leadbeater stabbed the air with his finger. "I locked this place down, nice and tight after the last shift. And I'm not the only one. Carey takes his job as Safety Officer seriously. There is no way he would have missed hearing that leak when he did his last check yesterday."

Sasha gasped again. "Then you're saying it *was* deliberate?"

"Okay, okay. That's it. Leadbeater, put a bloody cork in it!" Johnson waved his arm as if directing traffic. "The rest of you, clear off home until you're told to come back. I don't want a bunch of troublemakers hanging around this gate." He rocked back on his boots and swept a gimlet stare over the crowd.

"It's a capitalist plot," snarled Warren. "The tosser has had us working in unsafe conditions. We should sue."

The bloke had some real issues with management. But what if someone really had sabotaged the plant?

"Right. That's it." The older cop fronted the fiery union rep and growled, "I suggest you get back to your duties, Leadbeater, and stop stirring this lot up, or I'll haul you in for disturbing the peace and incitement. Everyone else go home. Stay away from here until you're notified otherwise."

Johnson brandished a key and proceeded to unlock

the gate then handed it over to Warren. Both he and his constable passed through.

Warren, his jaw clenched, secured the lock after them. Hands curled into fists, he swung away and, with his head lowered, he stalked back to the office. Despite the shouted questions from other workers, he ignored them and kept walking.

Shaking their heads and muttering to their neighbours, and with the police shooing them on like they were a mob of sheep, everyone soon dispersed.

A few seconds later, Sasha was left with the two police officers and the very interesting bloke holding her bike. She decided to try one last time. The notion of being thwarted in her quest for even a few hours at the office burned away the last of her earlier euphoria. Every minute wasted meant another day of imprisonment her uncle had to endure. "Sergeant, it's payday. I need to get inside the office, otherwise no one will get their wages."

Johnson shook his head and, by looking over his shoulder, managed to avoid eye contact. "My advice is go home and sit tight. Come on, Meredith, let's get back to the station. It's bitter out here and I've missed my breakfast." He gestured to his constable and together they marched to the highway patrol car parked further along the road.

Why did she get the feeling there was something more sinister going on? Sasha turned back to stare at the solid-looking padlock barring her entrance.

Outside the office, Warren leaned against the door, standing apart from the firies relaxing in their camp chairs. Overhead, a lone crow circled low, flapping its wide wings, its eerie *'Craw, craw'* sending another shiver along her spine.

"I've got a pair of fence-cutters in the back of my truck. Shall we?" a husky male voice murmured near her ear.

"Seriously?" She turned wide eyes on him and took a wary step backwards, holding her gloved hands in the air.

He chuckled and awareness frizzled over her skin. "Okay, you've got me. I was joking. I could do with a coffee or a cuppa to warm me up, though. It's bloody cold out here. Joe's Café opens at seven. Care to join me?"

She considered him while he handed back her bike with a slow smile that had her knees quivering. She was certain he was one of the local subbies who'd been contracted to work on the new extension to the mill. Maybe he could end up being a good source of information, especially about the town and in particular, her boss, Don Carter. But why was he singling her out? "You're after something."

"Yep. You got it in one. I know you're Sasha, the accountant here at Mindalby Cotton. I could do with a bit of inside info."

"I'm not the accountant or a gossip. I just handle data entry and admin."

He tilted his head and gave her the same serious contemplation she'd afforded him a few seconds ago.

By exercising extreme discipline, she refrained from whipping off her bike helmet and fluffing her hair. Instead, she fiddled with the bell, while her stomach muscles took flight like a flock of parrots drunk on fermenting nectar. It had been a long time since she'd experienced such a strong attraction to a member of the opposite sex.

Too long.

Still, she hesitated.

"You work in the office, you know things."

"I've only been there a few months." She managed a careless shrug, aware her heart was thumping like a runaway train.

"I'll settle for some friendly company, then. I'm Cole Mitchell." He extended his hand. "Offer is still on the table. How about it?"

F ifteen or so minutes later, Sasha pushed down her bike stand and unclipped her helmet before slinging it over the handlebars. She'd refused Cole's offer of a lift even though he had offered to transport her bike in the back of his ute.

She'd cited her need for exercise.

Only half a lie and far easier than admitting the truth: being trapped inside a moving vehicle would engender a panic attack.

She soothed a few stray strands of hair that had escaped from her short braid and opened the glass door of the cafe. Immediately a blast of hot air warmed her chilled face. The scent of frying sausages and bacon and strong coffee hit her nostrils and she inhaled deeply. Blinking at the sudden brightness after the gloom outside, she took a moment to look around the cramped interior. Its seventies décor of lime-green formica, hard plastic chairs and old brown lino were clean if out-dated.

It was apparent that a lot of the mill's employees now graced Joe's Café and were sipping hot drinks and talking nineteen-to-the-dozen.

The din was unbelievably loud and the glaring fluorescent lights made everyone's complexions appear pasty.

Or was anxiety the cause?

"Sasha. Over here."

She turned in the direction of the deep drawl and her gaze snagged and caught like a fish in a snare as she met Cole's blue eyes. Feeling she was being drawn in on a reel, she walked over to a bench by the side wall then slid into the seat opposite, shrugging off her satchel and parka as she did so.

Cole handed her the menu and she took it with a smile of thanks. After peeling off her gloves, she cast her eyes down the list of offerings. Anything to avoid that piercing gaze fixed so steadily on her face and the sizzling awareness of his very appealing body. Heat bubbled beneath the surface of her skin and she could feel it spreading. Why was he staring so hard? Did he suspect she was here under false pretences? Or could he be just as fascinated with her, as she was with him?

Shaken, she pressed her knees together; tried to ignore the flutter in her belly and the gorgeous curve of his mouth. It wasn't like her to have this reaction to a man and she found it quite unnerving.

A waitress sauntered over to them, notebook in hand and what looked like a chronically bored expression on her face. "Morning, Cole. Ready to order?"

"Hi, Beryl. A large flat white for me, please," his pleasant voice rumbled.

Willing the burning of her face to subside, Sasha glanced at the waitress. "Small flat white with soy milk, please."

"Rightcha. Be about ten." Beryl strolled off to the counter, a wiggle to her hips.

"Look, I'll be honest." Cole stretched out a hand and tapped her fingers gently. His gaze dropped to the puckered skin running over the back of her right hand then flicked back to her face.

Heart racing, she gently withdrew her hands, placing them out of sight in her lap and looked out the window. Hopefully, he'd get the hint and not ask gut-wrenching questions about where she'd received those scars. She wasn't ready to talk about her experience in the Middle East.

Maybe she'd never be ready.

Maybe she'd never deal with the guilt of having survived when so many died.

Cole continued in a quiet voice, "I need answers. I'm due three weeks' pay for welding I did on the extension. Any idea when that's going to happen?"

"You're not much for small talk, are you?" Her pulse steadied as the tricky moment passed. She turned back to face him. "I'm as much in the dark as you. I tried to phone Don twice on the ride over here. He didn't answer. I'm waiting for him to return my call."

Cole leaned back against the rear bench, a heavy frown furrowing his brow. "There's a lot of talk here already that the gas leak is a pile of crap."

"It can't be." She shook her head. "The fire brigade attended the scene and they had the gasfitter there. So the safety issue has to be legit."

His gaze searched hers. "You really have no idea?"

"No." What good would it do to fuel wild speculation with her doubts? She had nothing tangible to go on; just the union rep's reaction. And a niggling feeling that had nagged her constantly on the ride to the café.

"I'm guessing you wouldn't tell me anyway, even if you did know," he drawled.

She bit her lip, her gaze dropping from his for a second, and he laughed. But the bleak sound held little amusement.

"The town's hurting, Sasha. This drought ..." He sighed deeply and fell silent for several long seconds before he spoke again. "You haven't been here long. Maybe you're not familiar with local affairs."

"I know half the town relies on the mill for employment and that it's only seasonal work."

He nodded. "The rest of us work during planting and harvesting times on farms around the district or are self-employed. A few have steady, full-time jobs—they're the lucky ones."

"I guess the drought hasn't helped."

"Yeah, it's been a tough year. A lot farmers have had to borrow money to pay for extra water. It was either that or cut our crop size to suit. This season we've had to push our harvesting back a month. Normally we begin sometime in April."

He sighed. "Sasha, there's a lot of people here who have their livelihood tied up to Carter's mill."

"And what about you?"

"My granddad and I run Cotton Fields Glory. It's not a large farm, a little shy of four hundred hectares. We work a mixture of both dry and wet farming and rely on the Darling River for irrigation. This year, we had to truck water in or lose our crop."

"Hang on, didn't you say you're a welder?" She frowned.

"Second job and only on a casual basis. That's another thing about Mindalby. Most people here have more than one job to make ends meet."

Beryl returned to the table and placed two mugs on the table.

"Thank you." Sasha pulled the hot drink towards her and took a sip.

"Excuse me, miss?"

Surprised, she turned towards a man and woman standing beside her. "Yes?"

He looked vaguely familiar but she couldn't place him. About fifty-five or so, he was a lean man with a shy gaze and a blotchy complexion. The woman looked a few years older judging by the grey hair and heavily lined face. Her khaki jumper and black track pants were clean but baggy as if she'd lost a lot of weight recently.

"I'm Bob McDonald and this here's me wife, Esther. I work for Mr Carter. I do a few odd jobs like at the mill and his house." He cleared his throat. "You work in the office, don't you, miss? You're the one that pays us."

At his words, the other patrons ceased speaking to listen. Sasha could almost hear the twitching of their ears in the sudden hush. She lowered her mug then gripped her hands. "I record the timesheets and data and submit them for authorisation."

"Well, it's like this, see. We were wondering whether we'd be getting paid today." Bob and Esther exchanged the kind of glance long married couples often share, a way of communicating without the need for words. "It's rent day and Mr Carter promised I'd get what's owing to me. Four weeks, miss."

Sasha caught the gasp before it left her lips. That couldn't be right; his name wasn't in the system. She swallowed. "You haven't been paid for four weeks?"

"That's what he said," Esther said, her voice rising. "At first, Mr Carter said he'd pay Bob here off the books, then he said he'd have to put him on the payroll. We ain't seen no money yet and we're behind in the rent." Esther's lips trembled and she swayed, a thin blade of grass in a gathering storm.

"I'm sorry, Mrs McDonald. I honestly don't know.

I'm waiting on Mr Carter to phone me back. As soon as the office is opened, I'll ensure the pays go through."

"My Bobby isn't as young as he used to be," the older woman wailed. Her hands clenched over her woollen jumper. "He's not strong. It's his asthma, you see. And he's diabetic."

"Hush, Esther. The lass doesn't need to know our troubles."

"We need the money! We'll be turned onto the street. We'll be homeless!"

"See? What did I tell you? There's something shifty going on," shouted a male voice.

Sasha twisted around to glare at the four mill hands banging on the table with their fists.

Something hit the floor hard.

"Bloody hell!"

At Cole's exclamation, Sasha looked back. Esther McDonald was crumpled in a heap on the ground. Time slowed like frames in an old newsreel.

Cole leapt to his feet. His chair fell backwards with a clatter. His mug shattered on the lino, splattering coffee like rivulets of old blood.

Bob sank to his knees, clutching his head in his hands, crying, "Esther. Esther. Don't leave me." He seemed to shrink into himself.

Shattered. Broken. Like all those others.

Sasha's vision blurred at the edges.

Screams.

Blood.

Pleas for help ... That terrifying memory of not being able to move.

"Sasha, I need some help here. Call for an ambulance," Cole said.

Help.

She jumped, refocused as her training reasserted itself. Without further thought, she was out of her seat and beside the fallen woman, checking for a pulse, listening for breathing.

Nothing.

She began resuscitation.

Cole rubbed a hand along his jaw feeling the rasp of stubble against his palm. He stared down the road at the rapidly disappearing ambulance carrying Mrs McDonald and her husband to the ER. *Pisser of a way to start the day.*

"Do you think she'll make it?" He glanced at the woman standing at his side.

"It's hard to say without knowing her medical history but I hope so."

"You're certainly full of surprises. The way you rattled off the situation and the old lady's symptoms was impressive, not to mention how effortlessly you administered CPR." There was no doubt in his mind that she'd improved Mrs McDonald's chances of survival.

"I've picked up a few skills over the years." Sasha crossed her arms and turned away.

To avoid looking at me? He watched her march inside the cafe to their table then retrieve her coat and satchel. Before she'd jumped into action, she'd sat on that damn chair and just stared dead ahead as if frozen. Her face had bleached of all colour, her eyes wide and glazed. There'd been a remoteness about her stiff body that made him think she was in a different place, reliving an unpleasant memory.

Her reaction had rattled him. What the devil had happened to her? Whatever it was, it must have been quite an experience. But she'd risen to the occasion and thrown off whatever demon had caused her to freeze.

You had to admire a woman with that type of inner strength. Hell, a man would have to be blind not to admire her. Those glistening golden strands threaded amongst light brown hair reminded him of jersey caramels, his lolly of choice. Her cat-slanted eucalypt-leaf green eyes would catch the attention of any red-blooded man. Then there was the shapely way she filled out her yellow jumper and the long line of slim legs revealed by her faded blue denims as she walked towards him. His hands damn well itched like crazy to feel the warmth of her under his palms.

She reached his side, his nostrils flaring as he caught a whiff of her perfume—a mixture of citrus and jasmine. And his pulse ramped up. But whether it was the duration of his recent dry spell in the ladies' department or some crazy voodoo she'd cast over him, didn't matter. There was no way he intended to act on his attraction or even test the waters to see if she felt the same. Not with two kids to raise, a cotton farm to run and a bank manager breathing down his neck.

Sunrise washed away the darkness of the night and edged the clouds in the east with gold. While they stood in a silence he found hard to breach, a bloke in a purple hoodie and track pants jogged around the corner, his breath puffs of steam in the fresh morning air. Shifting direction, the jogger jumped onto the footpath and, in a few strides, reached them.

"Morning, Cuddlepie." The stranger stopped, beamed at Sasha, planted his hands on his hips and proceeded to swivel his upper torso from front to back, over and over.

Although he had a full head of steel-grey hair and a smoothly tanned face, Cole reckoned the bloke had to be in his mid-fifties. *Now where have I seen him before?* He flicked through his mental rolodex.

"Thought you'd be at work by now. Instead I find you on a date."

Heaving a mighty sigh, Sasha juggled her satchel and gloves while she pulled on her parka and groaned, "Dad."

"Baby-cake." Sasha's father sent Cole a wink, then began to jog in place and jab the air in front of him like a Rocky wannabe. "Who's the squeeze?"

"This is Cole Mitchell, Dad. He's a contractor at the factory." Sasha yanked on her gloves so savagely it was a wonder her fingers didn't poke holes through the tips. "And I am *not* on a date. The company had a gas leak this morning and is closed until it's fixed. Cole and I were just discussing the situation."

Punch, punch. Jab, jab. "No kidding?"

"Cole, meet my father, Obadiah Bernstein."

"Isn't she a peach? I hope your intentions are honourable."

"Seriously, Dad? Just ignore him, Cole. He loves to yank my chain."

Jab, jab. Punch, punch. "Is it working?"

Fighting his grin and failing miserably, Cole held out his hand. The older man stopped boxing the air to give him a mighty shake.

"Good to meet you, sir," Cole said.

"Please." Sasha's father waved a hand in the air. "Call me Obie." He peered around them at the cafe and inhaled noisily. "What's the coffee like, Sash?"

"I only had one sip but it was pretty good. A customer, an elderly lady, suffered a heart attack and I had to administer CPR."

"Poor woman." Obie shook his head and stopped moving, as if giving the moment silent respect. Obviously unable to stay still for long, he was off again, bending over and touching the ground then straightening and back down again.

Cole snapped his fingers. "I know where I've met you before. Yesterday, at Mindalby Primary. You performed free dental checks on my daughter's class. Year one."

Summer had insisted he attend as she'd been up for an award for *'good brushing technique.'* How could he refuse? Even if he hadn't been a single parent, there was no way he'd miss any golden moments in either of his kids' lives.

"Yes, I'm on leave from my own practice, travelling around Australia and thought, why not call in and see how my Cuddlepie is doing? Arrived on Saturday and staying at the caravan park. But I like being busy, so I volunteered with the local dentist to go with him when he did the rounds of the schools and pre-schools."

"Travelling? Sounds like a good life."

"Nothing like it, Cole. You should try it sometime. I bet I know which girl she is—long, brown hair with lots of scarlet ribbons and your unusual-coloured eyes. A cute little kid." Obie flowed into a sequence of martial arts movements, swinging his arms wide and nearly taking out the town's recently retired school principal, Ms Watson, as she attempted to enter the cafe.

The woman with her hair pulled back into a tight bun snapped off a snarky statement about traffic on the footpath, sniffed and stalked past.

"Morning, Ms Watson," Cole called after her, before addressing Obie. "Yes, that's my Summer. She's a sweetheart." His chest expanded at the thought of his gentle little girl, who was growing up way too fast. Both his kids were; there were days when he wanted to lock onto each precious moment and make it last forever. "Is that Tai Chi or Qigong?"

Obie balanced on one foot. "A mixture of both. I'm impressed you recognised the moves. Do you practise?"

Although slightly flushed in the face, Obie was breathing easy.

The bloke must be seriously fit. "Not me. I find footy training and coaching my kids' Little Athletics team sufficient exercise. My aunt Amber is into all kinds of alternative lifestyle stuff. She's a Wiccan and runs the Commune of the Golden Light, just out of town."

"What?" Obie froze. "A Wiccan? Here in Mindalby? And there's a commune? I'd love to visit. How do I get to meet this woman?" He spoke in a reverent whisper, his eyes sparkling as if he suddenly beheld the Holy Grail.

Sasha grinned. "Now you've done it, Cole. In an hour's time, Dad will have tracked her down and be following her about like a puppy. She'll never get rid of him."

Cole laughed, his gaze lingering on the impish smile on Sasha's face. "Don't worry. Aunt Amber can handle him."

"I practise a mix of Buddhism and Shamanism. Much to my Jewish parents' dismay." Obie flung an arm around his daughter and hauled her close. "And I love exploring new cultures."

Sasha smiled at him and there was such love

glowing in her shining eyes that Cole's throat clogged. "Yeah, every school holidays we were off on an adventure to some far-away place. I loved it."

Her father planted a smacking kiss on the top of her head. "What do you think, Cole? Isn't she one in a gazillion? Never one word of complaint about sleeping on the ground beside smelly yaks, or trekking over mountains with nothing but water, baked beans and Vegemite. You mentioned you have kids. Is there a Mrs Mitchell in the picture?"

"Dad!" A soft pink flared over Sasha's cheeks as she shrugged out of his hold. "You're as subtle as a sledgehammer."

Cole ran a finger around his zipped-up jacket collar. Damn that thing was tight. Should he admit he was a widower? Maybe he should say nothing. There'd be no need for any awkward explanations then. But he couldn't help his gaze from straying back onto Sasha's face and staying; especially when she snuck a peek at his left hand. "Single man, these days," he eventually croaked.

"Excellent." Obie rubbed his hands together. "Now, where can I find this wonderful Wiccan? I have so much to ask her."

Regaining his equilibrium, Cole pushed up his sleeve and checked his watch. "Aunt Amber should be pulling into the carpark of the grocery store in about fifteen minutes. You can't miss her. She'll be the one driving a wagon loaded with vegetables and pulled by two carthorses."

"A wagon! Oh my! This is meant to be. Circle the wagons, the Indians are coming!" Obie hollered and hauled Sasha close for another bear hug.

The hubbub flowing from inside the cafe hushed. Cole could only imagine the rubber-necking they were getting from the other diners.

"Dinner tonight, Cuddlepie? How about the *Ace in the Hole*?" Obie nodded towards the pub next door.

"Dad! You promised ..." Her voice trailed off and she bit her lip.

Her father tapped the side of his nose and winked. "No need to fret. I've got it covered."

Feeling more than a little mystified, Cole had to rein in his curiosity.

"If you're certain ... then sure, Dad. I'd love to."

"Be careful, Cuddlepie. Fantastic meeting you, Cole; I hope to see more of you." He gave a suggestive eye roll towards his daughter then sprinted off down the road.

"He can be exhausting sometimes, but he's the kindest man in the world." Sasha tilted her head and smiled.

Cole's heartbeat skipped and he quickly glanced away. It wasn't fair that a woman could have this much pull on a man. Especially in so short an acquaintance. He cleared his throat. "How long is your father staying in Mindalby?"

"With Dad, it's hard to say. He's always going walkabout."

"And you? What made you decide to come to our small town on the edge of the outback?" For a split second, he could have sworn dread flashed across her face.

She made a fuss over stashing her mobile inside her satchel. "I saw the ad for a position in accounts and thought, why not? I wanted somewhere quiet."

"There are a lot of quiet towns in Australia and none nearly as remote," he pointed out drily.

She shot back, "Why the interrogation?"

"I did wonder when you turned up in January, whether you might be one of Carter's cast-off lovers, intent on resuming your affair. He's had quite a few of them over the years."

"I don't know whether you're trying to be funny or trying to insult me." She fiddled some more with her bag.

He smiled but she remained stony-faced, staring back at him with those imperturbable cat-like eyes. He blundered on. "Now that we've spoken, I can see you're nowhere near his type. Carter usually goes for young bleached-blondes with big boobs."

Sasha zipped up her parka with something of a snap. "If I were you, I'd stop now before you dig a deeper hole and I bury you."

"Yeah, sorry." Longing for that hole to bury himself

in, he shoved his hands into his pants pockets. "You can tell I'm out of practice."

No sooner did the words leave his mouth, then his face burned even hotter. *Come on, mate, get a grip. She's pretty but so are lots of other women. And not one of them sends all my social skills scattering to the four winds like this.* He frowned, pretending to study the steady approach of a fuel truck powering down Burton Park Road.

A hand touched his tense arm before quickly withdrawing. He glanced down then looked at Sasha. She was smiling but it was a gentle smile and the cold frostiness in her eyes had been replaced with warmth. Although wariness lurked in the emerald depths.

Heat flushed through him.

"Hey. It's okay. I'm out of practice too." She stepped over to her bike and unhooked her helmet. "There wasn't any time for a social life where I lived previously."

"Oh? Where was that?" Curiosity burned bright.

Busy placing her helmet on and fastening the straps, she didn't look at him as she replied, "In my other life, I was a theatre sister with Doctors Without Borders. I spent sixteen months in Syria."

Holy ...! He sucked in his surprised gasp. Well, that certainly explained the professional assistance she'd rendered Mrs McDonald. Was that also the reason behind the scars on her hand? At the thought that she may have been injured or in danger, his gut rolled over. "And before that?"

"Various Melbourne and Sydney hospitals. I did a three-year stint in London and several years in Africa and the Middle East with the Red Cross. I've got my eyes on a post in the Philippines next."

A woman focused on her career.

What were the odds of that? The only woman who'd stirred both physical and emotional interest in him in the past five years was nothing like his wife. Denise had been a country girl through and through. Denise had loved this life as much as him. And in the end, it had been the remoteness of this life that had killed her.

Bolting the proverbial vault door against his contrary fascination with this woman, he pulled out a crumpled business card. "Here's my number. I'd appreciate if you could give me a call when the office opens. A text message would do. I need to know when I'll be paid. I've got an urgent matter that has to be settled within the next few days."

"Not a problem." Sasha stashed his card in her satchel.

Steeling himself against the temptation to linger, he walked away. Jaw clenched, he fought the urge to look back.

4

Midday came and went and still Sasha had yet to receive any communication from her employer. After arriving home from the cafe, she'd dusted, polished and vacuumed, then run the mower over the patch of weeds and straggly grass. Movement—noise—anything to drown out the voices of dread whispering in her ears. *That* and the realisation that a certain sexy guy apparently couldn't get away from her fast enough.

Fancy Cole insinuating she was having an affair with Don! Out of all the possible reasons for her to be in town, he'd locked onto the one reason that bore a semblance of truth.

Her hands trembled as she replaced a mug in the cupboard and recalled the past few months. Despite all his winks and smirks, Don had proved impervious to her charms.

The knowledge that she'd resorted to flirting in a suggestive fashion—which she had no intention of delivering on—churned her stomach.

Desperate measures. With Uncle Isaac's freedom on the line and all legal paths exhausted, she'd thought she had little choice. But so far working for Don had yielded nothing.

He and his witch of a wife kept their secrets well hidden.

And now he wouldn't return her calls.

She checked her mobile yet again as she looked out the kitchen window of the small flat she rented on Edward Street. The building had once been a two-storey house until a local bloke converted it into four flats—two on the ground floor and another two on the top.

When Sasha had arrived in town, she'd signed up for the vacant ground-floor flat the moment she'd seen the garden.

Filled with azaleas, camellias, bottlebrushes and grevilleas of various sizes, a carpet of *verbena bonariensis* with their clusters of tiny pink flowers, and clumps of lavender bushes, rosemary and agapanthus —she'd been sold before she'd even set foot inside the door. On this last day of autumn, most of the flowers had died. Come spring, this small expanse of heaven would be awash with colour. But by then, she'd be long gone. She would never see the garden, glowing with colour, the stems swaying in a gentle breeze, bees and butterflies hovering over the blooms.

For the first time, she toyed with the idea of living a different kind of life.

Movement caught her eyes. She leaned on the sink and stared into the branches of the stunted mulga tree near the fence, smiling when she saw six red-capped robins.

How lovely. Maybe one day she'd have a garden like this, brimming with native plants and trees that would be a haven for birds and insects. Maybe she'd grow her own vegetables and have a fruit tree or two.

Her phone rang and her breath caught when she saw the caller ID. She snatched the phone off the charger. "Hi, Mum. How's Uncle Isaac?"

"Sasha. I'm so glad I caught you. He's out of the prison infirmary and back in general population. Do you have any news?"

Her fingers tightened over her phone. On her mother's side, there'd only ever been Mum and Uncle Isaac. He'd played a prominent part in her childhood, always the gentle-mannered man with soft, shy eyes who'd listened patiently to her hopes and dreams. He was the one who'd taught her to ride a bike. When she was a teenager, they'd gone together on several charity rides.

There was no doubt in her mind whatsoever that he was innocent. When the property developer Uncle Isaac had been working for had gone belly-up three years ago, the news quickly emerged that funds had disappeared from the accounts to the tune of one point six million dollars. Her uncle had been charged and eighteen months later found guilty. Although no trace of the missing money had been found in his possession, he'd received a seven-year prison sentence with a non-parole period of three years.

He wasn't coping well and had been recently diagnosed by the prison doctor with severe depression.

"I'm sorry, Mum. I've been through every file in the office. I've found nothing at all that links Yasmin Carter with Uncle Isaac."

"Oh dear. I'd been hoping ..." Her mother's voice trailed off.

She said quietly, "Mum, maybe there's nothing to be found. I'm not certain I'd recognise any evidence even if I did find it. I'm a nurse, not an accountant or a detective."

"But you trained in accounting after high school before starting your nursing career."

"It was an accounts clerk diploma and working a couple of years for your charities didn't give me a lot of experience."

After their latest appeal for a re-trial had failed, her mother had hired a private investigator. He'd discovered that the woman Uncle Isaac had been seeing on a casual basis hadn't used her real name. Instead, she'd given the name of a girl who'd died at ten years of age. The next breakthrough had occurred when the private investigator obtained a copy of CCTV footage of a conference both Isaac and the woman attended. With a photo of the woman available, her true identity had soon been unearthed. Although her hair had been dark and not her current white-blonde, a clear shot of her face had given her away.

Yasmin Carter. A woman who hovered on the fringes of the upper echelon of Sydney society and the current wife of the CEO of Mindalby Cotton Company.

When this news had been relayed to Uncle Isaac, he'd suggested Yasmin must have obtained access to his laptop and hence the company accounts. However, with no concrete evidence tying her to the disappearance of the money, the police couldn't re-open the case.

"I know it was a crazy idea, but I'm desperate. I appreciate your efforts, I truly do, and I know how much you love your uncle. He's such a sweet soul. He doesn't deserve to be punished for something he didn't do. This self-harm attempt … Apparently, it was a miracle he survived. Oh, Sasha, I'm so worried. If he tries again …" Her mother's voice faltered into silence.

Sasha squeezed her eyes shut to ward off the sting of hot tears and the heavy thumping of her heart. After clearing her throat, she managed a quiet, "I'll keep looking."

"I know you will, darling. Please remember, no matter what happens, this is not on you. I just can't bear the thought of losing your uncle. He's all the family I have left. If only Sophie had lived, I may have had grandchildren by now," her mother said in a thick voice, referring to Sasha's only sibling who'd died of SIDS at three months.

"You still have me, Mum. And don't forget hottie Raphael," she teased, wiping her damp cheeks with the back of her hand, determined not to start *that* argument—again. Her mother knew her life plan didn't include children. "Dad sends his love."

Her mother snorted. "Your father. Always with his head in the clouds and his eyes on a new horizon. No wonder I left him. He's far too restless."

She noted her mother never mentioned her latest husband, Raphael, knowing his age was a sore point with her. He was barely six months older than Sasha! But she had to admit, he seemed kind and genuinely enamoured with her mother. And that was all that really mattered. "Sounds like Dad."

"I'm glad he's there, Sasha, keeping an eye on you."

"Mum. I'm thirty-four. I can look after myself. But it *is* great to have his company."

"Yes, he's a good man and I'm lucky we managed to remain friends all these years. You know I worry about you, especially after the explosion. Your poor skin. All those burns. That dreadfully deep wound in your back," her mother's voice cracked. "Some days in the hospital, I'd see this terrible expression in your eyes and worried that I'd ever reach you. The thought of losing my precious daughter terrified me. I never want to receive a phone call like that again."

"I'm fine now, Mum. I had a few dark moments and I'm sorry you were worried." More than a few moments, she admitted wryly to herself.

"Oh darling, it wasn't your fault. I have to be honest though. I wish you would settle down somewhere close. Get married. I used to dream of your wedding when you were a little girl." There was more than a hint of pleading in her mother's voice.

Sasha sighed, not knowing how to explain the compulsion that drove her to want to make a difference. "It's more than a job to me, Mum. It's a calling."

"You could have both. Plenty of women hold down a career and have a family." Her mother sighed heavily when Sasha remained silent. "In the hospital, the doctors mentioned something about survivor's guilt but you've always been this way. Always wanted to save the world. I'm so proud of your commitment to the victims of disaster and war. You're very brave."

Sasha gave a short laugh but there was little humour in the sound. "I'm not that brave, Mum. Most of the time I was bloody terrified. The conditions in the refugee camp were challenging. Lack of food and fresh water and dwindling medical supplies. And every day, the fighting got closer. The people donated blood, shared their food and water with us when our supplies ran out."

She closed her eyes, remembering. Recalling the

faces. "They were so grateful for whatever we could do, even when the only news we could give them was the worst possible kind. They are the true heroes."

Her mother said, "All I know is that I thank God every day that you came home to us. I'd better go. Raphael is taking me out for dinner to keep me occupied so I don't worry too much." Her mother bade her to take care and ended the call.

After re-placing her mobile on the charger, Sasha pressed her fingers to her aching forehead. It had been while she'd been recovering, attending physio and counselling sessions, that her mother had spotted the advertisement for an office/accounts assistant in Mindalby Cotton Company. It seemed the only course of action they had left.

When Don Carter had suggested they meet for dinner to discuss her application, she hadn't hesitated. He'd shown an interest that night that had led her to believe a little feminine persuasion could flatter him into indiscreet conversation.

But he'd proven harder to crack that night than anticipated, and when he'd offered her the position, she'd accepted. The perfect opportunity to do more sleuthing.

When her mother had been in the headlines, citing her brother's innocence at every opportunity, Sasha had been overseas. And since she'd kept her father's surname and her mother had re-married twice, their connection wasn't an easy one to make. All which led her to believe that Don had no idea of her relationship with the man his wife had framed.

And here I am. But so far, she had discovered nothing that could help her cause. And despite her best attempts at insinuating herself into Don's life in every way possible, she'd had very little contact with Yasmin Carter.

She'd tried the professional, hard-working approach—nope, nada. She'd kept up her feminine tactics. She knew the rest of the staff suspected her of making a play for Don; possibly even believing she was, as Cole had hinted, Don's latest fling.

Don was such a flirt, making smirky innuendoes to every female between the ages of eighteen and forty, that he needed little encouragement. However, despite his winks and smart remarks, not once had he crossed the line. And not once had she crossed paths with his wife while shopping, socialising or jogging down by the river. The woman was a ghost.

For the first time, she wondered why he'd employed someone who knew so little about accounting. She'd been so relieved to have won the job, she never thought too deeply about the why—she'd assumed Don had hoped to win her into his bed.

But now, given his interest in her had been so short-lived, what the hell had he been playing at?

She drummed her short-cut nails on the countertop.

And now the mill was closed. The company locking

the employees out didn't sit well with her. Having worked in some dangerous places, she'd often had to rely to on her gut feelings to survive. As the hours passed and she'd received no response from Don Carter, that nasty, nerve-biting clench in the pit of her belly told her there was more to the closure than a gas leak.

She had to find out what was really happening. This could be her last chance to help her uncle. She had to get back into that building. Or even better, inside Yasmin and Don Carter's home.

5

An announcement for a town meeting came over the local radio station after the four o'clock news flash. For a few seconds, Sasha couldn't believe what she'd heard. Placing her coffee mug on the sink, she rushed for her mobile then dialled Don's number. This time, amazingly, he picked up.

"Don? What's this about a meeting to address the closure of Mindalby Cotton?" Her palms felt damp with sweat and the phone almost fell through her noodle-limp fingers.

Don's heavy sigh came down the line, loud and clear.

Play acting. She was certain of it.

"It breaks my heart to have to do this but I've placed the company into voluntary administration."

"Oh no! When did this happen?" She prickled with sudden suspicion.

"Last night, actually."

"And you're only just telling people about it now?"

"The first announcement was before lunch today. Not that I consider it any of your business, Sash, when I tell my employees."

"What about the gas leak? Is that for real?"

"Come now. The police and the fire brigade were at the mill. You seriously think all those people would lie?"

"But …" She shook her head, trying to organise her whirling thoughts. Mrs McDonald's grey-hued face appeared in her mind. "What about the wages for this fortnight? And the end-of-month creditor payments?"

"What are you auditioning for? *Sixty Minutes?*" He laughed at his own joke.

She failed to see any humour in his response.

He blustered on, "It's all out of my hands now. I've got this woman, Felicity Robinson, who'll sort everything out. She'll need to speak to you, Sash. Since you're in charge of the accounts'"

"*What?* But I'm not the accountant. All I do is data entry and make payments you authorised," she spluttered.

"Doesn't matter. She'll still want to talk to you, so make certain you're available. I've given her your contact details." He hung up.

In disbelief she stared at her mobile. Had Don just dropped her head first into his mess? Her imagination went into overdrive. Had he planned for her to be in

Mindalby so she could take the fall? No. He'd never struck her as a strategist.

Still … she couldn't totally dismiss that line of thought.

Rousing herself, she filed away her suspicions and dug out Cole's business card from her satchel. She sent him a quick text message letting him know about the meeting. Like her, he may have missed the first announcement. *I'm just being friendly. No more. No less.*

Now who's lying? Grimacing, she checked the time before stuffing her mobile and wallet into her satchel and snatching up her bike helmet. Seconds later, she was out the door and on her bike.

People were filing through the front door of the community centre when she arrived. Built in the 1970s, it was a sturdy building of orange brick and terracotta roof tiles. A native garden flourished on both sides of the wide ramp leading up to the entrance.

She left her bike in the rack and, holding her helmet by the straps with her satchel over her shoulder, entered the spacious hallway. Passing by five small office-type rooms on her right, she walked into the main meeting room. Judging by the number of empty seats, she guessed a lot of people hadn't caught the announcement. Had it been a deliberate tactic of Don's to arrange only two radio announcements?

The hum of voices was subdued, almost drowned out by the dragging of chairs across the linoleum-covered floor. At the front, a woman aged around forty with wispy dark brown hair and a round face was standing, a sheaf of papers held in one hand as she waited.

This had to be the voluntary administrator, Felicity … Robbins? No: Robinson. Beside her stood a short, younger bloke with a receding hairline and thick glasses, his shirt buttoned up to this throat so tightly his blotchy skin looked like he was choking.

She grabbed a chair from the side and made her way to where Don's ex-wife, sat. She murmured a hello and nodded to the few other people she knew. Warren Leadbeater dropped into the seat in front of her and turned to glare at her so coldly she shrank back in her chair. He swung around and leaned forward to tap Tox Ryder, a burly tattooed ex-biker, on the shoulder and engage him in conversation. Sitting beside Tox was his wife, Wendy, who was almost as short as she was wide and who ran the family business Ryder Transport, with a *'take-no-prisoners'* attitude. She eyeballed Sasha narrowly before giving a sharp nod of recognition.

Sasha gave a perfunctory smile. Thinking of the current month's invoices sitting in her in-box, she was relieved when Wendy didn't begin to hound her for payment.

Heart fluttering and thinking this could be an opportunity to glean more background on the Carters, Sasha glanced at the woman beside her.

"Hello, I'm Veronica Carter," she said when their eyes met.

Pretending she didn't know the older woman's identity, she introduced herself. "I work for a Don Carter. Is he your husband?"

"Ex." The woman's face settled into an expression she couldn't interpret.

"Don't you own the women's boutique, *Bonnie's Country Threads*? I noticed a lovely evening dress in the window yesterday."

"The amber silk and cream lace." Veronica gave her the once-over. "It would suit you perfectly. You should come in and try it on."

Thinking of the scarring down her arms and over the right-hand side of her torso, she repressed a shudder. She'd taken care ever since her discharge from hospital to cover up her ruined skin, hating the thought of the pity or revulsion she'd face. "I'll think about it."

Two women edged along the row and sat on the other side of Veronica. "Hello, Mrs Carter," said the bone-thin woman with straight, chestnut brown hair and dressed in a too-tight skirt.

"Hello, Lesley. Do you know Sasha?"

"Yes."

Sasha frowned. "I'm sorry. I don't believe we've met."

"Hah! You should know me. I work in the kiosk at the mill. Lesley Thompson is the name." Lesley sniffed and said loudly to her companion. "I told you, she's a stuck-up cow."

Sasha froze in shock.

A mobile phone buzzed and Lesley dug around inside her handbag. Flicking it on, she turned her shoulder and muttered, "She's here. Stop hounding me. I know the drill." Her voice lowered as she continued for a few seconds before switching off her phone.

Veronica patted Sasha's hand, diverting her attention. "You haven't been here long, but I believe I saw you jogging through the park on Sunday with a distinguished-looking older man." The older woman's eyes were warm, her smile friendly.

"That would be my father. He's on holidays." She grinned.

Veronica waved to a woman who Sasha recognised as the lady her father almost knocked down outside the cafe that morning. "You're looking well, Ms Watson. I love your maroon jacket. It does wonders for your complexion."

Ms Watson murmured a greeting to Veronica and sat a few chairs along the same row. Two elderly blokes shuffled in and plonked down on one side of her and another old-timer book-ended her on the other.

Sasha had seen the old fellows in the Ace in the Hole pub last week. One of them, Max Dooley, the short one with the white moustache and bow legs, sometimes worked behind the bar.

She scanned the room. "There's not many people here."

"I noticed that too." Veronica sounded worried.

Up front, the microphone buzzed then Felicity spoke, welcoming everyone for coming at such short notice, adding, "My name is Felicity Robinson and the man beside me is my assistant, Dave Gresham. My company has been appointed as voluntary administrators for the Mindalby Cotton Company. Our objective is to save the company so it can continue trading rather than be placed into liquidation."

Ignoring the cries of dismay, she continued, "For those of you who don't know, our role is to take control and custody of all unsecured assets and assist secured creditors where necessary then evaluate the viability of the company's future. The first task is to ascertain whether the company can be saved. If not, we will endeavour to administer the company to ensure that the best possible return is awarded to the creditors and shareholders. A crisis counsellor will arrive in town shortly and can be contacted via the community centre. Please avail yourself of his services. Any questions?"

Sasha raised her hand. "You mention creditors but what about the employees' wages for the past fortnight?"

"Employee entitlements that arose prior to the date of voluntary administration are not normally paid during that period. Employees are viewed as unsecured creditors. How and when employees are paid will depend on the outcome of the creditors' meeting in five weeks. If we're able to ensure the company returns to the directors, all entitlements will be paid at that time."

"What if that's not an option?" Sasha kept her hand in the air.

"The terms of employee payments will be determined by the details worked out in the deed of company arrangement. Please be patient. These are early days."

"When you say creditors, do you also mean the subbies who've been working on the extension?" Cole said. "There's several of us here today, who are owed for the past month's work."

At the sound of his voice, Sasha looked over and found him standing with his arms folded across his chest, a heavy frown marring his face. He sent her a quick nod. But no smile.

Feeling rebuffed, she sank into her seat, remembering the glare the union rep had bored into her a few minutes ago. Did people blame her for this mess? But how could they? Her job was composed of data entry and paperwork, including payment of invoices and balancing account statements. She had little access to the company's financials beyond that, and none whatsoever to its bank account. Apart from a few cheque payments, the rest of the accounts were dealt with by the company accountants, an outside firm called Trove Financials Pty Ltd.

Don's sly words slunk into her mind. Perspiration began to bead her upper lip as her heartbeat quickened.

"Subcontractors' invoices will also be assessed as part of the review process. I would recommend anyone who hasn't sent in their claims or invoices to do so immediately and not to forget proof of purchase orders," Felicity announced.

"How long is this gonna take? We've got to put food on the table for our kids and pay our bills. How we gonna do that if we don't get paid?" Warren asked.

Felicity held up a hand to quell the rising wave of angry voices. "My assistant and I will work hard to expedite matters as quickly as possible. The first creditors' meeting will take place one week from today at nine-thirty am. All creditors will have the option of allowing us to continue with our work or appoint a new administrator. You will also need to decide whether to form a committee of creditors and who will be on that committee. If we're kept on, we'll complete our investigation and forward a report to each creditor. The report will table three options for the committee to vote on at the next meeting. One: the company could enter into a deed of company arrangement; two: go into liquidation; or three: be returned to the directors. The report will also include details of possible payouts to creditors."

Her voice rose to be heard above the rumblings of disbelief. "For those who don't know, a deed of company arrangement is where the company will pay all or part of its debts."

"You mean, we can still get paid what we're owed?" bawled Warren.

The woman hesitated. "That will depend on the state of the company's finances and whether all paperwork is in order. It's possible that only a certain proportion of what you're owed will be paid, or there might not be sufficient funds for any payments. All this information will be detailed in my report."

"Five weeks is a hell of a long time, Ms Robinson," said Cole. "Many of us don't have spare cash to fall back on. And what about the cotton already in the yard? I've got five hundred bales processed and ready to be transported, not to mention the four hundred modules waiting to be ginned. I'm not the only one in this situation. When will we have access to our own property? This is going to hurt us big time if we fail to meet our contracted delivery dates."

Murmurs of assent flowed through the room.

Ms Robinson tapped the microphone. "I reiterate, my colleague and I will do everything we can to work towards an early resolution."

"It's more than a bloody problem! It's our livelihood," Cody Nossiter yelled from behind them.

Sasha swung around to discover he had his beady, bloodshot eyes fixed on Veronica. His face appeared flushed and he stumbled as he pointed in her direction.

"What about you, lady muck? Living in your fancy house while the rest of us can't put food in our bellies."

"I have no input into my ex-husband's business

dealings, Cody." Veronica raised her chin but Sasha could see how tightly she gripped her fingers in her lap, and she reached out to pat her hand. The older woman sent her a grateful smile.

Tox Ryder called for everyone's attention. "The gin in Bourke may be able to take the rest of your harvest."

Mutters about organising additional transport and the price of freight these days filtered through the room.

"That's going to put more strain on our finances, Tox. Not all of us will be able to afford the extra costs." Cole walked between the rows of hard plastic chairs to fetch up beside where Sasha was sitting.

Tox shrugged. "I'm happy to transport modules to Bourke for the cost of the fuel."

"Thanks, mate." Cole chucked Tox on the shoulder. "I just may take you up on that offer."

Wendy Ryder shot to her feet, her double chins quivering. "Hold on a minute!" She planted her hands on her hips and glared at her husband. "Ryder Transport ain't no charity, Tox. We got wages to pay, just like everyone else."

"We need to do our bit for the town, lovey," Tox explained. "If the town goes under, then so do we."

Wendy swept her beady stare around the room then muttered, "I guess. But I'm adding ten percent to the fuel cost to cover insurances."

"That sounds fair enough," Cole said. "Thank you, Wendy."

Wendy rolled her eyes and sank into her chair while her husband pecked her affectionately on her cheek.

Voices rose again as everyone began to talk amongst themselves.

Cody took up his rant again, cutting through the chatter. "This is all well and good but I still say, lady muck here should ensure us workers don't lose out. We need to be paid. And what about her buddy there, Miss Mindalby Cotton Company accountant, sitting all prim and pretending to be one of us? She should have warned us."

Keenly aware of Cole's razor-sharp gaze fastened on her face, Sasha said as coolly as she could muster, "I had no idea any of this was going to happen."

Warren Leadbeater turned around, resting his elbow on the back of his chair and chimed in, "What a crock."

"What is wrong with you?" She returned his glare.

Surprisingly, Warren reddened. "As union rep I've gotta make sure my workmates aren't left holding the can for that gas leak. I've seen this happen before. The white-collar staff walk away, sitting pretty with their redundancies while the workers are shafted because of some poncy safety excuse."

"That's not going to happen here."

"Yeah? You sound mighty sure of yourself, for someone insisting she doesn't know what's going on."

"I was referring to payouts, Warren. I only meant that all of us are in the same position."

The foreman shook his head. "If you were any kind of accountant, you would have seen the writing on the wall ages ago. You should have given us the nod."

"I am *not* the accountant," she said through her teeth. *Geez.* What would it take to get that message through their thick heads? Her gaze swept the room. It seemed as if everyone was now staring at her.

Accusing her.

Heat flooded her face. Her stomach knotted. Was this how poor Uncle Isaac had felt? The sensation of being trapped rushed towards her, like a gaping black abyss yawning in front of her as she wobbled on the edge with no parachute. She shot to her feet, sending her chair scraping across the floor.

"What I will do is find out how we can all be paid as soon as possible. Excuse me." She pushed past Cole, stumbling in her haste to escape.

"That's it. Run away. She's hiding something, I tell you." Nossiter's hoarse shout followed her to the door.

A hand slipped under her elbow as she rushed headlong down the ramp. "Steady on," said Cole gruffly.

She whirled to face him, her heart thudding crazily. "You don't believe I had anything to do with the closure, do you?"

He shrugged. "Look, Sasha, the problem is, a lot of people will still think you must have known what was about to go down. Given your job and all."

She huffed out a breath. "For heaven's sake! I knew nothing about this."

"All I know, is that it looks like I'm not going to see my money any time soon." He ran a hand along his jaw, his gaze drifting to where a white Land Rover was parked under a street light on the opposite side of the road.

She peered past him. There appeared to be an elderly bloke sitting behind the wheel. A dark-haired little girl of about six was hanging halfway out of the rear passenger window, waving madly.

"Daddy. Come on! I'm hungry. Poppy says you're slower than a snail."

Cole looked back at Sasha, his brilliant eyes cool. "This is a bad day for Mindalby, Sasha. Let's hope for all our sakes this problem is resolved soon. I'll see you around." He walked off.

There'd been a note of warning in his deep voice that continued to vibrate along her nerve ends. Shivering, she watched Cole climb into his car before she turned away to retrieve her bike. He was right to be concerned. Desperate people often did desperate deeds. A fact she'd experienced first-hand.

A blustery wind sprang up, cutting through her woollen jumper as if it was no thicker than cotton. She mounted her bike and started pedalling.

Five weeks was a long time for people to wait to be paid.

In five weeks—anything could happen.

ole took a deep swallow of his beer, enjoying the cool rush of liquid down his parched throat and the yeasty scent in his nostrils. Leaning back in his chair, he gazed around the main bar of the Ace in the Hole pub, which was doing a roaring trade.

The predominance of timber panelling and vintage lithographs and etchings nailed to the wall gave the building an 'old world' ambience that he found soothing, even on what could turn out to be just about one of the worst days of the town's history.

After the town meeting, a lot of people had met up here to discuss, worry and rant about this disastrous event. Every now and again, the door would open letting in a blast of wintry night air and one more desperate person.

He'd spoken to a few mates since he'd arrived at the

pub. Everyone was busy speculating over the outcome and how the dickens they'd survive before some kind of solution was tabled. All he knew was that he couldn't afford for his cotton to remain inaccessible for that length of time. He'd already made phone calls to the businesses he was contracted to. While they were sympathetic, they had contracts to meet and now intended to source their cotton elsewhere. All in all, it was a screwed-up situation. He had the strong suspicion the workers and farmers were going to be screwed over.

Big time.

Flames roared up the chimney in the fireplace over on the far wall. The jukebox bleating out a woeful country and western song competed with the ebb and fall of voices. Normally, the place hummed with laughter and good-natured jokes as the locals relaxed after a hard day's work.

No one was laughing tonight.

A group of workers from the plant had their heads close together, as if they were plotting trouble. He recognised the foreman along with several others including old Hamish Easterby and the bloke now stabbing the air with his finger and yelling some crap about "We're not going to stand for it".

Cody Nossiter. That wanker, sure looked like he was doing his best to incite some kind of rebellion. What he hoped to achieve by this, Cole had no idea. The fool would be better off trying to work out another avenue of employment instead of stirring the pot.

People lined up over at the bar. Old Max Dooley was pouring beers like this was the only pub in the middle of the Simpson Desert. His two cronies, Chook and Harry, were perched on bar stools, like wrinkled old storks, whispering and nudging each other in the ribs, already three sheets to the wind.

He had no doubt they would be raffling off one of their bootleg bottles of home-brewed mead, 'honeyshine', in the carpark come curfew time. He only hoped the old buggers would show up on his farm tomorrow morning. They were three of the best and most experienced labourers in the district. Unfortunately, the old coots were not the most reliable.

"What do you make of this business going bust?" asked Cole's father, twirling his glass of neat whiskey in one hand.

Cole's mother sat bolt upright with her purse on her lap, looking like she'd prefer to be home snug in front of her television. But every fourth Tuesday night was when Cole caught up with his parents socially. Seeing his mother every school morning when she arrived to supervise his kids before driving them to school didn't count. He was usually out the door the moment she stepped inside. Tomorrow he planned to join his grandfather at eight-thirty and work until midnight harvesting another field of cotton.

"To be honest, Dad, I smell a rat." He took another

swallow. How much was Sasha involved? If at all? *And why the hell do I keep thinking about her?*

His father swirled his whiskey. "I knew Don from school. He always thought he was too smart for the rest of us."

"Wazza isn't helping, hanging around with Nossiter and his mates." Cole placed his beer glass on the table.

"He takes his job as union rep seriously, Cole. He's trying to look out for the workers." His father sipped his whiskey.

"Yeah, I guess." Cole wiped his mouth with the back of his hand. "We may not be able to make dinner next month, Mum. Cotton from our first harvested fields is locked behind Carter's gates until this problem's sorted and I haven't been paid for that welding job."

"Oh Cole." His mother laid her hand on his arm. "You know you can come to us if you need help."

"We'll be fine but thanks, Mum." He decided not to mention the wages they'd have to pay for the farm labourers and the contracted harvester. Or the bank overdraft they'd taken out after eighteen months of drought. When he'd received the inheritance from his maternal grandfather, he hadn't thought twice about asking his other grandfather—Pop—if he could buy into the farm as an equal partner.

Despite having lost half his leg in the Vietnam War, Pop had never allowed his injury to hold him back. Even at the age of seventy-four, he worked just as long and almost as hard as his grandson.

Cole loved his father but he admired his grandfather and the life he lived.

More importantly, Cotton Fields Glory was in his blood and he'd be damned if he allowed the farm to go to the wall.

His mother eyeballed his father calmly sipping his whiskey. "Where's your father, Roger? How long does it take to place a dinner order?"

"Now, now, Maisy. Pop will be along soon. Probably held up with Cole's kids changing their minds every six seconds." His dad winked at him.

His mother huffed. "A person could starve to death waiting."

"Afraid you'll miss tonight's episode of *True Crime?*" he teased.

His mother stole another piteous look at her watch. "I can't help it. I love that show."

"Do you mind if I join you, Cole?" a feminine voice said.

Glancing up, he found Lesley standing by their table, a broad smile on her face. Of its own volition, his gaze dropped to skim the hot-pink dress she wore. He immediately wished he'd refrained when her grin grew. That coffee they'd shared in Joe's Café several weeks ago had been a big mistake. Since then, every time he turned around, she seemed to be right there—in his personal space.

Recently, she'd turned up at the monthly SES meeting, citing how much she wanted to be a volunteer.

Then spent the remainder of the night badgering Cole with a million questions. It wasn't that he minded sharing his knowledge, only that he doubted her motives. Several times he'd caught her either yawning or looking bored when she thought no one was looking.

Without waiting for a response, she plopped onto the spare chair. "Don't mind me," she said gaily and held out her hand. "I'm Lesley Thompson. I work in the mill kiosk—well I used to. That's where Cole and I met."

She makes it sound like we're in some kind of relationship. All we've done is share a few cuppas—two at the most. He hastily introduced his parents and attempted to avoid the avid sparkle in his mother's eyes as if she'd downed half a bottle of champagne.

"Have you known each other long?" his mother asked, no doubt hopeful of a possible romance and probably planning a wedding already.

Ducking his head, he sculled his beer.

"Oh, we're old friends."

Like hell we are; I barely know you. Shifting in his seat, he glared at Lesley who blithely ignored him.

She babbled on. "Are you here for dinner? What a coincidence, so am I."

"Why don't you join us?"

"I'd love to. Thank you, Mrs. Mitchell."

"Please, call me Maisy."

Struth. This isn't good. Mum sounds like she's on the

matchmaking warpath again. Cole searched the room, looking for an escape route. "Pop's waving to us. Our table must be ready."

Pushing aside his empty glass, he bolted, leaving his parents and their unwanted guest to follow. He knew he was being rude but he couldn't help it. He had no interest in Lesley and every time he was in her vicinity, the hairs on his nape stiffened like a bristling echidna.

Entering the bistro area, he spotted his kids and his grandfather seated at a large table close by the fire.

Over in the corner were the Carey brothers and the bitter expression on Hayden's face reminded Cole of his best mate, Al Schumacher. The memory of the last time he'd seen him flashed through his mind.

The twisted metal.

The steam hissing from the engine.

The stink of burning rubber, petrol and fresh, ripe blood.

And his mate, or what was left of him: a crushed, broken bundle of bones jammed inside the cabin of his ute. Those poor bloody firies had had the job of cutting Al's corpse free from the wreckage. It had taken them a good four hours and everyone was damn well shaken afterwards.

He'd been called up as part of his duties as an SES member and the last thing he'd expected to see when he'd gotten the call, was Al's car wrapped around a tree. There seemed to be no reason for the crash—no marks to show he'd swerved and no other vehicles—it looked like he'd driven straight into the tree. No one should die like that—lost in such a despairing sea of depression they'd felt there was no other way out.

When the coroner's report came in, it was revealed that although the ute had reeked of alcohol, no trace had been found in Al's bloodstream. Mrs Schumacher, his invalid mother, and Daisy, his younger sister, had been devastated.

The day of Al's funeral, Cole had vowed to do something, anything, to raise awareness of the precarious state of rural mental health and had come up with a plan of action. Now, thanks to Mindalby Cotton Company's funds being frozen, he'd have to put his plans on hold.

"Daddy!" squealed Summer.

Shaking off his sombre mood, he made his way over to the table and drew out a wooden chair. "Hi, honey."

"What took you so long?" Summer wriggled closer on her chair until she could lean into his side.

He wrapped an arm around her small shoulders, breathing in the fresh strawberry scent of her shampoo, his heart swelling at the feel of his precious daughter so close.

His son, Toby, drawled, "It's been like five minutes. You really are a baby."

"I'm not a baby." Summer stuck her tongue out at her older brother who countered by chanting, "Baby, baby, baby."

"Okay, you two. Enough," he said as his parents joined them.

Lesley hurried to sink into the chair on his other side.

Cole sighed. "Lesley, this is my grandfather, Jasper Mitchell."

"Charmed." Lesley giggled and stuck out her hand. "How wonderful to finally meet your family." Her leg pressed against his.

Feeling a bit like a cornered rabbit, he leaned as far away as possible. Across the table, his grandfather's twinkling blue eyes met his. *You're enjoying this, you old rascal.*

A hand clapped him on his shoulder and a familiar voice boomed in his ear. "Cole. How wonderful to see you again."

Relief washing over him like he'd been facing a firing squad—of one—he smiled at Obie Bernstein. His eyes slid past to search for and find Sasha. His pulse roared into overdrive when their gazes met and her lovely pink lips deepened into a tiny smile. "Why don't you join us?"

"Don't mind if we do. Hoi, Cuddlepie! Grab your chair and come on over." Obie gestured madly.

"Have my seat." Gently dislodging his daughter from his side, Cole stood and waved for Obie to take his chair. Inwardly gleeful that he'd managed to put a buffer between himself and Lesley, he took the seat next to his grandfather.

His heart could have sung a song that reached the stars when Sasha pulled up a chair beside him. He peeked a sideways glance, absorbing how the gum-leaf green, woven dress with its long sleeves and high neck moulded her curvy figure. Her golden-brown hair hung loose to her shoulders and he suddenly wanted to feel its coolness brushing over his skin. She looked fresh, sophisticated and sexy as hell.

He shifted a little in his chair, wishing she'd lean her leg against his, and knew if she did, he wouldn't move away.

I've got it bad. Maybe I should ask her out to dinner. Maybe on further acquaintance, this dumb attraction will fade and I can forget about her.

At the opposite end of the table, his mother stared from one woman to the other as if she couldn't believe her eyes, then whispered something to his father.

Smothering his grin (it would never do for his mum to think he was amused by her not-so-covert interest in his love life or lack thereof), Cole introduced everyone, his shoulder muscles loosening as he began to relax. The evening was shaping up very nicely indeed with a tantalising invitation for him to mull over.

"Sasha Bernstein. The woman we all want to talk to." Lesley picked up a fork and rapped the side of her empty wine glass, garnering everyone's attention. "You all should hear what I found out today. Funds have disappeared. Mindalby Cotton Company has no money."

Her voice grew louder, more forceful with each word she spoke until it ricocheted off the walls like a spray of machine-gun bullets.

"This woman has to be involved. Not only is she responsible for paying the bills and us, but her uncle is a thief who is doing time for embezzlement!"

7

Later, Sasha swore she felt the impact of every person's eyes stabbing into her with the sharpness of knives.

Somehow, she kept a polite smile pinned to her lips and did her best to field the avid glances of Cole and his family. How on earth had Lesley ferreted out the information about her uncle? Had she recognised Obie then made the connection? As far as Sasha was aware, her father had never been contacted for an interview during the furore of Uncle Isaac's trial.

Her dad cleared his throat. "Well, there's no secrecy about Isaac. The poor blighter was headline news until the press found someone else to hound."

"It must be very hard for your family," murmured Mrs Mitchell, sending Sasha a sympathetic smile.

"Personally, I fail to see the connection, Lesley,

between Sasha's family and Mindalby Cotton." Cole set his glass down with a thud.

Lesley lifted her plucked eyebrows so high they disappeared beneath her fall of hair. "Hey, I'm doing my civic duty here."

"Yeah, right," Cole growled.

Apparently figuring she'd pushed him too far, Lesley pouted, folded her arms over her thin chest and slumped into the back of her chair.

Cole's father shot Sasha a quick glance before turning to Obie. "Do you play golf? I'm always on the lookout for a fellow enthusiast."

"Love it." Obie beamed around the table. "I've got my golf clubs in the back of my car, waiting for the opportunity. I had special protective covers made; they've all got my Cuddlepie's picture on them when she was two years old. Bald as a badger she was; didn't have a hair on her head until she was three."

Cole hurriedly turned his crack of laughter into a cough.

When everyone looked at Sasha's hair, heat flooded her face. *Way to go, Dad.*

"How about a week today?" Roger Mitchell said. "I've got an art exhibition in Sydney this weekend."

His wife frowned. "Are you still going, Rog? I would have thought after today's events, you would cancel."

"I can't see that my being here will help. Besides, aren't you going ahead with your lawn bowls tournament in Bourke?"

"It's the semi-finals."

"I rest my case."

"Honestly, Roger, you're impossible." Maisy glared at her husband who merely grinned. "This isn't a competition."

Roger winked across the table at Sasha. "Always is with Maise. She's the most competitive person I've ever met. But I love her anyway." He blew his wife a kiss.

"See what I have to put up with?" Maisy said, but her eyes glowed and there was a pretty flush to her cheeks. "What about you, Sasha? Are you married? And you, Lesley? Is there a significant other in your life?"

Before Sasha could open her mouth to respond, Lesley beat her to it.

All fluttering eyelashes, Lesley said, "Not yet, Maisy, but I have hopes." She sent a sidelong glance in Cole's direction.

Cole hid behind his beer glass, while his parents nudged each other and his grandfather tilted his head back and laughed. His daughter sat, wide-eyed, her eyes going from face to face while his son frowned and stared at Lesley.

The close bond Cole's family shared with each other was evident in their good-natured teasing, although Sasha fully sympathised with Cole over his not-so-subtle mother. It was obvious the lady would love nothing more than to see her son in a committed relationship and was keen to do whatever it took to foist suitable women on him.

How did Cole feel about Lesley? Was he interested in her? She certainly was attractive and appeared to be hell-bent on angling her way into Cole's family.

She snuck a peek at the other woman who had begun to question Mrs Mitchell about life in Mindalby. Maisy detailed an animated account of her parents and the huge cattle station they had once owned that sounded quite fascinating. Sasha wouldn't mind learning more about Cole's forebears and their history.

Pleating the napkin between her fingers, she frowned. What did Cole and his family really think about her uncle being in jail for embezzlement? Was it politeness that had led his father to divert the conversation away from the subject? A desire not to cause a scene? Or had they done so because they wanted to believe she wasn't involved in the mill closing?

Her skin prickled and she glanced over to find Cole's dark eyes examining her face. He smiled but she detected a faint reserve in his expression.

Her palms turned clammy.

He harboured doubts about her—it was etched in the tension sharpening the contours of his jaw.

The knowledge shouldn't hurt. She had only just met the man. And yet, disappointment was a heavy kick to her heart.

Summer slipped from her seat and trotted around the table to stand between her father and Sasha. "Do you like dollies?"

"I used to," she said promptly, happy to discuss

anything that would take her mind off her confused emotions. "My favourite doll was called Lily and had long, dark-brown hair."

"Really!" Eyes round with surprise, Summer clapped her hands. "Like my hair?"

"Yes, I guess her hair was a bit like yours." She smiled.

"Your daddy said you were bald." The tone was accusing.

Her lips quivered. "True, a long time ago. But I've got hair now."

"Hmmm." Summer cautiously lifted a strand of Sasha's hair and leaned closer as if to test it was real.

"Dad says you ride a pushbike to work," Toby said. "You should get a horse instead."

Sasha's fingers dug into her sweaty palms. *Please don't ask why I haven't got a car.* "I probably won't be here long enough and I don't know how to ride a horse."

"Seriously? Dad could teach you."

"She can ride Peanut," said Summer. "Daddy, when can she come and ride my pony?"

Toby snorted. "She needs a proper horse, not a horse for babies."

"Toby," warned Cole.

His son grinned while Summer's angelic countenance turned red and her mouth screwed up, giving the impression that the next second could well be tantrum time.

Sasha said quickly, "Peanut is a great name. Did you choose it, Summer?"

The little girl turned a suspicious gaze onto her and took a moment to answer; all the while her lovely blue eyes so like her father's scrutinised Sasha's face. "Poppy did, 'cause he said she was a little peanut when she was born."

She's a real little minx, this one. And obviously intelligent. Cole is going to have his hands full keeping up with her. Hiding her smile, she asked Cole's grandfather, "Did you breed Peanut, Mr Mitchell?"

He smiled fondly as Summer skipped to his side and leaned against his chair. "Call me Jasper, please. Not myself, but Cole's wife Denise was horse-mad. We've got five quarter horses on the farm and three ponies, Peanut being the last foal we bred. Three of our horses are getting quite old now."

Wife. But Cole said he was single—did that mean he was divorced? What had she been like? Why had she left such a gorgeous man and two cute kids? The questions Sasha so badly wanted to ask buzzed in her head like bees but she swallowed the words.

Keep your distance.

Don't get involved.

Her father piped up about how he'd never ridden a horse, before going into lengthy detail about the time they rode camels along the old Silk Road. Toby hung on his words, awe etched into his face as he listened.

The Mitchells joined in the conversation, adding in their own travelling experiences in Europe and the US.

Lesley sat quietly, her hands interlocked and resting on the table. Her gaze darted from face to face like she was memorising everyone's expressions.

Cole shifted closer to Sasha.

And Sasha promptly forgot about everyone else at the table. She and Cole could have been the only people left on the planet. All she could sense was his proximity. She could feel his body heat drawing her in. Her mouth went dry. When she looked up he caught her glance, holding it with those amazing blue eyes of his. The corners of his mouth curved just a little, causing thrilling tingles to course through her body.

He might have reservations about her actions, but there was no denying the powerful physical attraction surging between them. There was sufficient heat blazing in his eyes for her to combust at any second. His jaw worked, like he was battling inner turmoil.

Wanting to launch herself into his arms and beg him to understand, she wrenched her gaze aside.

Lesley was busy texting on her mobile, a smirk on her face. A second later, Lesley popped her mobile into her handbag. "Here's our food. Thank heavens because I'm starving." Then she laughed.

THE SHATTERING of glass roused Sasha from an uneasy sleep. Hand to her throat, she stiffened. Her heart slammed against her ribs with every beat. Her fingers eased under her pillow, closing over the knife she kept hidden there.

A man's voice yelled a string of profanity, then shouted, "Where's our money, bitch? You'll soon get yours!"

Another man laughed. Footsteps pounded on asphalt, followed by the slamming of car doors. An engine revved then roared off into the night.

Gingerly she pushed herself upright, the weapon clenched in her right hand, her body tense, poised to strike at the first indication of danger. Her bedroom was at the back of the old house, away from the street, and only the weak light from the moon illuminated her surroundings. Holding her breath, she listened for any unfamiliar sounds that meant she was no longer alone.

But apart from the ticking of the clock in the hall and her own breathing, she heard nothing. Finally satisfied, she shoved her doona aside and slipped from the bed to pad over to the window. Ensuring she stood side-on, she pressed against the wall while inching aside the heavy curtain to peer out into the night. Nothing moved in the small backyard.

Heart pounding, she snatched up the small torch lying on top of the chest of drawers and with the help of its bright LED light made her way to the living room where she paused in the doorway. Her gaze searched for intruders as she flicked the torch beam around the room. Everything was normal.

She was alone.

Her pulse eased its frantic pace.

Releasing her pent-up breath, she went to step further into the room when she saw the broken glass scattered over the carpet below the front window.

And a brick.

"Idiots," she muttered crossly and snapped on the light before flicking off her torch. She checked the road outside but found no sign of anyone loitering. Not that she'd expected to after hearing the car take off. After confirming all the windows were locked and the front and rear doors were bolted shut, she took photos of the damage with her mobile then set about clearing up the mess.

She was lucky she'd decided to lock her moped in the rear shed, rather than leaving it on the front porch. It could have been damaged. Apart from her bike, it was her only means of transport.

Finished, she sank into an armchair, aware her knees were shaking. She phoned the local police station and reported the vandalism, adding how she was certain she'd recognised one voice: Cody Nossiter. The constable she spoke to yawned and requested her to come first thing in the morning to make a statement.

She hung up, drained from the adrenaline rush and more than a little annoyed. A headache throbbed behind her forehead and she pressed her fingers to the offending area. Since the accident, she often suffered from insomnia and after this brick episode, she knew she'd be wasting her time trying to sleep. Instead, she pulled socks over her bare feet and snuggled into a thick dressing gown before returning to her bedroom.

She closed the door to keep out some of the cold night air wafting in through the broken front window despite the plastic bag she'd taped to the glass. Then she settled on the bed with her laptop and a notebook and pen. Guided by the soft glow of her bedside lamp, she fired up her computer and googled employee entitlements. May as well be productive, she thought after checking the opening time of the glass repair company. She emailed Asher who worked at the real estate office, to advise her of the situation and request her to arrange authorisation for a window repairer to come over as soon as possible.

Her thoughts wandered even as she browsed the internet, returning to the evening before and dwelling with a sense of wonder over how much she'd enjoyed being in Cole's company, that of his family and his two utterly charming children.

She didn't know quite what to make of that realisation. Interacting with kids on a personal level was usually not her thing.

Toby had confided to her his love for electronics and how he pulled apart old computers and phones to see how they worked, while Summer had chatted about her dog's escapades in the vegetable garden.

Irritated at how easily her mind kept returning to Cole and co, Sasha scowled at the screen. It hadn't been all flowers and smiles. It was obvious that Lesley's nasty announcement had chiselled doubts in Cole's mind.

Her gaze darted to her mobile. Should she explain? But if she did, how much should she confide? Would he understand her passionate need to exonerate her unworldly uncle? And how far she would go to protect those she loved?

Cole had already indicated he had little time for Don Carter and obviously despised the man for his extramarital affairs.

But she had never went that far. She would have drawn the line … Wouldn't she?

Every second of every day, people were forced to take ruthless actions in order to survive.

Take Mindalby. The people here would soon be desperate to hang onto the lives they'd worked so hard to attain.

Lesley's declaration was no doubt responsible for the louts damaging her window. Every patron in the pub's bistro must have heard her strident voice and by now the news would have spread throughout the entire town.

Who knew what would follow in the days to come?

But how had the woman made the connection? Had her dad's arrival in town been the catalyst? She didn't strike Sasha as that intuitive, so where did that leave her?

She had nothing. Nothing to help Uncle Isaac. Nothing on how Lesley knew she was his niece. Maybe coming here had been a huge waste of time.

Shaken, her headache gained force as she returned to her research.

A couple of hours later, she yawned and stretched, rubbing her heavy eyes. Certain that she'd now be able to sleep, she shut down her computer and pushed aside her notes. Dragging the doona up over her shoulders, she closed her eyes and allowed Morpheus to drag her under until her alarm sounded.

After an hour's yoga workout, which always helped to lower her anxiety levels, she showered and consumed a breakfast of fresh fruit and rolled oats. Then Sasha found Warren's phone number in the contact details of the company's website and phoned.

He took a while to pick up, his greeting brusque.

"Warren, it's Sasha Bernstein here."

"What's up?"

"I've found the details of a couple of sites that may be helpful to the workers. There's government assistance available but you have to meet certain criteria and there's a waiting period."

"Huh, typical."

Willing herself to remain patient, she ploughed on. "If anyone needs help applying, I can be at the commu-nity centre for a few hours this afternoon. The wi-fi connection is fairly reliable so we can make applications online without too much trouble."

"Thanks. I'll let my boys know." Whether they were male or female Warren always referred to the workers as his *'boys'*. He paused then said almost reluctantly, "You said a couple of sites."

"Yes, I've found a lawyer who specialises in fighting for workers' rights in similar situations. Actually, I've got the details of more than one and thought I could have this info printed out into leaflets that you might like to pass on."

"Sounds to me like you trust these nobs as little as I do. Being an accountant and all, I suppose you already know we're going to get stuff-all on the money side of things."

"Warren, I am *not* an accountant. I'm actually a nurse." Sasha tapped her nails on the countertop. Unbelievable. "This is totally new to me."

"Whatever. I appreciate your help." He rang off.

Shaking her head, Sasha paced to the kitchen window and looked out into the garden. The grey overcast sky seemed to mirror the gloomy state of her mind. It was obvious the union rep entertained reservations about her motives; not to mention her honesty.

She drummed her fingers on the window sill fighting her growing dread at facing the people of Mindalby. At seeing the accusation and disappointment in their faces before they turned away from her.

This is how Uncle Isaac must have felt: alone, defence-less, desperately searching for a way out of his nightmare.

She could only imagine how depressed he must be. She made a mental note to send him a care package and a long letter of her 'doings'—well, a carefully constructed letter.

Outside the wind rustled through the branches of the mulga trees, sending the leaves shivering and whip-ping a few off the spindly branches to twirl through the air. The day looked bleak. Probably almost as cold as it was inside her house. She hoped the repairman wouldn't take too long to fix the window.

A quick glance at her mobile showed eight-thirty. Was it still too early to phone Cole Mitchell? The last thing she wanted to appear was overly eager for contact. *I'm being helpful. That's all. Yeah right; like you can't wait to hear those gravelly tones of his again.*

She paced through the small flat, peered through the broken window, paced back to her bedroom and decided she'd take her laptop with her. Gloves, helmet, parka; all ready and laid out on the bed.

Snakes alive. What could it hurt to phone him?

Before she could second-guess herself, she found the text she'd sent yesterday and rang his number.

8

He picked up on the sixth ring, just as she was about to hang up. "Cole here."

She quivered, her tummy flipping over as his voice rumbled through her. Clearing her throat delicately, she said, "Um, it's Sasha."

"Hey, how you doing?"

The warmth in his tones heated her cheeks. "Ah, good thanks. I had a spot of bother during the night when some nutter decided to throw a brick through my window."

"No way! Are you alright?" He sounded concerned.

Nothing to indicate he doubted her—just genuine—and probably just neighbourly—concern.

"Oh, yes, I'm fine apart from some broken glass." She squeezed her eyes shut, exasperated at how breathless she sounded and tried for cool. "I hope I haven't caught you at a bad time. I've done some research and thought you might like to know what I've discovered."

"That was kind of you. Are you sure you're okay? I can come over once I've got the fellows sorted. We're harvesting the south field today and tomorrow. I can disappear for an hour or two."

Her toes curled as her tummy lurched. Play it cool. "It's fine, thank you. The real estate agent will organise the repair. So you're still going ahead with harvesting?"

"Have to otherwise we'll lose our crop and won't have the fields ready for the next planting. Plus, I can't miss my slot with the harvester, Silvano. These blokes bring themselves and their equipment all the way down from Queensland. As a rule, they're totally booked out while they're here then they move onto the next cotton region. But this year the weather wasn't on our side, so Mindalby is last on their list. I know Silvano is eager to get back home. Unless we can pay him double, he wants out of here on the due date."

"Oh, I didn't realise."

She squirmed inwardly. Anything to do with farming was completely foreign to her. She'd grown up in the city, where the only wildlife she saw were a few sparrows and pigeons. Both her parents were well-off. Sasha had never known what it was like to worry about how to pay the rent or live week to week.

"Why would you?" His voice was easy, no condemnation or derision at her lack of knowledge. "The main thing is you weren't hurt. Did you report it to the cops?"

"Yes. I'm supposed to go in this morning and sign a statement. I doubt it'll get anywhere though as the constable didn't indicate he'd come over and look. Plus, I never saw who it was although I think I recognised Cody's voice."

"I'm not surprised. The bloke's riding for trouble."

"What I wanted to tell you, well actually, I just thought I'd run this past you. Apparently when a company goes into voluntary administration it doesn't always mean they shut up shop and stop trading."

"Yeah? Then what happened here?"

"I don't know but I suspect, and mind you, this is only coming from what I found on the web last night, is that there isn't any money. I think your friend Lesley is right. The business is insolvent which makes sense, otherwise why would they close the gates?"

Cole fell silent for a few seconds.

Sasha couldn't help wondering whether he was considering Lesley's accusation and whether there was any truth in the Chinese whispers game the woman had started.

"Bloody hell. Looks like we may as well kiss our wages goodbye."

Her fingers trembled. So he had no intention of asking her outright. Maybe he preferred not to know whether she was involved. "Is this ... will this mean a lot of problems for you financially?"

"We'll take a hit," Cole admitted. "But I've got a little bit of my inheritance left from my mum's father put aside. I did have other plans for it but it looks like I'll have to use it to pay our workers and this month's overdraft."

"I'm sorry, Cole."

"Things will be tight but if I can still meet my contracted commitments for this year's cotton harvest, we shouldn't get too far in the red."

She frowned. "You need to get your cotton out of the yard as soon as possible."

"Yeah. You got it in one."

"There's a few solicitors' firms I've found – one of them may be able to help expedite matters." She rattled off their details. "I really recommend you seek legal advice as soon as possible."

"Mmm, we've got a good solicitor already in town. Penny Fordham and her firm have handled our business for years. I'm not sure I'd want to go with an outsider."

"Well, that's up to you. I just thought I'd pass it on."

"Listen, about what Lesley said last night ..."

There it was. How much should she reveal? As little as possible, her innately cautious-self warned. She didn't know this man. For all she knew, he could be best mates with Don Carter. Swallowing over her constricted throat, she forced out the hoarse words. "She was right. My uncle is in prison but he's innocent."

"Isn't that what they all say?" He laughed but the sound rang hollow. When she remained silent, he ended up muttering, "I'm sorry, that was insensitive of me. I admit I don't know anything about his case."

"I bet the entire town knows by now," she said bitterly.

"Probably," Cole admitted. "Rumours spread fast in small communities and unfortunately can get out of hand. My mother has a lot of pull with the older residents. I'll see what we can do to quash any wild speculation."

"Thanks, Cole. I appreciate that."

"This town doesn't need any more fuel when its already sitting on a powder keg."

So much for feeling warm and fuzzy. That was telling her exactly where she stood in his eyes. He was looking out for his town. Not for her. In the background, she heard someone call his name and decided to wind the conversation up. "If I hear anything else about the closure, I'll let you know. Have a good one."

She rang off before he had time to utter another word and tossed the phone onto her bed where she glared at it for several minutes. She felt dissatisfied but wasn't sure why; only that the call left her feeling restless.

And, snakes alive, why was she crying?

Snatching a tissue from the box, she blew her nose. Was it because he hadn't pressed her for details? But then if he had, would she have opened up to him, or brushed him off? Maybe he hadn't asked because he just wasn't that interested in her life or her. Maybe that was what was really upsetting her.

She didn't need this kind of complication in her life. Her chin lifted. A bike ride was just the ticket to warm her blood and shed these silly ideas where a certain cotton farmer was concerned. She had a job to do and, regardless of the consequences to herself, she intended to carry through. The thought of an Italian coffee and the lure of a sweet pastry from the bakery helped galvanise her into action.

Ten minutes later she was pedalling down the road. This time of the morning the small town began to come alive. Kids with laden backpacks were jostling each other as they walked in small groups on their way to school. Cars drove along the road. Two young mums jogged past laughing, pushing their babies snug inside prams. An elderly couple walked hand-in-hand on the opposite footpath, a fat dachshund panting and straining at the leash.

For some odd reason, she found the sights soothing, an affirmation of the continuation of the cycle of everyday life.

Especially since, so far, no one turned and pointed in her direction.

No Chinese whispers then.

She rode past the high school and turned right onto Louth Road, preferring to take a back street rather than the main thoroughfare. When she reached Trappers Lane, she turned left and pedalled along the narrow strip of tar past a carpark and the back of the RSL club until she came to the next intersection. On the other side of Burton Park Road, the street turned into Markers Lane. After ensuring the road was clear, she crossed over to the other side and stopped outside the bakery. The rich scent of brewing coffee, freshly baked bread, hot sausage rolls and meat pies wafted out to tempt her. Despite having eaten, her stomach rumbled.

Being the sole customer, she was immediately served by Nan Henderson who ran the shop with her foster daughter. Today, Nan appeared drawn, her face pale despite her makeup and pink lipstick. There were dark smudges under her eyes as if she hadn't slept well. She pushed at her softly curling, short white hair with a trembling, lined hand marred by age spots. Using a pair of small tongs, Nan slipped a chocolate croissant into a brown paper bag.

"You work at the factory, don't you?" She popped the bag on the counter and stepped aside to work the espresso machine.

"Yes."

"My daughter's husband works there too. Do you know when he'll be paid?"

Biting back her sigh, Sasha said, "No, I'm sorry—but there is government assistance available if you meet the criteria. I'll give you the details. There's a waiting period though."

Nan frowned. "Maybe this is all some kind of mistake. Maybe things will be back to normal tomorrow."

"I guess that's possible. If I hear anything, I'll let you know." She fished out her notebook and pen from her satchel. Tearing out a sheet of paper, she explained quickly about possible government assistance and wrote down the details of the site. She pushed the slip across the counter and added, "Hopefully, it'll all be sorted soon."

"Thank you for this, I'll pass it onto Sharlene." Nan placed the disposable cup on the counter. "Seven-fifty, please."

Sasha handed over the correct change and left the warmth of the shop. Once outside, she pushed the pastry into her satchel, having lost her appetite, and took a sip of the hot coffee. Next to the bakery was an empty shop and alongside that a hardware store. A ute roared down the road and swung into a vacant parking spot. She glared when Cody Nossiter climbed out of the car.

Her thoughts full of the damage to her window, Sasha left her bike outside the bakery, and strode quickly along the pavement. She fetched up beside Cody just as he was hitching up jeans over his skinny arse and about to step inside the hardware store.

She planted herself in front of him. "I know it was you last night. I've reported your stupidity to the police."

" 'Ere, what's off with you?" Cody flicked a dismissive glance up and down her body.

"My window. A brick. Last night. Remember?"

He tipped back his head and laughed, like she was a world-class comedian. "Prove it."

A car door slammed. "What's going on, Cody?" growled an older man with greying black hair and a pronounced beer belly. He advanced, crumpling a beer can in one fist.

Cody smirked. "It's that bitch accountant, Ham."

"The one who refuses to pay our wages." The bloke, Ham—which Sasha suspected was short for something else—belched a fetid stream of beer fumes then spat onto to the ground. Right beside her feet.

She stood her ground even as her eyes watered. "You're mistaken. I don't have anything to do with the company's problems."

"Not what I heard." Ham lumbered closer, his blood-shot eyes glazed, a bitter twist to his mouth. "I heard you made damn sure you got your money's worth out of the joint."

Cody jumped from foot to foot, crowing with delight. "Yeah, you show her Hamish. Show her what we're talking about."

Sasha's heart leapt into her mouth.

The older bloke raised his fist.

Did he seriously intend to hit her? She danced backwards.

He lurched forward and chucked the beer can.

She ducked. The bloke was spun sideways and shoved hard by a man in a purple tracksuit. "Dad!"

"You okay, Cuddlepie?" Her father had his fists raised in a boxer's stance and stood directly in front of her.

The drunk reeled on his feet, his eyes almost bugging from his head.

"I'm fine, Dad. Thanks." Drawing a shuddering breath, she indicated the can lying on the pavement. "He missed."

"Doesn't matter. He intended to hurt you and I'm going to report him." Her father pulled out his mobile one-handed, keeping his right hand fisted a couple of inches from Hamish's nose.

"Come on, mate. It was an accident," blustered Hamish, all aggression blanked from his face. He staggered backwards, tangling his feet together and went down on his knees, howling as he hit the concrete. "Oi! Me ankle!"

"Assaulting a woman with a can and threatening her is no accident," snapped Obie. "I'm calling the police."

Hamish stared in a bleary fashion up at Obie as if he had no idea where he was or what was happening.

"No need, we're leaving." A heavy scowl on his face, Cody stepped out from where he'd been lurking near the entrance of the building. Well out of any firing line. He helped the older man to his feet, all but shoving him into the car. After giving Sasha and Obie the finger, Cody rushed around to the driver's side. He yanked open the door and thirty seconds later was screeching down the road.

"What a charmer." Her father pocketed his mobile and turned around to eye her critically. "I still intend to make a complaint, baby-cake. That fellow is a drunken bully."

"Then let's walk around to the police station together. I need to see them anyway." She gave a brief account of the incident during the night, omitting how the single act had left her shaken and uneasy. They reached where she'd left her bike and she released his arm.

"I don't like how all this is unfolding, Sasha. I want you to go back to Sydney."

"To Mum's place? Dad, I haven't lived there since I left university." Her heart sank.

"Don't play semantics with me. You know full well your mother keeps a bedroom in her house ready for you. No, if this problem with the mill isn't resolved soon, the town could ignite like dynamite. It isn't safe for you here."

Hoping to deflect him, she quipped, "Like the Middle East was safe?"

"Don't remind me."

When her father compressed his lips, she knew he was seriously upset. "Dad, I'm fine and I promise I'll be careful. I have you here now to watch my back." She reached over and kissed his cheek.

"Baby-cake." He sniffed. "You can't blame me for worrying. We came too close to losing you, Sasha."

"I know, Dad." She held his gaze. "Nursing is my life, Dad. I'm not changing my mind about joining a new team as soon as I'm cleared as mentally fit. You and Mum need to accept my decision. But I'm not walking away from here either. Not until I'm one hundred per cent certain there's nothing I can do to clear Uncle Isaac."

"You've always known your own mind."

"Both you and Mum taught me to follow my heart and to pay forward some of the blessings of my life." She smiled fondly at him.

"I must have had rocks in my head," her father grumbled.

"No, you're just an awesome dad."

They crossed the road to the police station in silence, Sasha pushing her bike, her father strolling along, hands in his trouser pockets and studying the ground. He was plotting something.

"There's only one thing for it," her father finally said in a thoughtful tone. "I'll arrange for someone else to keep an eye on you when I can't be around, especially at night. That Cole fellow is the perfect candidate. You got his number, Cuddlepie?"

9

Two hours later, Sasha's cheeks still burned every time she recalled her father's declaration. And—she had to be honest—that was often. The notion of Cole protecting her during the night certainly had her feeling hot and tingly and sending her imagination into orbit.

One day, I'll ... really I don't know what I'll do! Sasha grumbled to herself as she rode her bike towards Don Carter's house.

Damn her father for voicing the fantasy she'd been doing her best to block. It was a go-nowhere situation anyway—what with her intention to resume her career elsewhere and his doubts over her integrity. Plus, for all she knew he may not be officially divorced. They could be separated—working out their differences—having a break ...

She shook her head. She needed to concentrate on Uncle Isaac and how to help him. Not waste her time daydreaming over gorgeous blue eyes, the way Cole's lips curved when he smiled, the shivers that trembled over her skin at the sound of his voice and how much she wanted to glide her hands over those magnificent wide shoulders of his.

Sasha! Focus, woman.

She passed Mindalby Memorial Park and the entrance to the golf club on her right then slowed her frantic pedalling. The last thing she wanted to do was front her employer looking all flustered and out of breath. When she reached the front drive, she stopped and pushed her kickstand down. Removing her helmet, she took a few minutes to comb her flattened hair and straighten her clothes. She added a slick of tangerine lipstick to her mouth then decided she was as ready as she'd ever be.

Pushing her bike, Sasha walked down the stencilled drive to the front of the two-storey house. The number of bare glass windows fronting the drive made Sasha think of a fish bowl. The building was certainly large enough to house a family of eight but to Sasha's knowledge only Don, his second wife Yasmin and their housekeeper lived there. The chunky, rough-looking bricks and the balconies with their wrought-iron balustrades gave the impression of age and history. But it was apparent to Sasha, peering in through the glass, that the house was architect designed, with a mixed décor of both antique and modern furniture and built within the last ten years.

A middle-aged black-haired woman of Hispanic descent answered the door and ushered Sasha inside. She led the way along a wide, granite-tiled hallway. Leafy plants in urn-shaped terracotta pots lined the walls. She stopped outside a room on the left, knocked, then after giving Sasha a smile, indicated she should enter.

The study was of an impressive size with plush carpet underfoot and a stone fireplace against one wall. Bookshelves lined the walls along with cabinets displaying rows of trophies. On one wall hung a huge portrait of a racehorse.

Sasha crossed the room and, without waiting to be asked, took the armchair facing the desk where Don Carter was seated, his nose buried amongst a massive sheaf of papers.

"Where the devil is it?" he muttered, not lifting his head. He turned a page over and frowned. "What are you doing here?"

"I know why you called in a voluntary administrator," she declared and paused. *Come on. Come on. Look at me. And then I might be able to tell if you're lying.*

"What? What's that?" He glanced up.

She snatched his gaze and held it. "You've got no money left to pay the bills."

A rich flush spread over his face. The veins in his neck above his white polo collar bulged alarmingly. "What the devil … Sash, I can't have you waltzing about sprouting such rubbish."

"It's not rubbish, is it, Don? Tell me the truth," she urged.

"Or you'll what?" He gave a harsh laugh. "It doesn't make a difference now anyway."

"Rubbish." She tamped down her rising outrage.

"The factory workers deserve to be paid as do the contractors and local suppliers. If there'd been money left in the till, you would never have ordered the business to shut down. Is that what you're hiding?"

Where a moment ago his face had been red, now it blanched of all colour. His jaw sagged before he snapped it shut. "What the devil are you implying?"

"I'm thinking some kind of misappropriation of funds. You know, I always wondered why you gave me the job. There must have been more qualified applicants yet you offered it to me, someone with limited accounts experience. And I'm an outsider. The perfect dupe."

Carter dropped the papers and leaned back in his chair. "You think you have all the answers. You don't. That Felicity woman wants to see you. Today. Make sure you turn up or she might think you're the one with something to hide."

She bit her tongue on the threats she wanted to

throw at him. Didn't he have a conscience? Didn't he care that people were hurting? The huge fallout the business closure would have on his workers, his friends, his neighbours—the whole damn town?

She swept a hand out indicating the luxurious furnishings. "You could make some payments from your personal assets. At least, meet the workers' past fortnight's wages."

He laughed. "This is business, Sash. Get used to it and get out of my house." He pointed to the door.

Feeling she'd made a right mess of things, she pushed to her feet at the same moment the door opened.

"Have you seen my iPhone, darling?" came a cool feminine voice.

Rising to her feet, Sasha turned, forcing a smile. "Hello, Mrs Carter." She held out her hand and took stock of the other woman.

Two or so years younger than herself—although Sasha suspected the woman would prefer to be burned at the stake than admit it—Yasmin Carter stood tall and willowy slim with white-blonde hair beautifully cut to frame her slightly angular face. Dressed in a lacy candy-pink top that clung to breasts way too big for her slender frame, and a cream linen skirt falling to her knees, she posed on a pair of blood-red stilettoes.

Yasmin extended a hand as limp as a dead fish and murmured a disinterested "Charmed" but her eyes had hardened to snake-like flatness as she gave Sasha the once-over. Yasmin switched her gaze to her husband. "Don? Did you hear what I said?"

"Not now, Yas. Can't you see I'm busy?"

A tiny wrinkle appeared on Yasmin's too-smooth brow, as if she was trying to frown but couldn't pull it off.

"I wouldn't be here if it wasn't important." Her tone was glacial and remained so when she flicked a disdainful glance in Sasha's direction. "I believe you were leaving."

There was no point in staying any longer. Sasha doubted she'd get anything out of Don who obviously didn't give a toss about his workers.

No one spoke as she walked out and along the hall-way. A furtive glance around the foyer revealed no sign of the housekeeper. Holding her breath, she retraced her steps closer to the study and pressed herself against the wall, listening.

"My phone …"

"Forget your bloody phone."

"Don. I need that phone. It has all my … well, my contacts. Did you take it with you yesterday when you went to the mill?"

"How the hell would I know? Maybe I picked it up by mistake. Who cares? This is your fault, you stupid cow. I should never have listened to you. Now I'll have SafeWork down on me, bleating about unsafe conditions. If they find any fault whatsoever, I'll be more than bloody fined."

"Don't take it out on me. You're the one who wanted to use a gas leak as an excuse. I told you to wait but no, you rushed in without checking with me first. And what was *she* doing here?"

"Some rubbishy sentiment about me forking out to pay the workers."

"I don't believe you. She's snooping around, Don. I don't like it. Why on earth did you employ her in the first place?"

"Hey? How was I to know she's related to that nerd? Her name is all legit 'cause I checked out her references and birth certificate."

"You're such an idiot. You didn't go deep enough. How many times have I told you to triple-check every single fact?"

"Yeah, well, we aren't all like you, babe."

"I don't like this Don. I don't think it's a coincidence that she applied for that job. She suspects us."

"More likely she suspects you. I found her perfectly charming."

"God, you're a fool with nothing but crap for brains."

"And you're a two-timing bitch. Still sniffing around farmer Mitchell? Good luck with that one. He's not that desperate."

"I know you've been playing away. So don't act the betrayed husband with me."

"Damn you, Yasmin."

Something slammed into the wall, shattering like broken china; from elsewhere in the house, a door slammed.

Sasha raced to the front door and down the steps. Not bothering with her helmet, she mounted her bike and headed down the driveway. Her skin prickled.

She looked over her shoulder, her gaze sweeping the expanse of glass until she found Yasmin staring out the window. At her.

Did Yasmin know she'd overheard their conversation?

Heart thumping uncomfortably hard, she continued along the road. When she reached the boundary of the park, she paused to catch her breath. With a screech of brakes and an ominous engine whine, a kombi campervan with a flaking orange paint job pulled up outside the Carters' driveway. Then, trailing petrol fumes, the van travelled towards the house.

After the other night, she'd recognised that brown hair and the narrow face of the driver anywhere: Lesley Thompson. What business could she have with the Carters?

From somewhere in the park, a child shrieked with laughter. Sasha stood still, helmet in hand. Wondering. The penny dropped and her pulse raced with elation.

Yasmin's phone.

A link to her contacts; maybe even her emails.

If Sasha found it, who knew what information the

device held? Maybe something that could exonerate her uncle.

Don had mentioned he may have taken Yasmin's phone by mistake. She must have searched the house for it, otherwise why accuse him? What if he'd dropped the phone at the mill?

What if it was still there?

SASHA CAME across Felicity Robinson entrenched inside one of the small meeting rooms of the community centre, looking as if she was there for the long haul. Surrounded by stacks of binders and ledgers, the woman was hunched over a tablet, ticking off a list on the paper next to it. She looked up with a tight smile when Sasha entered then returned her attention to her work.

Her sidekick Dave, was busy pulling out more folders from archive boxes and placing them on another desk. He sent Sasha a shy glance over the top of his glasses and indicated she should sit.

"Thanks for coming. Sasha, isn't it?" Felicity said, her pen poised mid-air.

"Yes. I'm happy to help in any way I can."

"I'm glad to hear it. I understand you're the accountant for Mindalby Cotton Company."

Sasha gripped the back of the chair and inwardly groaned. "No, I'm not. My duties include data entry and paying what I'm authorised to pay. The accounting side of the business is dealt with by an outside company called Trove Financials Pty Ltd."

The woman pursed her lips and adjusted her glasses over the bridge of her nose. "That's not what I've been led to believe."

Perspiration formed along her spine and she repeated, "Trove Financials. Not me." She indicated the boxes and folders. "Surely, Don told you?"

"Mr Carter did mention that firm but said he only used them for personal business." Eyebrows raised, Felicity laid her hands on the desk.

"Well, he's either lied to you or you've misunderstood. I have no qualifications as an accountant and no access to the company's bank accounts. Any payments I made were done by cheque and only after authorisation by either Don or Trove Financials. And … if you look at my employment history, you will see that I've only been here since the end of January."

"We've already established that fact. You sound on very friendly terms with Donald Carter. How would you define your relationship?"

"Employer and employee." Face hot, she recalled the three coffee meets and the two late-night dinners she'd shared with Don before he'd offered her the job. What if her suspicion was correct? What if he *had* hired her, only to set her up to take the blame? But that kind of forward-thinking didn't fit with her assessment of his character.

Then a terrible thought hit her. Could Yasmin be repeating what had worked so well for her in the past? Setting up a fall guy—her! Head reeling, her legs giving way, Sasha flopped onto the chair, hoping her face didn't reflect her horror.

"Have you had a great deal of contact with Mr Carter? How often did he come to the office?" Felicity asked.

Sasha drew a deep breath, willing herself to remain still beneath that gimlet stare. "We met once or twice in Sydney before I was offered the job. In the months I've been working here, I haven't seen much of him. He rarely came into the office."

"I see. And Mrs Carter?"

"I met her for the first time today."

"You've worked for their company for almost five months and never met her before?"

Sasha firmed her chin, keeping her gaze steady. "That's correct."

"Then why today?"

She shrugged. "I went to Don's house to ask if he'd consider paying this week's wages using his personal funds. His wife entered the study while I was still there."

"I find this all very interesting." Felicity removed her glasses and rubbed her forehead before replacing them.

Over in the corner, papers rustled as Dave turned pages.

"May I call you Sasha?"

She nodded.

"I'm telling you now that what we've discovered so far looks suspicious."

Snakes alive but this woman's stare could bore holes through concrete. Sasha traced her fingers along the zipper line on her satchel then froze when Felicity dropped her gaze for a split second. "How so?"

Felicity's razor-sharp eyes raked Sasha's face. Then she nodded, like she'd come to some inner decision. "We've got reams of paper here but nothing of any real use."

"It's smoke," inserted Dave, coming up for air from bending over a box.

Felicity repeated, "Smoke."

"I don't know what that means," Sasha said slowly.

"I'm going to trust you and insist you keep what I'm going to say confidential," Felicity warned. "It's possible there is more than one set of company accounts. What we've been given isn't worth the paper its printed on."

Felicity tapped her finger against the tablet. "We need to find the true financials and hope that we're retained to finish what we've started. My firm has a good rep, Sasha. We're solid and deliver the best results possible for everyone involved in situations like this. We will not allow the wool to be pulled over our eyes. In circumstances where someone is responsible for a business going under, we do our best to ensure their culpability is brought to light. Is there anything you can tell us? Anything you know or have heard in passing? Especially, since you appear to be on very friendly terms with the major shareholder."

'Very friendly terms ...' Sasha swallowed over her suddenly dry throat, wondering whether it would raise a red flag if she asked for a glass of water. Why were they being so forthcoming? Were they attempting to trap her into an admission of guilt? Hoping their friendly manner would lead her to offer up information? But she didn't know anything! If only the woman would stop staring.

"As I said before, my job consisted more of data entry than anything else." She gestured at the folders and hoped the other woman didn't notice her trembling hand. "I could see if there's anything I don't recognise as having been put through the system." And she might find something that she had overlooked—something that could help her Uncle Isaac. Or documents deliberately planted to incriminate her.

"Good. I hope you don't have any plans over the next few days." Felicity gave a grim smile. "You'll be paid of course. Your hours will be added to whatever is owed to you by the company."

"I'm busy this afternoon." Sasha hesitated, wondering whether she should tell the administrator she intended to spend a few hours helping fellow employees apply for government assistance. But the moment was lost.

"All right. We'll see you here tomorrow at eight-thirty sharp."

Sasha nodded. "Can you tell me when the employees and subbies are likely to be paid, Ms Robinson?"

"No, it's early days, however what we've discovered isn't good. The company is bust and I recommend anyone who is owed money retains a good lawyer."

10

Grubby and sweaty after a long day harvesting his fields, Cole cast a look at the darkening sky and stretched his back. Time for dinner break. He called to his casual labourers and gestured to Silvano, the guy working the John Deere 7460 cotton stripper. The bloke held his thumb up, indicating he understood and shut down the machine.

Cole clapped Max on the back. "Good day's work."

Max planted his gnarled hands on his spindly hips and eyed the modules of cotton stacked on the small flat-top truck. The harvested cotton would be stored in the shed for now. "What you intend to do with this lot, boss?"

"We're going to take up Tox's offer and ship the lot to Bourke. The gin there is expecting our load late Friday arvo."

"Rightio, boss."

Harry and Chook came ambling over, pulling off their heavy work gloves, big grins wreathing their wrinkled faces.

"Beer time," said Chook, smacking his lips.

"Not tonight, boys, we've still got more work to do afterwards. Let's get cleaned up. Dinner should be on the table." Cole always fed his workers when they put in a twelve-hour stint or over. In his mind, it was only fair, even though he paid good wages. His crew seemed to appreciate it and probably by now expected it, so there was no way he'd stop—no matter how tight money became.

They walked to the homestead where they took turns washing in the outside shower. It was bloody chilly with no hot water. But the scrub-up would make them reasonably clean for the dinner table. A tradition his grandmother had put in place, saying the smell of man-sweat put her off her food.

Cole grinned as he remembered his outspoken gran. Her broad Texan accent had never diminished over the years. She could ride a horse, shoot a snake and work the fields alongside the best of men. She'd been taken from them by a stroke five years ago and Cole knew his grandfather missed her every single day.

His grandparents only had the one child, Cole's father, and he'd never taken to the land. His passion lay with a canvas board and paintbrush. His grandparents had encouraged his father's career choice; but they couldn't hide their joy when Cole developed a love of the land and farming.

He stepped onto the back verandah and, after dumping off his mud-caked workboots onto the old floorboards, pushed open the door leading into the kitchen.

"Daddy!" Feet pattered across the floor as Summer rushed to greet him.

"Hello, princess pea." Smiling, Cole swept his daughter off her feet and up into his arms. He carried her to the table where he tousled his son's hair.

Toby ducked and weaved but shot him a grin. "Yo, Dad. What's up?" He raised his clenched knuckles in the air.

Cole imitated him and their hands smacked together. They gripped each others' fingers then released.

"That's no way to greet your father," admonished Cole's grandfather. He opened the oven door and the succulent scent of roast lamb and vegetables filled the kitchen. "In my day, a man got the respect he deserved from his kids. Why if your gran was here, she'd be sitting you down in that there corner and there'd be no dinner for you until you learned to speak to your elders properly."

"He's cool with it, aren't you, Dad?" Toby said, sounding a tad anxious. Lately, he'd been as hungry as a starving locust and always appeared to be hanging around the pantry scrounging for things to eat.

"All good, son." He sent his son a wink and gestured towards the stove.

Toby scrambled to his feet. "I'll give you a hand, Pop."

"That's my boy. You can take this plate of vegies and come back for the gravy."

Food was soon on the long table and everyone pulled up a chair then dug in. Conversation lagged while the serious business of eating was attended to, leaving Cole free to ponder a certain green-eyed woman. And how much that broadside Lesley had delivered the other night had shaken him.

Hell, it had damn well shocked everyone in the pub. The other diners had craned their necks to stare. Then the whispering had started, accompanied by frowns and suspicious glares. His family had done their best to smooth over the awkward moment but the damage had been done.

Talk about poking a stick at a snake's nest!

Blasted woman. What had Lesley hoped to achieve? He rubbed a hand over the back of his neck then forked a morsel of roast lamb into his mouth. By now, half the town would believe Sasha was involved in Don Carter's shenanigans thanks to Lesley's vindictive innuendoes.

He wished he'd never had coffee with her. Maybe then, Lesley wouldn't have believed their casual encounters could morph into something more serious.

He chased peas around his plate, hating the sliver of

doubt slinking through his mind. What if Sasha *was* involved?

She'd certainly appeared out of nowhere a few months back, sliding right into a job that could well have been filled by a local. And now for her father to turn up as well. What exactly where they doing here?

He'd had the chance to ask earlier today but he'd baulked, telling himself it was none of his business.

He couldn't rid himself of that corrosive suspicion. Because he remembered only too well her reaction to his dumb comment outside Joe's Café when he'd joked she was Carter's latest squeeze.

She'd ducked her head to fiddle with her helmet or was it her bag?

Either way, she'd certainly taken her time in responding. Time enough to compose her expression and think of an answer.

Nothing like fooling himself. If he didn't keep his distance he'd fall hard. Whether she was involved in a relationship with Carter or up to her pretty neck with that jackass's problems, or simply filling in time before she returned to her city life—she wasn't the woman for him.

She didn't belong in Mindalby.

No way was he going to put either himself or his kids through heartache again. Hell, his kids were still struggling with Denise's death five years ago. Toby especially, as he had memories to both sustain and grieve over. But his little girl—she'd lacked a mother's love since she was a year old.

But that attack of vandalism on Sasha's flat worried him. If the bad feelings in town escalated into a mob mentality, there was no saying what could happen. She could be in danger.

"Dad? *Dad!*"

Shaking himself free from his unsettling thoughts, Cole looked at his son who was scowling at him from across the table.

"You haven't forgotten about the school camp, have you? It's three days at Wooraroogan National Park. You said you'd come with us as a supervising parent. Coupla kids' dads pulled out today and one of them was a paramedic." Toby showered his meal with pepper. "Mr Doherty says, if we haven't got a first-aider on board the camp will be cancelled. That totally sucks. He's going to approach the hospital to see if a nurse is interested."

He *had* forgotten. Cole rapidly searched his memory. "Er … that's two weeks away, isn't it?"

Toby rolled his eyes and groaned, "Dad! The camp's a week this Thursday, the ninth of June and we come back on Saturday."

"Right. The ninth. Sure." He nodded while he mentally rearranged his schedule for the next few weeks. This coming Saturday and Sunday were already full, what with Little Athletics, the farm accounts to attend to, going over the harvested field and readying it for the next planting. Then working out how much water they'd need in the coming months if it didn't rain soon and digging another channel from the river to his property. He also vaguely remembered promising the kids a horse ride along the riverbank to visit his Aunt Amber at the Commune.

"Can I come? Can I come? Daddy, I want to go, too!" cried Summer.

"Babies aren't allowed." Toby grinned then shovelled a heaped forkful of roast potatoes into his mouth.

At least his son chewed with his mouth closed.

"I'm sorry, honey, the camp is for the older kids." He sighed as he waited for his daughter to bring the house down, demanding to go. His little girl could twist him around her little finger usually. But there was no way he could include her. He was probably too soft with both of them, but it was hard travelling the parenthood road alone and not over-compensating. If only kids came with instruction manuals.

His little princess burst into loud sobs, tears spilling down her cheeks. She collapsed on folded arms, her forehead on the table and bawled into the checked tablecloth like her heart was breaking.

Sending her hunted glances, Chook, Max and Harry fairly bolted down the remainder of their dinner. His grandfather began to berate Toby for his thoughtless comment. Toby turned surly, shoving his plate across the table before stalking from the room.

Summer wailed louder as their two dogs howled

from the back verandah. Toby's bedroom door slammed and a few seconds later they were blasted with loud heavy-metal music. Gran's prized china chinked and wobbled on the sideboard in unison with the *doof doof* pounding up through the old floorboards.

Only Silvano appeared undisturbed by the uproar. He helped himself to more lamb and poured a sea of gravy over the top. Shrugging, he met Cole's gaze. "I have six daughters. Eldest is seventeen and the rest want to be seventeen."

Six. Cole shuddered then, leaving his dinner to congeal, he set about consoling his little girl. There were days when he wondered whether he'd survive parenthood without losing every hair on his head.

This was one of them.

THE NEXT MORNING, Sasha rose at her usual time: half an hour before dawn.

She'd risen several times throughout the night to pace the flat and examine the windows and doors. There'd been at least three times when she'd shot up in bed, sweating, her heart pounding so hard it was a wonder it didn't explode from her chest. Her psychologist had warned her OCD—obsessive compulsive disorder—could be a residual outcome of her post-traumatic stress syndrome, and lately she'd been unable to control her constant checking of locks.

Having the flat vandalised hadn't helped. Now she had to check the bloody windows as well.

Each time she staggered back to bed, it had proved harder to fall asleep.

She wasn't getting better. She clenched her fists then began to deliberately relax her body, one muscle at a time, willing her mind to block the memory of the cries and pleas of those trapped in the wreckage, as buildings crackled and burned around them.

But the memories bombarded her. *She was unable to move, something heavy across her back where she'd sprawled over her patient. Saad's wide staring eyes beginning to glaze over.*

The blood.

The smoke.

The stench of burning flesh.

Searing pain each time she regained consciousness. The interminable waiting, wondering if they'd be caught in the crossfire which raged on and on.

It had taken four long hours before a contingent of soldiers arrived to evacuate her and the other survivors. Most of her memories of what happened were fragmented: shadowed faces peering at her, voices speaking in another language, the jostling of her body as she was moved. And the blood from Saad's broken body splattered all over her. The waves of pain that kept coming and coming.

All in the past.

After five minutes of deep breathing, her pulse

calmed. Still shaking, she went into the bathroom and washed her clammy face and hands. She avoided the mirror, already knowing what she'd see: pallid skin and dark circles under her red-rimmed, shadowed eyes.

Think of the present, she admonished herself. But that wasn't any better. The slim gap of opportunity was slipping through her grasp. Less than five weeks before the VA hands down her report on the business then she would no longer have a reason to stay.

New images and thoughts ping-ponged inside her head. Cole's crinkly smile, Uncle Isaac, her looming health assessment, Yasmin's iPhone, the missing company accounts, Cole's brilliant blue eyes which seemed to see right through to her soul, Felicity's warning to get a solicitor.

Cole … just Cole.

Despite Sasha hanging around the community centre for most of yesterday, few people had turned up, which made her wonder whether Warren had passed on her message. Perhaps they'd decided on a 'wait and see' tactic, hoping they'd soon return to their jobs.

She'd spent her time by making up flyers with the information about the government's Fair Entitlements Guarantee and the FEG website, and the contact details of the solicitors she'd discovered, in particular a Ms Adrianne Sheldon whose biography for some reason had resonated with Sasha. After tacking up a boldly printed poster and laying the flyers in neat piles on a table, she'd departed.

The memory of Cole's deep laugh echoed in her mind. She quivered, her knees turning to mush. Gripping the basin, she wondered if she should just sleep with him. At least, that would assuage one craving.

She'd recognised the mutual attraction burning in his eyes. It wouldn't take much to seduce him despite his suspicions of her involvement with the mill's closure. She could be up-front, telling him she wasn't looking for anything serious, then neither of them would get hurt. She could lose herself for an hour or two in his strong arms, assuage her curiosity about the temptation of his lips on hers.

Then she could move on.

And concentrate on what was important.

A tiny voice whispered inside her head that Cole wouldn't be an easy man to forget.

Squaring her shoulders, Sasha straightened and pushed away from the bathroom vanity. What rubbish. She had her life plan all worked out: a career devoted to helping others. A committed relationship or a family of her own had never interested her. Until now.

She marched into the bedroom and snatched up her mobile, deciding the foreman needed to know about what she'd overheard regarding the gas leak. Maybe he'd be able to ensure none of his workers were blamed. At the very least, he'd know how to instigate an independent inquiry.

Another swing past Mindalby Cotton was in order before she headed to the community centre. She had to investigate the remote possibility that Yasmin's iPhone was somewhere in the mill. She could do a little recon and check if there was a way to get inside.

A little before eight o'clock, dressed in a pair of blue jeans, sturdy boots and her parka, Sasha pushed her bike outside and locked her front door.

When the gates of the mill came into view, the only reaction she experienced was the lurching sensation in the pit of her stomach.

No mind-numbing flashbacks.

No urge to run.

No sharp, twisting pain in her chest like her heart was a stick of C4 with a detonator attached.

Deep in thought she barely registered this knowledge as she took in the scene in front of the gates. She'd hoped to find the place deserted. Unfortunately, there was a group of people standing about with hands shoved in pockets, shoulders hunched against the cold.

She greeted the few people she recognised then propped her bike against the fence and examined the layout, taking note of the CCTV positions. Dimly, she caught snippets of conversations; words like *'picket-line'*, *'we're not gonna stand for this'*, *'there's that woman who hasn't paid us'*.

Those she'd said 'good morning' to had muttered a gruff response, but she hadn't failed to notice how their gazes had slid from hers or how quickly they moved away.

She was *a pariah*.

Sasha thought of her broken window. Her fingers curled into her palms. She hoped that was the only intimidation that would be aimed in her direction. One bloke grabbed the wire fencing in both hands and shook it roughly while another guy hurled a rock over the fence. Don could well end up with a riot on his hands.

Turning around, she took note of the faces in the crowd. A woman in her late thirties with green-dyed dreadlocks, wearing a hot-pink puffer jacket and shabby blue jeans, and clutching a smart phone, eased out from behind the knot of men.

"Are you Sasha Bernstein?" she called out in the hoarse voice of a long-term smoker.

Fiddling with her bottle cap, Sasha gave a wary nod.

"I'm Jo Johnson, local DJ from MO83 Radio. How you doing?" The woman smiled toothily.

"Fine thanks." Was the woman related to the town's head police officer? If so, then she probably already had access to way more information than Sasha. Sasha hesitated wondering whether she could do her own interrogating, but another glance at the avid eyes glittering like a predator had her rethinking that idea. Screwing the lid on her bottle, she strode toward her bike, hoping to give the impression she was on a mission.

The DJ kept pace. "I hear you work for Don Carter in the office. Any chance of an interview? I run Chat Hour at midday, Monday to Friday."

"Sorry. I'm not interested." She strapped her bottle to the bike then rammed on her helmet.

Jo Johnson waved her phone in the air. "Mind if I record this? It would be great to get your perspective on the mill closure. Straight from the horse's mouth, so to speak."

About to mount her bike, Sasha frowned. "What do you mean? And no, you can't record our conversation."

Jo's smile vanished. "Rumour has it, that you're having an affair with Don. Have you met the second Mrs Carter?"

Longing to hurl a furious denial into the other woman's hard-as-stone face and knowing that whatever she said could be twisted into a different meaning, she forced through gritted teeth, "No comment."

Hands trembling, she gripped the handlebars and pushed off, ignoring the DJ's calculating stare.

It took enormous willpower but she forced herself not to look back as she pedalled around the perimeter of the mill yard. Once out of sight she exhaled loudly.

She'd expected the DJ to home in on the angle of her uncle. But no, the woman had run off on a totally different tack. The knowledge this rumour was circulating shook her. Was this another Chinese whisper generated by Lesley Thompson? Or had someone else fed the town gossips with this spicy titbit?

What if Cole heard about it? She remembered how he'd joked she was involved with Don. The thought of the condemnation she'd see in his eyes was like a phys-ical pain ripping through her chest.

She didn't know him. Not really. She shouldn't give two hoots about what he thought about her. But she did. With gallows humour, she decided that would be one way to sever the attraction between them.

Just past the locked exit gates on Forbes Street, she stopped then chugged down more water, as she studied the high security fence. Her gaze snagged where wire had been pulled off a steel fencepost, close to the ground and almost hidden behind a wild rosemary bush. If she hadn't stopped she would have missed it. The gap was big enough for an animal to pass through —or a slim woman if she was lucky.

Adrenaline fizzed in her veins.

Helping Uncle Isaac was the reason she'd come here and he was her priority. She rammed the lid back onto her bottle. Tonight, she was going in.

11

Dressed totally in black, Sasha crept closer to the fence. She snuck a quick glance over both shoulders then, satisfied the road was empty, pulled on the wire until she'd levered a gap sufficiently wide to allow her to pass through. She had wriggled her upper body through when her mobile rang, its strident tones cutting through the quiet night.

Her heart leapt to her throat.

She attempted to reach her pocket but couldn't manoeuvre her arm back through the wire. A jagged end snagged her jacket sleeve and the material ripped. She pulled, she tugged, but the wire held fast while the damn phone rang on and on. *Seriously?*

The phone stopped. Her voicemail pinged.

One vicious yank and she was free. Sweat prickled her scalp beneath her beanie as she military-crawled another metre.

Her phone went off again.

I don't believe this! Her hand went to her pocket while she scrambled forward until she reached the first row of cotton bales. Peering around the side, she searched the area for any sign she'd been made, her pulse drumming in her ears. Nothing stirred.

"Hello," she whispered, gulping air.

"Why are you breathing so hard?" demanded Cole.

"Oh, Cole. Gosh, it's you."

"I'm coming over. What's your address? As soon as I hang up, phone the police."

She squeezed her eyes shut. *This means nothing. He's just being neighbourly.* "No, please don't," she hissed. "I'm fine. Nothing's the matter."

"Then why are you whispering?"

Biting her lip, she debated how to respond. She'd already sunk in his estimation, so a little break and enter couldn't matter. Hell, he might even join her. The thought of his solid company while they stole through the cold gloom might keep her nightmares at bay.

She eyed the black writing on the yellow-covered cotton bales next to her. *Property of Cotton Fields Glory.* "I'm in the south-western bale yard of Mindalby Cotton. The good news is no one has stolen your cotton," she added flippantly, her composure returning at the prospect of shocking him.

"You want to run that past me again?" His voice turned frosty.

She smiled to herself. "I'm inside the factory yard."

"Yeah, I thought that's what you said. What the hell are you doing in there?"

"A little snooping."

"Are you crazy? Place is off-limits. I bet that Felicity woman has requested police patrols to ward off pissed-off farmers thinking about stealing back their cotton."

"Keep your hair on. I'm just going to take a little peek around the gas cylinders." She relayed what she'd overhead at the Carters' house omitting any references to herself. "I know it's clutching at straws but if Don had his wife's phone, he could have dropped it somewhere in the yard."

"Women are a complete mystery to me. Why is someone else's missing phone so important you'd risk a break and enter charge? No, don't tell me. Don't move an inch. I'll be there in twenty."

The phone went dead.

Limp, she flopped against the closest bale as her heartrate settled. He was on his way—no doubt, riding to what he believed was her rescue. Problem was, she didn't need rescuing; she needed him to believe in her.

He was going to want answers and, for the life of her, she had no idea how she'd respond.

She shivered when icy wind smacked into her face, chafing her lips and making the tip of her nose ache. Until now she'd been too high on stress and adrenaline to register the cold but, alas, no more.

Hunching her shoulders, she slipped lower in the

hope that the cotton bales would protect her from the storm front thundering in from the south-west. She hugged herself, rubbing her arms up and down to warm her blood.

Why had Cole phoned? Had he heard the latest gossip and wanted to hear her side of the story? Would he believe her, if she attempted to vindicate herself? What if he'd been going to ask her out on a date? That thought made her feel all toasty inside.

She rolled her eyes at her reaction, high on hormones and excitement, as if she was a teenager experiencing her first crush. But despite her admonishments to grow up, she couldn't quite quash her rising anticipation.

It felt as if six hours had passed—but from constantly checking her phone she knew it had only been eighteen minutes—when a set of headlights appeared at the end of the street.

Hopefully Cole and not the police. She'd have a lot of difficulty in explaining away her actions. She switched on the torch in her phone and flashed it three times to indicate the gap in the fence, feeling a little like some dorky sidekick in a spy movie.

The vehicle approached then stopped. The head-lights died. The overhead light in the cabin bloomed briefly to reveal Cole's dark head as he opened the car door.

She waited until he was closer to the fence before

leaving the protection of the bales. Bent against the wind, she staggered across the tarmac and lit up the hole in the wire with her phone.

Thirty seconds later he was standing in front of her. "You want to tell me what this is really about?"

"Later. I promise. Let's move before the storm hits and my toes get frostbite."

Cole, bless his cotton socks, didn't ask any more questions. He simply slung his arm around her shoulders, pressing her to his warm, hard body. "There'll be more cover from any passing cars if we go this way."

Lighting the way with a high-powered small LED torch he held in his free hand, he led her around the furthest end of the cotton bales. Huddled together, they paced along the rear fence until they reached the grassed area where staff sometimes spent their lunch breaks.

"I thought you were harvesting this week," she whispered as they crept past the textile mill towards the crib block.

"We were but the harvester broke down."

"Oh no!" Genuinely concerned, she tried to make out his features in the dark.

His voice betrayed his fatigue when he muttered, "Yeah. Couldn't have happened at a worse possible time."

"What are you going to do?"

She felt the movement of his taut muscles as he shrugged. "What we always do: deal with it. Silvano has sent off for a spare part. Harry and Chook are working on fixing up something temporary until it arrives. We might get lucky and finish the field."

"It's a hard life, working on the land." She fiddled with the torch strap.

"It's not for everyone and it's tough on families. Divorce rate is high out here. Every year we see more and more kids head off to the big smoke in search of an easier life, one where you get paid a decent wage for your time and effort. A man can end up trapped, owing too much then forced to sell, walking away with nothing more than the clothes on his back to show for a lifetime working twenty-four seven."

Was that what happened with his wife? Had she left, unable to cope? The need to know trembled on Sasha's lips but she snatched back the words before she could utter them. *Don't get involved.*

Cole stopped and indicated the sky with his torch. "This storm isn't going to help."

A car drove slowly down the entrance road, stopping where Sasha estimated the front gates were, engine running, headlights still on. "Do you think they saw us?"

Cole snapped off his torch.

The wind howled around the buildings and somewhere in the distance metal creaked.

She sucked in a sharp breath over her thundering pulse. "Did someone just open the gate?"

Cole whispered, "Shush. Wait."

A few seconds later, a car door slammed. An engine started up. Gravel crunched under tyres and the sound of the engine diminished as it moved away. The creaking metal she'd heard must have been the wind blowing against the fence.

"Probably the police checking there hasn't been a break-in." Cole's voice was dry.

Hand to her tight chest, she gave a nervous snicker.

"This way." Switching on the torch, Cole led her across the narrow yard to the mill building.

Lightning jagged through the sky illuminating the yard briefly. A rolling rumble of thunder followed. As she stepped from shadow to shadow, she muttered, "I think it's going to pour any second. Will the rain damage the bales you have here?"

"No, they're sealed. It's the remaining third of our crop waiting to be harvested we're worried about. Our first year at trialling a new type of cotton too and contracts with different merchants. We were hoping for a decent profit."

"We, as in you and your grandfather? He seems a lovely man."

"He is. You would have liked Gran, too. She was the sister of a Yankie mate Pop made during the Vietnam War. His mate never made it home and after his tour of duty Pop visited the bloke's family. Fell for Gran the moment he clapped eyes on her. Married her and brought her to Mindalby where they bought the farm and decided to grow cotton. Gran was a stayer and met every challenge head on. Strong, determined and never took bull from anyone. Pop adored her. Their marriage was the kind I'd hoped for."

Flexing her cold fingers inside their gloves, she chewed that over for a few minutes before prompting softly, "I take it you weren't so lucky." So much for keeping her distance.

He sighed. "Denise … well, we both thought we were in love. We grew up together, same school, same circle of friends. We got married not long out of high-school. Then about thirteen months after Summer was born, Denise's appendix burst when she was out riding. She'd had some pains off and on in the weeks before but figured it wasn't anything major. She died on the operating table."

She shivered at the lost note in his voice. "Oh, I'm so sorry. What a terrible thing to happen."

"We'd been drifting apart for some time before she died. I'd like to think we could have found our way back together again, if we'd had more time. But now, I don't know. We seemed to be turning into two entirely different people."

"Your children must miss her."

"I know Toby does. He remembers her. With Summer, its more she feels there is something missing in her life. I see her looking at her friends with their mothers and my heart breaks. She looks so bloody wistful."

Tears burned her eyes. "You could always marry

again."

"If I ever do head down the aisle again, it will be with my forever woman – a woman who will be content and eager to live a life with me."

"Someone like your grandmother?"

"Yeah."

Sounded like a hard act to follow. Her spirits low, she walked silently by his side for a few minutes.

They crept around garbage bins, Sasha holding her breath at the ripe stench. Suddenly, the wind blew off one of the lids with a loud clatter that made her jump. She cut her eyes in all directions, straining to see into the blackness.

"Okay, Sasha?" Cole asked, sweeping the torch light over the ground in front of them.

His deep voice washed away her momentary panic and she sucked in a shaky breath. Relax, it was the wind. Not a gunshot. She croaked, "I'm fine."

"Watch where you step. There's a stormwater grate in front of you."

"I see it." Knees feeling like jelly, she walked around the metal grate and wrenched her thoughts back to the present.

She slid a considering glance in his direction. Lightning lit up the sky outlining his profile.

Nice. Very nice. And he seemed like such a kind guy as well. The next Mrs Cole Mitchell, if there was one, would be a very lucky woman. If she could ever compete with a ghost. No, make that two ghosts. His wife and his gran. Whoever Cole set his sights on would have to be loved by his kids as well. And there was no way he'd ever bring a woman into their lives who couldn't love them too.

They skirted the corner of the crib building and stopped.

"The gas cylinders are next to the side door." Cole played his torch along the side of the cotton ginning building.

"I remember." She shook free of her unsettling thoughts, eased out of his hold and switched on her mobile torch. "I'll go this way if you'll go the other?"

"No sweat." He moved off. The light from his torch soon dwindled.

A clap of thunder sounded overhead and she started, heart pounding. When she glanced up, a fat raindrop plopped into her eyes. Then her forehead, then her cheek. She wiped the moisture from her face. They didn't have a lot of time before the storm hit. That made finding the phone even more imperative.

An hour later, the icy rain was falling steadily. Her face felt whipped raw from the wind and her back ached from peering beneath scraps of timber and amongst the long grass. This was a lost cause. After sending one last regretful glance at the mill and factory buildings, she texted Cole then trudged back to the fence-line.

Thunder rumbled and the rain fell harder. Cole caught up with her just as she was wriggling through the gap in the wire.

When they were both through the fence, she said, "Thanks. I really appreciate your help, especially coming out in this weather and after working all day."

He wiped his wet face with his sleeve. "You owe me an explanation; one I intend extracting as I drive you home. Plus, I need warming up."

His voice was deeper, gravelly.

Heat flared under her skin. Did he mean …? "No! I mean, no thanks,' she stuttered, as her stomach lurched, edgy desire and panic wrestling in a sickening fashion. Oh how she wanted to say 'yes, please'. But she simply couldn't get in his car! "I want to ride back so I can think."

"You'll be soaked in three minutes flat."

She forced a laugh and flapped her arms, shaking water in all directions, to demonstrate her point. "I'm already wet."

Moving quickly, she found her bike in the darkness and strapped on her helmet. "About that explanation? I'm absolutely bushed. Can I take a raincheck?"

"I like the pun." His teeth flashed white as he grinned. "No worries. And Sasha, take it easy riding home. Text me when you arrive, so I know you're home okay?"

For some stupid reason, her chest tightened and a salty tear mingled with the pelting rain. "Sure."

"I'll catch you later." He turned and strode back to his Land Rover.

Shivering and frozen to her marrow, Sasha mounted her bike. All she could think as she rode through the rain was *I wish I'd said yes.*

Morning dawned, damp and soggy. While sipping her coffee and gazing at the sodden yard through the kitchen window, Sasha's thoughts centred on last night. It had been sweet of Cole to help her, although their covert activity had yielded no results. Sweet and protective.

Apart from her father, no one else had ever looked out for her. She'd always stood alone. *And that's how it must stay. I have a job to do, then I'm back where I belong.*

She swallowed the last mouthful of coffee, finding it bitter on her tongue. The idea of sneaking into the Mindalby Cotton yard again for another search didn't arouse a lot of enthusiasm. Yasmin could have found her phone by now.

She needed to move on. Sighing, Sasha considered today's agenda. A long, and no doubt frustrating, day spent within the confines of the community centre.

But she couldn't refuse what could well be her last opportunity to help her uncle.

Setting down her mug, she wondered whether she should take the administrator's advice and phone her family solicitor. But would the news then reach her mother's ears? No, not a great idea. Her mother would have a meltdown. And she didn't need any more stress.

No, she would sit tight and see how events pan out. She knew she was innocent. All she had done was manoeuvre her way into that job. But would Cole also view her actions the same way?

Drat the man. If only she could get him out of her head. A knock came from the front door.

She opened it.

Jo Johnson beamed at her from her porch, a scarlet woollen beanie crammed over her dreadlocks. The smile did nothing to soften the stony look in her eyes. "Morning."

Sasha stiffened, not bothering to return the greeting, her fingers digging into the timber doorframe.

"I know you said yesterday, you weren't interested in an interview, but I thought you might have reconsidered." Jo cocked her head to the side. "This is a small town where people stick together in a crisis. Giving your side could go a long way to soothing public opinion."

"Just what are you saying?"

Jo gave another toothy grin but Sasha wasn't fooled. "There's talk you're Don's mistress. So working in the accounts section of a business that just put half the town out of work and will affect the livelihood of local farmers is bound to stir up trouble. People are asking questions. Tell me your side of what happened. It could soften public opinion."

"That sounds like a threat."

"I'm pointing out the obvious, Ms Bernstein. *And* I'm giving you an opportunity to help yourself."

Sasha narrowed her eyes. "I'll pass on the interview. But you can tell your listeners one thing: I'm not in a romantic relationship with Don Carter, nor have I ever been, nor have I any wish to be."

Jo pushed back her dreadlocks and gave a disbelieving snort. "I'll be sure to pass your comment on. Make sure you listen in—midday."

After closing and locking the door, Sasha leant back against the hard timber and squeezed her eyes shut. Perspiration beaded her hairline as her heart raced. The notion she was being manipulated into a trap took hold. Someone was feeding misinformation to the press, as well as to the town.

Who could it be?

Lesley Thompson? Don Carter himself? His wife? *Who?*

But more to the point, what could she do about it?

As the hours crawled towards noon, Sasha grew more anxious, torn between wanting to know what the DJ would say and wanting to remain oblivious. Seated at the desk she'd been allocated in the community centre, she picked up yet another file.

The work certainly didn't help. It was so mundane and boring. So far, she had little to show for her efforts. Certainly, she'd been unable to spot anything that might be fishy in the mounds of paper and folders she'd been given by Dave Gresham who was busy picking through digital records from the company computer.

She'd thought her clerical job mind-numbing but the knowledge it was only short-term had kept her focused. Plus, she'd negotiated her hours to ensure she'd start early and finish around two in the after-noon, leaving her with the remainder of the day to work out at the gym or attend physiotherapy at the hospital clinic.

"Sasha! Sasha." The high tenor voice of Dave Gresham broke through her dismal musing.

"Sorry, Dave. You were saying?" She tilted her head and smiled at the PA who stood near her desk, a paper clutched in his hand that he'd just taken off the printer.

"Felicity said to give you this list of companies. If you come across any mention of them, let her know immediately." Dave handed the page over.

She frowned and scanned the list. "Does Don have other businesses?"

"It's a possibility we're investigating. This is a list of companies that assist people to hide assets and/or money from either their relatives or to avoid paying taxes."

"What people do to hold onto their money." She sighed and shook her head, her mouth turning down.

"You'd be surprised at how far people will go." Dave's voice was dry. "Sometimes, as far as murder."

"Murder?"

"I've seen it happen before." He checked his watch. "Lunchtime. Come and join us. Felicity and I will be out in the courtyard. We intend to listen to the local radio. Apparently there's a chat session on soon. You can pick up a lot of gossip that can prove helpful in our line of work."

Repressing her shudder, she politely refused, saying she had some personal calls to make and pretended to study the document he'd given her.

After he left, she scrambled to find her phone and tune in to the radio station. Heart pounding, she listened to the remainder of the news and weather. Then the live chat session started.

Any appetite she'd felt vanished. The DJ populated her talk with innuendoes about Sasha's character and lack of morals in a way that bordered on slander while she answered on-air calls. Unable to listen any longer, Sasha switched off her phone. Elbows on the desk, she propped her head in her hands and battled her anger and disbelief.

Her mobile rang; the *Rocky* theme ringtone signalled it was her father.

"Hello, Dad."

"Sasha, have you heard what's being said on the radio today?"

"Yeah, I copped some of it."

"I'm phoning our solicitor immediately. I'll have him issue a statement on your behalf, that it's a pack of lies and that we intend to sue."

"Dad, let it go. If we punch back, they'll swing harder. If I say nothing, they'll have no ammunition to argue against." As long as no one discovered those dinner dates with Don!

"But they're implying you're in a relationship with a married man. And in on his plan to escape paying his debts and his workers! The town will be out for your blood."

"It's not going to come to that, Dad. I'm sure people will realise this is pure speculation. The DJ hasn't mentioned any facts, just aimed darts in different directions."

"I dunno, Cuddlepie. People under pressure tend to react first and think later. What if your squeeze hears this rubbish?"

Biting her lip, she blinked back the hot thrust of dismay crowding her heart. "What of it, Dad? He's only a guy that I've spoken to once or twice."

Her father's snort came over loud and clear. "I'm

not blind. I've seen the way you two look at each other. The chemistry between you two is undeniable."

"A passing attraction, that's all it is."

"If you say so." His tone clearly indicated he didn't believe a word of her protest.

She didn't blame him. She wasn't that certain she believed it either.

Hurried footsteps along the corridor had her ending the call. "Have to go, Dad. Talk soon." She placed her mobile onto the desk at the same moment Felicity barrelled into the room.

The other woman planted her hands on her hips, a forbidding scowl hardening her flushed face. A serious-looking Dave rushed in behind her. "Care to explain yourself? I've suspected all along you were hiding something. Now I know you've lied to me."

"I am not in, nor have I ever been in, a relationship with Don Carter."

"Show her, Dave." Felicity stepped aside while her PA shuffled forward as he scrolled through his phone.

Dave showed her the screen which depicted an invoice.

"I don't understand." Sasha shook her head, wondering what was going on. She'd thought the woman had charged in for an explanation of the rubbish spawned by the local DJ. "It's for the purchase of clothing."

"Lingerie." Felicity thinned her lips and added, "From an online store that sells sex toys and provocative underwear. If you look a little closer, you'll notice the delivery address is your previous address in Sydney."

Sasha's gaze shot back to the small screen. Her throat closed as the details burned into her retinas. Her blood cooled as her pulse slowed to a heavy thump.

"Dated early January, ordered by a D Carter and paid for by Mindalby Cotton Company," Dave murmured accusingly.

"How did you get this?"

"Dave found the receipt on the company computer."

"I don't know what to say. I remember a package arriving but as I hadn't ordered it, I returned it to sender. Unopened." She switched her defiant gaze to the woman's face. "You are welcome to check with the store."

"I deal in facts," said Felicity.

"Facts can be created to mislead people."

Felicity paused, as if considering the possibility. "This receipt is pretty damming when combined with what we just heard on the radio however I'm prepared to listen to your version."

"It's not my version. It's the truth. I applied for a vacant position. Met Don Carter and discussed my job application over dinner. I had no idea he sent me lingerie which, by the way, I would never accept. If this invoice is related to the package I returned to the store, then the store should have a credit voucher. Or details of the return." Jaw clenched, she snapped the folder she held shut with an air of finality and stood.

"What are you doing?" asked Felicity, sharply.

"Leaving. I don't imagine you want me here any longer." She began to gather up her belongings.

"That's where you're wrong, Sasha." Felicity turned to leave. "I want you to stay."

"Why?"

The older woman glanced over her shoulder and gave a grim smile. "I know when someone is withholding information. Until I find out what it is and whether you're telling the truth about having nothing to do with the Carters or their company, I want you where I can keep an eye on you." She marched from the room, Dave in her wake.

Alone, Sasha slumped back into the chair. What a mess. At least she still had free rein with Don's files and an ever-narrowing chance to help her uncle. Was she doing the right thing in holding back the true reason why she was here? But if she came clean Felicity could well throw Sasha out on her ear.

She couldn't risk it. Her family were depending on her.

She returned to sifting through the mountain of files. For the remainder of the afternoon Felicity and Dave left her alone, for which she was grateful. Time was her enemy. At any moment, she could be shown the door.

As she worked, she kept checking her mobile for any messages or missed calls from Cole.

What had he made of her insistence on searching for another woman's missing phone? But her uncle's predicament wasn't a matter she could easily discuss with a stranger.

Had he heard the rumour circulating about her and Don Carter? The question gnawed at her mind relentlessly.

To be honest, she *wanted* Cole to phone. She wanted to see him again.

But so far—zip.

A big, fat nothing.

The only bright spot in a long, miserable day was the fact her broken window had been fixed.

SATURDAY MORNING FOUND Sasha manning a free sausage-sizzle stall with her father. He'd met Cole's parents on Thursday afternoon at the golf club and Maisy had mentioned that she and her Country Women's Association members were deliberating on how they could help lift people's spirits in the town. He'd suggested the free sausage sizzle. It hadn't taken long for Maisy to organise the donated food and then rope Obie into working the barbecue for the day.

As she buttered slices of bread, Sasha wondered whether Maisy now regretted inviting them to participate. Last night she'd expected the woman to phone and cancel, but her mobile had remained silent.

She looked along the main street. Her father had chosen the busiest section in town to place the long trestle table and set up the barbecue. While the small community hardly imitated the bustle of a city, there were quite a few shoppers about and it wasn't long before people began to queue for their free meal.

By the avid way they scrutinised Sasha, she wondered whether they were here to ogle her rather than to eat. Despite the furtive glances and brief thanks, no one levelled any direct accusations. Although several women hung around in small groups, sneaking looks at Sasha and whispering behind their sandwiches.

As the morning passed, she relaxed sufficiently to enjoy the crisp breeze bringing with it the after-rain freshness. She sniffed, inhaling the succulent scent of hot, vegetable soup from Amber Stanworth's wagon parked across the road.

The very second Cole's aunt had arrived, her father had grabbed Sasha by the elbow and hustled her over to introduce them. Sasha had been quietly impressed with the way Amber Stanworth handled her boisterous father. The woman had an air of unquenchable authority about her; one that put her forcibly in mind of an old-fashioned nursery governess. Whatever magic the woman wielded, she certainly appeared to have enthralled her father. All morning, he'd done nothing but rave over her copper-red hair, her love of travel and her well-informed mind—his words.

Around midday, Maisy Mitchell appeared hauling a bulging personal-shopping cart behind her. After giving Sasha a brusque nod, she enquired how the food supplies were going.

"We've got a few loaves of bread left and about three kilos of snags," said Obie, waving his tongs in the air.

Maisy neatly sidestepped a spatter of meat grease that landed near her feet. "Excellent. I do hope no one is giving yo u any trouble after yesterday." It was obvious what the woman was referring to.

Cheeks burning, Sasha said, "Everyone has been very polite."

To her surprise, Cole's mother refrained from mentioning the previous day's radio talk show or grilling Sasha over whether or not the rumours were true.

Instead Maisy marched around the side of the table to unload the contents of her trolley. "Our CWA members have been busy. We've got homemade cakes and biscuits to give away. I'm sorry I wasn't here earlier. Saturday morning I'm at lawn bowls."

Which Sasha easily interpreted to mean that nothing less than an apocalypse could change the older woman's bowls schedule. Smiling, she moved over to lend a hand and they arranged the plastic-wrapped food onto one half of the table.

"Come and get your free cake!" Maisy shot a dark glance across the street and sniffed. "I see my sister thinks she can outdo us. Let's see who can get rid of their food first." A rich flush washed over her face as she raised her voice even louder, hollering, "Free cakes and cookies!"

On the other side of the road, Amber Stanworth bawled, "Homemade hot vegetable soup! Take some home today!"

Maisy shouted, "Treat your children to yummy homemade cakes!"

Amber bellowed, "Nutritious soup! Made from organically grown vegetables!"

Exchanging an amused look with her father, Sasha figured it was going to be a long day.

13

Sunday morning was a repeat of the day before, even down to the weather: cool and cloudy. Having food left over from yesterday, both Sasha and her father decided to set up the barbecue again and lay out the remaining cakes.

There were fewer people around today and they decided to keep at it until lunchtime or they ran out, whichever came first. As Sasha buttered yet another slice of bread, she wondered how she'd be able to search the Mindalby Cotton offices. Before the controversial chat show had aired, she'd asked Felicity if she could retrieve personal items she'd left in her locker, but after one long minute the answer had been 'no'.

She'd have to make her own opportunity. And that had led her to asking her father about picking locks. As a consequence, it seemed like every time she turned around—there he was. He'd even insisted on sleeping in her spare room last night. Whether he was concerned she'd do something crazy or whether it was born from the vandalism at her flat or her confrontation with the drunk guy, she couldn't tell.

Her brush with death in Syria had not only altered her life, it had changed her parents' acceptance of her chosen career. When she was finally cleared to return to work, she knew she was going to have a battle on her hands, regardless of the fact she was thirty-four.

She turned back to reach for another loaf of bread.

"Here she is," intoned her father in a voice bordering on awe, referring to Amber.

Smiling, Sasha waved at the red-headed woman driving a wagon drawn by two chestnut draught horses.

"Amber! How wonderful of you to return to the battlelines." Sasha's father tossed off his purple apron. He bustled past the trestle table to greet the woman, his arms outstretched as if he intended to embrace her.

"Still cooking flesh, I see, Obadiah." Amber Stanworth heaved on the wagon brake, jumped lightly to the ground then dodged Obie's hug by striding to the rear of the wagon. She shot the bolts then yanked down the rear tailgate.

Her father's arms dropped to his side and he turned forlorn puppy-dog eyes on Sasha who'd followed him over.

She grinned, calling out, "Good morning, Miss

Stanworth. Unfortunately, we haven't any vegie burgers although we do have a few homemade cakes."

"I suppose we all have to start somewhere." Amber set up a small folding table then hoisted out a large esky.

"Here, let me help you." Obie rushed forward.

"No need to fuss. I've got everything under control.' She heaved the esky onto the table, which rocked under its weight. Next, she loosened the horses' girth straps then half-filled two buckets with water, placing it near the animals. "If you want to make yourself useful, Obadiah, fetch me that basket of bowls."

"Yes, ma'am." He bounded to the wagon then returned almost completely obscured behind a massive wicker basket which he placed reverently at Amber's cloth-sandalled feet. He tutted over her bare toes. "You must be freezing. That wind is bitter. Sash, get those spare gumboots from the boot of my car. I'm certain there's socks in there as well."

Amber held up a hand as if marshalling a platoon of tanks and Obie froze in his tracks. "I rarely feel the cold; besides, I like to be as close to the earth as possible."

A disapproving frown formed on Amber's tanned, weather-beaten face as she stared pointedly at his hand-tooled leather boots. "One can't possibly feel the spirit of mother earth through the soles of your feet when wearing a barrier made from slaughtered animals. It interrupts the flow of energy."

Before her father decided to throw off his boots and set them on fire, Sasha jumped in. "Dad, I need your help. There's a group of people heading our way. Looks like they've been to church and are looking rather hungry."

He sighed gustily but trudged back to the barbecue where he briskly rescued the well-cooked sausages and scooped a pile of shrivelled onions onto a tray. Every so often, he'd cast glances to where Amber was pouring hot vegetable soup from a thermos into clay bowls and exchanging pleasantries with the few people lining up in front of her.

Sasha noticed two grizzled old men nudging each other and scowling in Amber's direction. Whispers reached her ears: *'witch', 'devil-worshippers', 'druggies', 'bloody hippies'*. It seemed not everyone in town was happy they had a commune on their outskirts.

Two hours later, with their supplies depleted, Sasha and her father packed up. Together they carried the trestle table to Obie's car where they strapped it onto the roof rack.

"What now, Cuddlepie?" Obie peered past her to where Amber was readying the horses for the journey home.

Sasha could only describe his expression as yearning. "Dad, if you want to ask her out, do it!" She gave him a gentle push on the arm.

"No, no. I'm happy to keep you company." But his tone lacked conviction.

"Liar." Chuckling, she crossed over to Amber. Ensuring she gave the huge horses a wide berth, she said, "Are you busy this afternoon, Miss Stanworth? My father and I were wondering whether you'd care to join us at Joe's Café."

The other woman smiled as she pulled an oilskin from beneath the bench then pushed her arms into the sleeves. Whatever mental image Sasha had entertained about Wiccans had evaporated the moment she'd laid eyes on Cole's aunt. She'd had a vision of a woman wearing lots of beads and a long flowing gown. Amber Stanworth preferred thick cotton-drill pants and a black and blue checked flannelette shirt over her grey woollen jumper.

Clapping an old floppy hat onto her head, she slid a shy glance in Obie's direction before meeting Sasha's gaze. "Sorry, prior commitment. We've got an initiation ceremony tonight to prepare for but why don't both of you come with me? One of our members can drive you back to town after the ceremony finishes."

Obie clasped his hands together and inhaled sharply.

Not wanting to disappoint her father and also because she was curious, Sasha smiled. "We'd love to. I'll ride my moped though. Dad, are you driving or going on the wagon?"

"The wagon. But I need to take the table back to the CWA hall first."

The sun chose that moment to break through the

sullen clouds but the brightness was nothing compared to the excitement shining in her father's eyes as Amber said how she'd pick him up from outside the hall. She exchanged a grin with Amber. "I'll cycle back to my flat and catch up with you along the road."

Several minutes later, she caught up with the wagon as it clattered past the caravan park. She eased off on the throttle to fall in behind as they crossed Woodburn Bridge where the sluggish grey-brown waters of the Darling River lay beneath.

Heads down, the horses clopped along. Her father and Amber's voices as they chatted were all but obliterated by the rattle and squeak of the wagon and the steady purr of her moped engine.

Raising her right arm in the air, Amber gestured for Sasha to move forward.

After checking for no oncoming traffic, Sasha motored up alongside.

Amber hollered, "We're coming to the south-eastern boundary of Nambaring National Park. You and your father should take time to visit while you're in town. The land used to be a grazing station until sold to the government who then gave it back to the First Nation people to manage. The original homestead and outbuildings are available for holiday stays. Or there's camping grounds. All this area—" Amber waved her arm in a mighty sweep "—is floodplains and turns into the most amazing wetlands after a decent rainfall. The birdlife and wildflowers are fantastic. There are brilliant sunsets and you won't find a clearer sky at night."

Sasha yelled back, "It sounds lovely. What are the walking trails like?"

"Hmm, I'd say on the easy side. If you're looking for gorges and slightly more challenging walks, you're better off visiting Wooraroogan National Park. That's the one on the eastern side of town. Wooraroogan has a good crop of ridges and a mountain that offers spectacular views. Not that Nambaring isn't pretty. Just depends what you're looking for." Amber speared a sharp glance at Sasha who blinked in surprise.

Was there a hidden message in those words? "Does the commune flood?"

"Although we're situated close by the river, we're on higher ground than the town, which copped the brunt of flooding before they built a levee. Of course, nothing was spared in the one-in-one-hundred-years flood we had a while back. Not even my mother."

"Oh, I'm so sorry."

"Were you here at the time, Amber?" Obie said.

"Yes." One word and yet it resonated with pain.

Obie patted Amber's hand that held the reins. "Tell me about the commune."

Amber shrugged. "There isn't a lot to tell. We had a cattle and wheat property that had been in our family since 1911. But we fell on hard times what with the Great Depression and two world wars. Our little empire diminished in both fortune and kin. My father was the only male Stanworth left and he sold up after the floods of 1985 when my mother died. She was thirty-nine years old."

"That must have been terrible for all of you," Obie said.

"Yeah." Amber stared dead ahead, her profile grim. "Mindalby lost five people in that flood. My mother had been in town shopping and was trying to get home. She drove across a causeway and her car was swept downstream. Cole's grandfather was heading home to Cotton Fields Glory when he spied the car floating down the river. Jasper drove along the bank for ages until her car became stuck within the branches of a fallen tree. He and Max Dooley managed to winch the vehicle from the river. But they never found her body."

"You must have been young." Obie turned a sympathetic face towards Amber.

"Nineteen and in love with a very unsuitable young man. Niels was a Norwegian backpacker travelling the world. He'd worked on our station for six months and both my sister and I thought he was God's gift." She shook her head. "My, how Maisy and I fought over him. Maisy, being the eldest, thought she should have first pick of everything in those days. But I was the one who really fell for him. He left town after the flood and I never heard from him again."

Amber slapped the reins on the horses' rumps, stirring them into a trot and signalling an end to the topic.

"The turn-off to the commune is around that bend, although we still have a way to go before we reach the settlement."

Sasha slowed down to follow behind the wagon again. A few moments later the clopping of horses' hooves against the hard tar changed to soft clomps when they moved onto a narrow dirt road. Dust rose from behind the wagon; coughing, Sasha slowed to increase the distance between them. She looked about with interest, taking in the sturdy timber post-and-rail fencing which bordered the property and lined the entrance for fifty or so metres, ceasing at the cattle grid.

Small coolabah woodlands, clumps of mallee trees and a few red river gums dotted the paddocks on both sides of the track. This area had been only partially cleared and a mob of red kangaroos raised their heads to stare inquisitively before returning to graze amid knee-high grasses. A couple of donkeys trotted up then followed the wagon before veering off and heading towards a large dam. A windmill stood on the banks, its wide arms etched dark against the fluffy white clouds covering the sky.

In the paddock on Sasha's right was a row of wind turbines, barely spinning in the gentle breeze. She admired the few late-blooming wildflowers then with a start realised she'd fallen behind and sped up.

Over a crest, she stopped again. Before her was a slight valley of gently rolling plain. On her left, a track branched off the dirt road and wound through a tiny farmlet.

She cast a quick glance towards the disappearing wagon then decided a quick detour wouldn't hurt and turned off the main road. She soon came to a small wooden bridge over a narrow creek bed. Ahead lay a large red-timbered barn with an iron roof and several outbuildings built from timber and mudbrick.

After crossing the bridge, she motored past the barn on the right. Here the land opened out to the north-west revealing ploughed paddocks and rows of neatly planted vegetables. Several people worked in the fields. Shade trees lined the dirt road and under many there were timber benches, providing a welcome, shady place to shelter from the heat of the day. The layout reminded her of several small farm villages she'd seen when travelling through England; perhaps this area had been designed with that effect in mind.

She drove towards the barn, passing an orchard of stone fruits on her left, then another orchard of citrus trees.

Around the corner of a mudbrick dwelling strode a stout figure covered in a beekeeper's outfit and carrying a metal bucket. A feminine voice said, "Hello there. Are you lost?"

Sasha stopped her moped, leaving the engine idling. "Err, no. I'm here with Amber Stanworth," she said.

The dark haired woman gave a pleasant smile. "I'm

Wanda. Perhaps I'll see you at the initiation ceremony tonight." She disappeared inside the building.

Sasha rode back the way she'd come then turned onto the main dirt road which ran a few hundred metres before opening out into the main settlement area.

14

By dint of waking before the birds—or, as his Pop always said, before sparrow's fart—Cole completed his daily chores leaving a few hours free in the afternoon for the promised horse ride with his children. They took the track through Cotton Fields Glory to the riverbank then followed its winding path towards the commune.

The riverbank was sheltered from the chilly breeze and it wasn't long before Toby unzipped his parka. "Let's go for a swim, Dad."

Cole shuddered at the thought of the icy water. "No way, son. None of us have a change of clothes or a towel."

"We can borrow towels from Aunt Amber," Toby argued.

Summer turned a pouting face towards him. "My

hair will get wet. I don't want my hair to get wet. I don't want to go for a swim."

"You don't have to, sweetheart." Cole smiled at his daughter then rolled his eyes when his son kept baiting her.

"Babies can't swim."

"I'm not a baby."

"Prove it. Go for a swim."

"I want to go for a swim, Daddy."

Cole smothered his grin. "I didn't bring your bathers."

"Why didn't you?" Summer wailed.

Toby kicked his palomino gelding into a canter, yelling over his shoulder, "Because you're a baby."

Summer let out a screech that sent a flock of white corellas soaring into the air with indignant squawks. She flicked her reins and sent her pony chasing after Toby who was whooping loudly as his horse thundered down the track.

Cole wasn't worried. Both kids were good riders and familiar with this area. He knew he'd catch up with them soon enough. Easing back in the saddle, he tilted his face towards the weak warmth of the sinking sun.

He inhaled deeply, filling his lungs with the earthy smells of the bush: horse, leather, eucalypt, bush rosemary and muddy river water.

This was the life for him. A life of hard, physical and yet rewarding labour. A life surrounded by his children and his family. A life where his roots were embedded in the history of Mindalby.

His thoughts switched to Sasha and his complacency of a moment ago was wiped out as if it never existed. She disturbed him, this woman. Especially after that little escapade in the middle of the night. What the devil had she hoped to achieve? Why had she been so hell-bent on finding a phone belonging to a woman she barely knew?

When he'd asked for an explanation, she'd fobbed him off. Was it because she didn't want him to know the truth? Or had she simply wanted to be rid of him? Maybe she just wasn't interested in him. A notion that didn't sit well with him on any level whatsoever! Damn the woman. Why couldn't she be a country girl, content with home and family? *What am I thinking?* He didn't need a woman with secrets complicating his life.

Sighing, he leaned forward and rubbed his horse's neck.

Who was he kidding? He still hadn't made up his mind whether he should act on his attraction and that irritatingly growing need to know she was safe. Or keep distance between them and protect his heart.

She was definitely hiding something from him. He hated the growing certainty she was involved on some level with Don Carter. Lesley Thompson hadn't helped, turning up at the farm yesterday with a casserole, yakking on about what she'd heard on the local radio.

Wanting to hear Sasha's explanation, he'd phoned

this morning, then when she didn't pick up, he'd sent three text messages. But she hadn't replied.

Was she in trouble again?

He shook his head. No, it was dumb of him to think she'd be waiting by the phone for his call. She was no doubt busy; she could even be with another man.

Don Carter for example.

That thought twisted his gut with unexpected savagery. A little shaken, he tugged the brim of his Akubra lower over his forehead then ducked to avoid a low-hanging branch. His kids were nowhere to be seen. He kneed his mare into a canter, turning her onto the dirt track that led to the commune.

"I BET Dad just loves this place," Sasha muttered to herself as she looked at the yurts made from varying materials, including timber, mudbrick and canvas.

There were also several mudbrick houses, three still in the throes of construction and a caravan with a canvas annex. Every dwelling had one or more water tanks to capture the rainfall off the roofs. The landscape was mildly undulating, and here and there were several dirt tracks meandering off in different directions. Whoever had designed the Commune had left quite a few shade trees intact and it was obvious that over the years many more had been planted that weren't native to the area.

Sasha recognised jacarandas, Algerian oaks, several large Poplars and Liquidambars which she knew made excellent fire breaks, and in the distance a clump of shady Moreton Bay fig trees. A few homes had herb gardens planted out front. From an old bathtub situated not far from a massive timber yurt, a couple of dogs and a black-bearded goat slurped noisily.

She parked her moped next to where the wagon was stationed. Her father and Amber had already unhitched the horses and were now relieving them of their harnesses.

"That's our main communal area," Amber said, jerking her chin in the direction of the timber yurt. It had been modified to accommodate the Australian climate with wide verandahs on all sides.

Slipping her satchel over her shoulder, Sasha leaned over to sniff a few blooms on the gardenia bush. "The gardens are beautiful."

"Are you interested in gardening? We could certainly use more help." Amber planted her hands on her hips. Her hopeful smile softened her strong features.

"I'm afraid I know very little about it, although I wouldn't mind giving it a go." Sasha smiled ruefully.

"No time like the present." Amber turned back to the horse and slipped the bridle over its head, slapped its rump then hoisted the harnesses over her shoulder as if they weighed no more than a backpack.

Obie looked on, admiration smeared over his face like butter over bread.

"I hear you've lost your job along with others at the factory." Amber turned away and began to stride across a wide expanse of mown grass. "This way. Hurry up."

Chuckling to herself, Sasha jogged after her father and Amber. Tails swishing, the two carthorses ambled off towards the water trough.

Amber was still talking. "There's plenty for you to do here if you need to keep busy. Personally, I can't abide idle people. It's a recipe for trouble. Let's see … There's planting for next season's vegetables or quilting if you can sew. Every year we enter the Mindalby Cotton Festival quilting competition. This year I'm determined someone from the commune wins the first prize trophy. If Maisy wins again, I'll demand an independent judge be brought in. It's not right that the judges are her minions from the CWA."

"Cole's mother seems to be very immersed in the town's affairs, Miss Stanworth."

"Call me Amber. It's true, my sister has the town's best interests at heart. If you can drag her away from her lawns bowls, that is." Amber sniffed loudly.

"I hear she's quite the champion bowler," ventured Obie.

"Personally, I can't see the point spending all day tossing a heavy ball over some grass. Much more satisfaction if you can see the fruit of your labours." Amber's smile lit up her face like sunbeams as she stopped outside a tiny mudbrick building with a thatched roof. "Get it? Fruit? Labours?"

Obie chuckled while Sasha grinned. Lordy, they were made for each other.

Seemingly satisfied her humour had been appreciated, Amber shouldered through the plank door and re-emerged a few seconds later minus the harnesses and bridles. She dusted her hands briskly.

"I've heard of the festival," Sasha said. "I wonder whether it will go ahead if the mill stays closed.'

Amber frowned. "Hard to say. It'll be a real shame if the organisers decide to can it. The town needs something to look forward to. This way. I'll make us a hot cup of ginger green tea."

Beckoning for them to follow, she pattered up the wide timber steps onto the verandah then passed inside an open doorway.

Sasha followed and caught her breath when she entered. "Oh, how lovely. All this timber and I love how it's all one big living space."

Turning slowly on her heels, she absorbed how each wall was made up of a ceiling-to-waist-high window and a lower panel in rich mahogany. Waist-high bookcases sat beneath the windows, jam-packed with books. Two squishy-looking lounges bookended a hand-carved coffee table that made her mouth water with longing. Brightly coloured hand-woven rugs covered the timber floor. On the far side under an open window sat a Japanese bed, its futon mattress covered with a white crochet throw. The gauzy curtains lifted and billowed with each puff of breeze while wooden chimes clunked together in a soothing symphony.

Waving a glass jar filled with herbs, Amber beamed from behind a narrow kitchen bench. "Thank you. I designed and built most of it myself. There is a small bathroom behind the kitchen pantry if you need it. Our electricity is a mixture of solar and wind power. We do have a backup generator for emergencies. Most folk here use candles after dark and we go to bed early."

From a cupboard, Amber retrieved three clay mugs and placed them on the counter, then filled the mugs with a dark liquid taken from a pot simmering on the stove.

Sasha murmured her thanks and took a cautious sip of the hot tea. Her brows arched. "Wow. This is different. It's quite refreshing."

Amber nodded. "It's a great pick-me-up. Better for you than loading your system with coffee." After drinking from her own mug, she put it down and glanced at Sasha's father. "Now, Obie, you were asking me about the initiation ceremony we're holding tonight for a local woman. Sasha, you may know her. Lesley Thompson, she worked at Carter's mill."

Not wanting to re-hash the conversation from the other night at the Ace in the Hole, Sasha mumbled something noncommittal then buried her face in her mug. It seemed try as she might she couldn't get away from the woman.

Amber said, "Our Rede is to be at one with the earth and all living things …"

"I love it." Obie perched on a stool and clapped his hands.

Sasha glanced from him to Amber, who was acting as if having a man gazing at her so adoringly was an everyday occurrence.

What if her father had fallen in love? Sasha had assumed his fascination with the Wiccan was borne from his insatiable curiosity. Now, after sneaking a peek at the warm glow in his eyes, she wasn't so certain. In many ways, her father was oblivious to the world around him, his attention always fixed on a new adventure or experience. But this time, there was no dazzled glaze in his expression. Just something honest and real—and Sasha's heart sank. What if Amber couldn't reciprocate his feelings? Another reason to do the job she was sent here to do and leave ASAP. And taking her father with her!

With that thought, she set her mug down. "Thank you for the tea, Amber, but we really should get back to town."

"But we've only just arrived!" Her father's astonishment didn't deter her.

"The drive out here took longer than I thought and I prefer to be home before dark."

Obie's chin lifted. "Then you leave now and I'll follow later. Amber said someone can drive me into town. I don't want to miss the ceremony."

"You're welcome to stay, Sasha. No one in need is ever turned away from the Commune of the Golden Light."

"I'm not in need," she snapped then immediately felt ashamed by her rudeness. She shuffled her feet, feeling awkward, but the other woman remained unruffled.

"Obadiah." Amber placed a hand on Sasha's father's arm. "Sasha may feel our ways conflict with her personal beliefs."

"What rubbish. I brought my girl up to think outside the box and never to judge. She's got a phobia about being in vehicles; that's why she rides her bike or moped everywhere."

Sasha's heart jumped hard against her ribs. *"Dad!"*

Obie slapped a hand against his mouth, his eyes big and filled with self-reproach when he looked over at her. "Sorry, Cuddlepie," he mumbled. "I spoke without thinking."

"Long ago, I made the mistake of not seeking help for my social anxiety. Life is too precious to waste. I should know, it took me until I was forty years old before I realised I needed help. Afterwards, I made a vow to reach out and help others in need. I purchased this land and began the commune." Amber's smile radiated kindness. "Here at the Commune of the Golden Light, we offer meditation and self-help classes. Or simply a safe haven."

Sasha sent the woman a tight smile. "Thank you for

your hospitality, Amber. I'll think about your offer but I need to be on my way."

Picking up her satchel from the couch, she walked to the door in carefully controlled steps. The urge to bolt was strong. Only her desire not to cause her father any distress stayed the panic roiling in her chest.

Her father followed her, catching up as she stepped onto the verandah. "Sasha, I shouldn't have opened my big mouth."

"It's okay, Dad." She kissed his cheek. "I know you didn't mean any harm. Unfortunately, I'm not comfortable with sharing my phobias." She grimaced.

"Oh baby-cake, it's more than a phobia and I'm a total klutz. But my lips are sealed from now on. I promise." With his fingertips, he mimed zipping his mouth before wrapping his arms around her and squeezing hard. "Now. I feel wonderfully energised after drinking that tea. There's a bo-staff fighting technique exercise in fifteen minutes. I believe I'll join in."

"Uumph, you're squashing me."

He let her go and they grinned at each other.

"Maybe I should stay and keep an eye on you. Who knows what sort of spell Amber's cast on you," she said.

He snickered and rubbed his hands together. "I may be initiated as well. The thought of dancing naked by the full moon has put all sorts of ideas into my head. Not to mention what it's done to my libido."

"Eww. Dad, that is way too much information." She narrowed her eyes, noticing how the love-lorn puppy eyes now had quite an anticipatory sparkle. "Actually, Dad ..."

"Your father will be safe with me, Sasha." Amber came up behind, startling her. "You need to let go, child. Not hide in the shadows of your past. Remember, you will always be welcome here."

About to turn away, Sasha swung back, frowning. "What have you heard about me?"

"Nothing. But I recognise suffering when I see it." Amber sighed softly then stared past her. A broad smile spread across her face, softening the sharpness in her eyes. "The passage of time usually helps but I'm a bigger believer in the healing power of love."

Amber stepped off the verandah her hands outstretched. "Cole, you're just the man to persuade Sasha to stay longer. Are the children with you?"

15

"Welcome!" Obie bounded forward and wrung Cole's hand with fervour. "Be at one with all living things and the earth," he boomed.

Cole prised his hands from Obie's strong grip. Seemed like the bloke had really taken the commune's mantra on board. If only his daughter would greet him with half as much enthusiasm. He flicked Sasha a quick glance, taking in the heightened colour on her cheeks. Tiny worry lines bracketed her mouth as her polite smile fell away, leaving her lips drooping at the corners. There was a glazed expression in her eyes that reminded him of that moment in the cafe when Mrs McDonald had collapsed. Had his aunt upset her? He'd certainly been close enough to overhear his aunt's words. If it wasn't hard enough having a mother wanting to matchmake it appeared even his aunt had gotten on board!

Sasha's gaze jerked from his face and flitted around the settlement. Her hands fiddled with the straps of the satchel she always seemed to have slung over her shoulder. She gave him the impression she would bolt at any second.

"My word! Is that the time? I have to get ready for the bo-staff class." Throwing his daughter a wink, Obie propelled Aunt Amber off in the direction of the meeting yurt.

Amber called over her shoulder, "Cole, help yourselves to drinks and food. There's plenty for all of you." Her eyes flicked to Sasha.

"Thanks, Aunt." Turning at the sound of approaching horses, he grinned. "Hey kids. Where have you been?"

He noted how both his kids' eyes went straight to Sasha and his brows knitted together. They were both excited at seeing her again. Was that a good or bad sign?

"We went to the farm first, Dad. Summer wanted to see the piglets." Toby smiled shyly at Sasha. "Hi. Are you going to live here with Aunty Amber?"

"Hello, Toby, Summer. No, I'm visiting with my father and we're only here for a few hours. I've got my own flat and Dad is staying at the caravan park." Sasha looked towards where her father and Amber were entering another yurt. "Actually, I'm about to head home."

"Oh no!" wailed Summer, flicking her reins and causing Peanut to amble forward. The pony stretched out its neck until its muzzle was a few centimetres away from Sasha. Peanut blew out a gusty, wet, grassy breath from his nostrils and Summer giggled. "He likes you, Sasha. He wants you to say, hello."

"Errrrr, hello." Sasha arched her back a trifle as Peanut leaned closer.

Cole smiled. "Give Sasha a little space, kids. She isn't used to horses."

"But I can ride a camel and I've been on an elephant several times," Sasha said as if to atone for what she must have thought were perceived short-comings.

"An elephant." Summer's eyes bulged and Toby's jaw dropped. Cole felt pretty impressed himself.

"I remember, your dad told us about the camels." Toby gave a satisfied smile, like Sasha had passed some kind of test. "But an elephant, that's way cool too."

After slipping her right foot free of the stirrup, Summer slid to the ground, handing Cole the reins. He absently patted her pony's neck.

"Sasha. Look. This is Princess Ariel and this is Princess Merida and this is Princess Elsa ..." Summer said, pulling doll after doll out of the large bag strapped to her pony's saddle and shoving them into Sasha's hands.

"Summer, how about you introduce one doll and

save the rest for later." Cole's arm rested lightly on the pony's rump as he grinned at his daughter.

Summer paused to consider his words then frowned at Sasha. "But you said you liked dollies."

"Oh, I do but I'd hate to drop them and get their pretty clothes dirty."

"Hmmm." Summer scowled at a small cloud of red sand that rose as she kicked the dirt with her feet. "S'pose." She heaved a mighty sigh. "Poppy is always growling about having to wash them."

"Dad. Have you asked her yet?" Toby, still astride, nudged his horse into motion and then stopped it when Sasha jumped back. "Sorry. I didn't mean to startle you. I forgot you don't like horses."

Sasha smiled wryly. "It's not that I don't like them, only that I haven't been around them before."

"Camels are big animals," Cole pointed out.

"I know." Sasha paused, her eyes glinting with suppressed laughter. "They spit and have big teeth, as I found out when one decided he wanted my banana. Nipped my finger." She shrugged. "I was only twelve."

"Sounds like you've led an interesting life."

"Holidays with Dad were never boring. Mum could never understand why I'd sleep for a week when I returned home." She chuckled.

He smiled, his body tightening, his chest expanding at that joyous sound. He could feel her laughter wrap around his heart with a soft, gentle warmth. If he made the wrong move, he strongly suspected she'd take flight like a wary black cockatoo. *She's trouble, remember?*

"Holy cow!"

At his son's expletive, Cole dragged his gaze away from Sasha then swung around to see what Toby was goggling at. His own eyebrows shot up and he had to clamp his lips down hard over the curse that charged up his throat.

Strolling towards them, her face wreathed with a smug smile, was Lesley Thompson. Practically stark naked. The dress that fell to her bare feet was so sheer it was blatantly obvious she wore no underclothes. Seething that the woman could stroll around like that when there were kids about, Cole turned his back on her then held his hands out for the reins. "Toby, hop down and take your sister inside Aunt Amber's house. Stay away from the windows."

"Sure thing, Dad." His face red, Toby dismounted and took his sister's hand.

"I want to stay with Sasha," whined Summer.

Sasha took one long look at Lesley before glancing at Cole. A smile tugged at her lips. "I'll go with them."

"Thanks. I appreciate it," he muttered as he shifted position in an attempt to shield his kids from the approaching woman.

One arm full of dolls, Sasha placed a gentle hand in the small of Summer's back. "Let's go inside for a drink. I'm sure you're thirsty. I know I am." With brisk efficiency, she shooed his kids up the steps and inside the yurt.

He spared their departing backs a regretful look. What he wouldn't give to go with them but it was too late.

Lesley reached his side and slipped a hand into the crook of his arm, leaning heavily into his side. "Cole, you came to my initiation ceremony. How sweet."

"Hi, Lesley. No, sorry, I knew nothing about it. I'm here to see my aunt." He stepped away, positioning himself between the horses, leaving no space for her to wiggle into.

Lesley's smile did nothing to soften the speculative glitter in her eyes. "No matter. You can come now that you're here."

"Sorry, I've got plans." He dipped his chin, but ensured his eyes never strayed lower than Lesley's face. 'What do you think you're doing, wandering about dressed like that? There's kids here for heaven's sake."

"Duh. This is a commune, where conventions don't matter."

"I think you've got the wrong idea about this place. Aunt Amber may be broad-minded but first and foremost she is all about creating a respectful sanctuary for her community. And that get-up is definitely not showing any respect to anyone."

"You're such a prude. Who would have thought it?" Lesley laughed.

"I'm sorry, Lesley, if I gave you the wrong impression. I've not that interested in you." He looked past the woman to where his aunt was striding towards them.

"Really? I suppose it's that uppity Sasha Bernstein you've got your eyes on." Lesley's voice turned as hard as concrete.

Cole slid her an uncertain glance, and shifted his weight.

"Lesley!" Aunt Amber caught the other woman by the wrist. "You need to change into the initiation robe that was laid out for you. What you're wearing is unacceptable."

"You can't be serious!"

Stony-faced, Aunt Amber simply crossed her arms.

Obie bustled up to join them—or rather, Aunt Amber, by standing squarely by her side.

"I am almost always serious," Amber said drily.

Lesley's expression turned ugly, her frown thunderous. "I never took you as being a judgemental old fuddy-duddy."

"Come with me. I'll show you the initiation room and get you a cup of herbal tea." Aunt Amber looped an arm around Lesley's waist and steered her away like she was a contrary donkey who'd baulk at any second. Obie followed.

Alone, Cole heaved a heavy sigh and shifted his attention to the horses. He secured them to a railing within reach of the water trough.

Rubbing the back of his itchy neck, he wondered what was bothering him. Had it been Lesley's comment about Sasha? Or the note of warning in her harsh voice?

WHEN SHE HEARD Cole's firm tread on the steps, Sasha rose from the stool beside Summer and Toby and moved to the refrigerator. She'd spotted a partially filled bottle of some type of rose-coloured wine when she'd fetched the homemade lemonade for the kids. She suspected Cole might prefer a stronger drink after his encounter with Lesley. With all the windows wide open, their voices had drifted inside although the words had been muffled. But the anger in Lesley's voice had been unmistakable.

Both kids looked up at their father when he sat beside them.

"Dad, is that lady okay?" Frowning, Toby pinched his bottom lip with his finger and thumb.

Summer crammed a cookie into her mouth and mumbled, "I think she's cold. I'd be cold if I didn't have any clothes on."

"Don't speak with food in your mouth." Cole smiled when Sasha set a glass of wine down in front of him. "Thanks, Sasha."

"No problem." She settled onto a stool the far side of Summer and swiftly changed the subject. "Toby mentioned the school camp taking place this Thursday.

Apparently, you need a nurse or a first-aider or the camp will be cancelled."

Cole raked a hand through his hair. "Yeah, a lot of people have pulled out."

She linked her hands together. What she wouldn't give to smooth those tousled strands. "Because of the closure?"

Cole nodded. "Lack of funds, I suppose. Plus, those who managed to find other work probably can't afford to take time off."

"I'll come. My qualifications should ensure the camp goes ahead."

"Really?"

Her pulse sped to full throttle in the space of two seconds at the delighted grin on Cole's face. Maybe he hadn't heard the latest gossip after all. Unable to speak, she nodded.

"That would be fantastic."

"Yay!" Tobie high-fived his father. "It's gonna be a blast, Sasha. We'll toast marshmallows over the fire and there's this great gorge. Mr Doherty says we can climb to the top. I can't wait."

"Daddy! I want to go too."

"Sorry, sweetheart, we talked about this, remember? There'll be plenty of times Toby won't be allowed to go on your school excursions."

"Like I would *want* to go on baby stuff," scoffed Toby.

"Tobe … geez. Give it a break, mate." Cole rolled his eyes.

Sasha stifled her smile as Summer scrunched up her face and let out an almighty howl. Toby sniggered which only made his sister bawl louder. Raising her voice to be heard over the din Sasha said, "I have an idea."

The Mitchell clan turned as one to study her. Toby with his mischievous grin, Cole with amusement and exasperation warring on his face, Summer in full flood of crocodile tears that she'd obviously perfected to twist her dad around her little finger.

Under that combined onslaught of crystal-blue eyes, something caught hold of Sasha's heart with such a firm grip she wondered whether she'd ever be able to break free.

She cleared her throat. "If you're a good girl and forget about your brother's camp, I'll help you make a quilt for your dolls. Say, the weekend after the camp? Would you like that, Summer?"

Tears evaporating like a summer shower, Summer was all sunny smiles. "Yay!"

Toby swung his feet. "If Sasha comes to the farm, we can teach her to ride a horse. Can't we, Dad?"

"I want to teach Sasha too."

"You can lend her Peanut, sis. He's a good horse for Sasha to learn on," Toby said, pushing his fist towards his little sister who giggled and rapped his knuckles with her own. "Let's see if Wanda is home and will let us take Alice to feed the piglets. Aunty Amber has some scraps we can use."

"Okay. I like Alice. She's cute and Wanda might give me more beads for my hair." Sliding off her stool, Summer raised her small arms towards Sasha.

Slightly startled, she bent down to receive the hug.

"Thank you, Sasha. You won't forget to come?" Summer's eyes were big and solemn.

"I won't. I promise."

Satisfied, Summer followed her brother who'd retrieved a metal bucket and was walking towards the door. She watched, feeling amazed as brother and sister linked hands as if they'd never been arguing only minutes ago.

"Don't worry. They're very close. Toby likes to tease and Summer thrives on drama," Cole said, laughter rich and deep in his voice.

Her belly quivered in response.

He stood, glass in hand, and took a few sips before saying, "Are you certain you're able to give us a hand?"

"Yes. I'm helping Felicity on a casual basis. Really, my time is my own now that I'm one of those without employment. Is learning to ride a horse mandatory?" Quirking her eyebrows, she drank her cold tea.

"Hey. You'll love it. If everything goes according to plan, you can join our marathon horse-ride."

"Sounds interesting but I'm leaving town soon."

"That's a pity." Face averted, Cole leant his elbows on the kitchen counter.

His tone was polite rather than friendly, the previous warmth he'd shown when she'd volunteered for the camp now cool. Had it all been an act? She was such a fool. Of course he'd be happy his son's camp wouldn't be cancelled. Such a friendly, generous guy was bound to offer something in return. Although, she could do without horse-riding lessons. She dropped her gaze to the mug in her hands as an awkward silence fell.

Eventually, Cole turned to face her, leaning back against the counter. "The first official creditors meeting has been called for this coming Tuesday. We're going to vote for members to sit on the committee and advise Ms Robinson of our decision about her staying on to finish the job she started."

"It's a shame matters have come to this." She eyed him cautiously, noting the tense line of his wide shoulders made bulky by the jacket he wore, and cleared her dry throat. "I hope Felicity and Dave find a way for the company to pay everyone. Have you had time to seek legal advice?"

"Kinda. I contacted Penny, our solicitor, however she suggested we find someone who could offer more specialised assistance. She reviewed the companies you found and agreed the one you recommended, Sheldon and Bragg, would be the best bet. I've reached out but haven't heard back yet. Will you be at the meeting?"

She shook her head. "I'm not sure. I thought it was only for creditors."

"I'll give you an update, if you like. Well, time is marching on and I need to get my kids home before dark." Cole straightened. After gathering up all the glasses and mugs, he walked to the sink where he rinsed them. Turning around, he said, "Would you have dinner with me Tuesday night, say six-thirty? The Fat Buddha has a few Australian dishes if you're not into Chinese or Vietnamese food."

Her heart slammed against her ribs and a rush of heat sizzled through her body. A date! He was asking her out on a date. Hoping she wasn't grinning like a loon, she mumbled, "I love the name and Asian food." She took a deep breath, feeling like she was diving over a cliff face. Head first. "I'd like to have dinner with you very much."

"We can discuss the results of the meeting."

He was hunting for information, not asking her out on a date. Her euphoria deflated and she raised her chin. "Of course."

"We'll need to discuss details for the camp, too." He grinned and her heart did a silly pitter-patter dance. "I'll pick you up at your flat."

"No. I'll meet you there."

The sparkle in his eyes dimmed at her sharp response.

She stuttered, "I'm sorry, it's nothing personal. I'll … I'll explain later."

Shoving his hands into his pockets, Cole frowned. "Will this include that raincheck you mentioned the other night?" The wary expression in his eyes told her loud and clear she had more than one explanation to cover.

He was a man used to responsibility and appeared to shoulder it with ease. He certainly had the build for it. Maybe it was time she sought outside help. *Liar. You just want him to like you.*

"Yes." Flustered, she scooped her satchel off the floor. "I'll meet you out the front of the restaurant at six-thirty."

"No worries." He moved closer, proffering his arm and raising his eyebrows in a suggestive fashion. "Are you staying for the initiation ceremony? I understand your father is keen to show Aunt Amber his dance moves later tonight."

"That is definitely one experience they can have all to themselves." She gave a theatrical shudder and laughed as she slid her hand into the crook of his arm.

Together they walked to the door, their bodies brushing against each other and sending thrills of awareness prickling over her skin. Despite the chill of the waning day, inside she was all warm and cozy.

The prospect of spending more time with him, the sensual curve to his lips and the mischief in his eyes, had her heart spiralling into the clouds.

And the last of her defences melted like snowflakes in summer.

The bleak day had fallen into a frosty night when Sasha jogged up to Mindalby Cotton Company's gates. She didn't know what she expected to find; all she knew was that she desperately needed to get inside those walls. If she didn't? Then she could wave goodbye to her last chance of helping her uncle.

Thankfully, there were no anxious employees or disgruntled subbies hanging around. No doubt cold and hunger had driven them home, given it was close to eight o'clock and the gusting wind was bitter.

What did surprise her though was finding the gates unlocked with one pushed ajar. After a quick check to ensure she was alone, she slipped between the gates and ran towards the shadowy buildings.

A glaring floodlight revealed an unknown ute

drawn up around the corner of the admin office and the sliding glass door open.

Feeling a little like she was a fly and a nasty spider waited inside, she hesitated a few seconds. She flicked on her mobile torch and slipped inside the reception area.

She edged past the four plastic visitors' chairs fronting the narrow counter that separated the entry from the reception area. Old black and white squared lino, faded yellow painted walls and the row of metal filing cabinets along the far side of the wall, did little to alleviate the utilitarian décor.

The sweep of her light sought out the shadows in the rectangular room but revealed no one else.

Floorboards creaked overhead.

Sasha stared at the ceiling. Someone was on the first floor, and whoever it was must have let themselves in with a key as there'd been no sign of forced entry.

Don. It had to be him.

But why creep around his own building in the dark?

Unless he was up to no good.

Well she could either hide down there and wait for him to leave and then continue her own search. Or take a peek and see what he was doing up there in the main office area.

Where her desk was situated.

Heart thudding, she switched off her torch and sneaked up the carpeted stairs. She paused a few steps from the top, straining her eyes and her ears.

He was moving around. Not taking any trouble to hide the noise he made opening cabinet drawers then slamming them shut.

A chair squeaked as if someone had sat down.

The noise sounded faint and she surmised it came from the far side of the room – right where her desk was situated.

What was he up to?

Crouching down, she inched further up the stairs then poked her head around the corner. On the far side of the large room, a wall light had been turned on. Her heart skipped a beat when she spotted the figure with a hoodie drawn over his face, seated at her desk.

The person rifled through the top drawer. Slammed it shut, then opened the next.

Searching for something but what?

The computers had already been taken away by Felicity and Dave. With a muffled curse, the person stood.

Sasha ducked, scrunching her body as low as possible to the top step.

Then she heard the grating sound of a filing cabinet being shifted.

She risked another glance.

The person was pulling the cabinet away from the wall before flicking on a torch to reveal a small safe.

A safe she had had no idea existed. She frowned as she got a better look at the other intruder. Whoever it was, it wasn't Don. This person was quite thin, nothing like her well-fed boss.

A few seconds later, the figure had the safe door open, which seriously surprised Sashs and made her wonder whether it had been locked at all or if they had a key of their own, and was reaching inside the cavity. Sasha caught a brief glimpse of a black rectangular box, like an external hard drive, before they stuffed the object into their jacket pocket.

That could be the second set of accounts Felicity mentioned.

Without thinking it through, Sasha stood and shouted, "Don't move. Police."

"I doubt it," drawled Yasmin Carter. She turned around and pointed. "You're trespassing."

"I could say the same about you. No one's allowed to enter this building."

Yasmin simply raised an eyebrow then turned back to shut the safe. "I'm retrieving my personal belongings. What's your explanation?"

Rubbish!

"Same." Sasha's fingers twitched. Should she call the police? But how would she explain her own presence?

As if discerning her thoughts, Yasmin laughed. "Snap! Now get out of my way." She stalked forward. "Oh and don't forget to lock up after yourself. Not that there's anything to find."

She shouldered past Sasha and jogged down the

stairs. A few minutes later, an engine roared to life then gravel crunched as the vehicle moved off.

Alone in the building, Sasha knew she had seconds to make herself scarce before the police arrived. The first thing that witch would have done was call the cops and spew some lies about seeing lights inside the building.

Frustrated, Sasha rushed for the door. There went her last chance of searching the office and quite possibly the last chance of the true company accounts ever coming to light.

Mid Tuesday morning found Sasha entering the meeting room in the community centre. She'd spent the majority of yesterday sifting through files while worrying about what Yasmin had retrieved from the safe and whether she should mention it to Felicity. Afterwards she'd endured a heavy workout at the local gym, which really was little more than exercise equipment in some bloke's shed. But it was the best the town had to offer and Dale was a good trainer.

Discreetly rubbing her aching thighs, she paused on the threshold and glanced about the room. The place was packed. Of their own volition, her eyes sought and found Cole leaning against the wall.

She drank him in: his dark silky hair, the line of his jaw, the natural curve of his sensual lips, the way his folded arms seemed to emphasise his firm pectorals, how his close-fitting faded denim jeans moulded over strong-looking thighs. She couldn't drag her eyes off him.

He turned. A delighted smile raised sexy to new heights, and he walked over.

She sighed.

He did more than walk—he poured new meaning into the word. His long legs moved an easy grace and a slight swing from his lean hips. All the moisture evaporated from her mouth.

"Sasha. This is a surprise." His hand reached out.

Without conscious thought, she placed hers in his and stared into his crystal eyes.

He swung her hand gently to and fro, while people pushed past.

She had to make a conscious effort to focus. "Warren said since I know about the government assistance, I should come."

Heat flooded her face.

Wickedness sparkled in his eyes and he grinned, tugging her closer. Any closer and her breasts would brush against his chest.

Breathless, she pulled away, putting distance between them and hopefully cooling her tingling body.

Cole squeezed her fingers before releasing her. "I'm hoping the meeting won't last too long. Pop and I have got to get back to the farm and finish up the west field, if I'm to make our dinner date later."

She shrugged, not knowing what to make of his casual tone. Maybe he'd had second thoughts. Her pulse steadied and she found her voice. "We can take another raincheck if that's easier." *Or never.* Her nails dug into her palms while she waited for his response.

He took his time, his eyes examining her face. "Sasha love, I've been looking forward to tonight. But would you mind if we pushed it back another hour? Say seven thirty?"

She nodded.

His lips quirked. Then, he leaned close to her ear and whispered, "Is that a promise, that you'll … come?"

Hating the blush flaming her skin, she stepped away and glared.

Cole chuckled. "Sorry, I couldn't resist." But he didn't sound the least bit sorry.

Cheeky monkey.

"If I can have your attention, please!" hollered Warren from the front of the hall.

"Pop's this way." Cole led her around the side then in between a couple of rows about mid-way down the room.

Jasper Mitchell beamed a welcome. "It's a pleasure seeing you again, Sasha."

"Likewise, Mr Mitchell." She looked around. "Where's Toby and Summer?"

'With my son and his wife. Roger is giving them an art lesson and, hopefully, keeping them out of trouble. We'll pick them up on the way home." He shot a glance at Cole then back to her from under his beetling brows. "Call me Pop."

"I'd like that, Pop, thank you." Touched, she plopped onto her seat and resolutely turned her attention to the stage.

The meeting began with Warren Leadbeater announcing the names of those heading up the creditors' committee. He was interrupted a few times by several blokes jumping to their feet, waving their fists in the air and threatening retribution to the company shareholders.

With the doors closed and the heaters going flat out, it soon became quite warm and the smell of beer turned Sasha's stomach. A good number of attendees must have come from the pub. She hoped the alcohol wouldn't further inflame the tinder that was the crowd's mood.

Warren had phoned her only an hour earlier, asking her to repeat the details of possible government assistance and her pulse picked up as she waited for her turn to address the crowd. The fear she'd be accused of misconduct again ate into her confidence.

When it was her turn to speak, she declined to speak from the stage, instead stood beside her chair. When she'd finished, she flopped back onto her seat.

Felicity walked onto the stage and read a brief statement prepared by the creditors' committee confirming her own appointment. She reiterated her assurances that she and her team would work diligently to find a satisfactory solution.

While the administrator spoke, Sasha sat back and allowed her thoughts to drift. As seemed to be the norm these days, they settled immediately on the hunk beside her.

Her delicious daydreams ceased abruptly when everyone began to stand. The meeting had finished. Few people left immediately. Most stood about talking in huddles and throwing dark glances now and then towards where she still sat attempting to marshal her thoughts.

Warren waved to her and edged his way along the row. "Before you leave, I'd like a word." He sank into the vacant chair next to her.

Leaning forward to include Cole's grandfather in the conversation, he said, "I've been doing a little asking around. You know Cody Nossiter?"

"Yes."

"Yeah well, I know he's a tosser but he doesn't have the brains to think up anything that hasn't been spoonfed to him."

"What are you talking about, Waz?" Cole frowned.

"The gas leak and the hint Sasha here gave me about who was responsible. According to Cody, he was stumbling home that morning after a serious drinking session down by the riverbank, which as you know, Cole, is beyond the alcohol-free zone. He stopped near

Mindalby Cotton to … well you get my drift." Warren reddened.

"Bodily functions. Alcohol. A perfectly natural necessity." She nodded.

Warren continued gruffly, "Cody reckons he saw Carter's car parked near the rear exit an hour or so before the first shift was due. Everyone knows that tosser never turns up at the office until after lunch."

"What are you doing about it?" Cole asked.

Warren rasped a hand over his bristling chin. "I told the cops and the SafeWork nobs but I don't know if they took my report or Cody's claim seriously."

"True. Everyone knows Cody's been mouthing off about Don since the closure," said Cole.

"I don't want Herb to get the blame for something he didn't do once they get wind of his OCD issues. It's his job to check everything else is turned off at the end of the shifts."

"Did Cody give the police a written statement? Either way, I'll let Felicity know. It could have a bearing on her investigations," Sasha said also thinking about what she saw the other night.

"Nah, Cody gets the hives if he goes too close to the cops. They've attempted to contact him but he's ignoring their calls." Warren clapped his hands down hard on his thighs. 'I thought you should know."

"We appreciate the heads-up, Waz. Thanks." Cole held out his hand and shook Warren's.

"Most of this lot are going to the pub." Warren

shook his head. "Thought I'd go and talk the lads into only having one or two. I can see tonight ending badly if they hang around too long. We've got a lot of worried people here. Who knows what will happen once they get their bellies full of grog."

With a jerk of his head, he indicated the bottleneck at the doorway where a bunch of people were attempting to exit the room all at once, jostling each other in a snarled tangle.

No good-natured banter could be heard—only curses and dark mutterings.

And the frequent mention of Sasha's name.

The sun had fled the cold day, ducking below the horizon at five-thirty. When Sasha left her flat, the evening was ice cold, still and dark, with no wind and no moon. Shivering, she walked briskly along the road. She tugged her hood lower over her face then dug her gloved hands into her parka pockets.

Her footsteps rang out loud in the empty street. With curtains drawn against the bleak night, little light spilled out from homes. The shadows lay deep between the widely-spaced street lights. The hairs on her nape prickled and she stopped, positive a footfall sounded behind her.

She listened. Nothing.

Glancing around, she studied the street. There were a couple of kids shooting ball through a hoop attached to a house garage a few doors down but no one else on the pavement.

Shrugging, she continued, but her hand clenched over the pocketknife she always carried. She looked behind several times, positive she could feel eyes watching her, but saw no one.

Her anxiety raising its ugly head again? Or was she really being followed?

Either way, she was relieved to see the bright lights glowing out the front of the Fat Buddha restaurant.

Bang on the dot of seven-thirty, Cole climbed out of the Land Rover he'd parked alongside the kerb. One hand was held behind his back. As he approached in that long-limbed graceful stride of his, he whipped out an offering of flowers wrapped in gold paper and tied with white and gold ribbons.

Sasha buried her nose in the blooms, inhaling the delicious scent of paperwhites, daffodils and cream and yellow calendulas amidst a spray of emerald green fern. "These are beautiful. Thank you, Cole."

She pushed to the toes of her knee-high brown boots and placed a gentle kiss on his cheek. His skin was smooth and warm to the touch and the contact sent her pulse skipping with delight.

"Shall we?"

"Yes, please."

He opened the door and ushered her in where he was greeted by name by a smiling Vietnamese woman, Kim Nguyen, who led the way to their table.

Sasha smiled a little as he held out the chair for her, appreciating the courtesy. She shrugged out of her parka while sweeping her gaze over the red and gold walls. "I like the wallpaper."

Cole took off his heavy jacket, revealing a navy-blue dress shirt and dark grey trousers. He looked gorgeous and fit and she was glad she'd taken time over her own appearance.

"With your green dress, I'm reminded of Christmas."

She grinned and handed her parka to Mrs Nguyen who bore their outer garments and the flowers off to a cloak room. "I like Christmas."

"So do I. I never realised how much though until tonight." His eyes crinkled at the corners, his smile wide. No hint of any reservation in his expression; he was the epitome of a guy eager to enjoy her company.

She could feel the answering tug at her lips and the magical surge of her heart wanting to open and welcome him inside. How had he remained unattached again for so long? Gosh, he only had to glance in her direction and she was a puddle on the floor. It was more than his sexy good-looks. It was the deep love he had for his children and family that called to her. The integrity in his steady gaze. The ease with which he appeared to shoulder responsibility.

He was a forever guy.

More than a little shaken, she fiddled with her spoon. Should she run while she still had the chance?

Before she could make up her mind, Mrs Nguyen reappeared with menus.

And Cole looked over and smiled.

I want this night. Decision made.

After consulting with Sasha, Cole gave their order then requested a bottle of sauvignon blanc from a nearby boutique vineyard.

She said, "Well, here we are; having that raincheck."

"I do have a few questions." He quirked his brows in a self-deprecating fashion.

She was glad he'd broached the subject. It was time to clear the air—well, as much as she intended to divulge. "The other night at the mill, you must have thought I was crazy. I'm not sure if I thanked you or not, but I did appreciate your support."

"After the brick episode, I didn't like the thought of you wandering about in a storm at night by yourself," he admitted slowly.

"I was glad you were with me." She drew a deep breath and placed her hands on the table. "Fire away."

He shook his head, reached out and covered her hands with his. "Now that we're here, all I want to do is look at you and savour the moment."

His warmth embraced her. The ardent heat in his eyes took her breath away; sent her belly quivering on a roller-coaster of dizzy emotions. He was such a gorgeous guy, inside and out. *I want him. I want all of him.* A little overwhelmed, she dropped her gaze to her hands, where he gently traced the puckered scarring with his forefinger, not saying anything. With the majority of her nerve ends severely damaged, his touch hadn't registered. He was giving her an out. Letting her know she didn't have to spill her fears or bare her soul. Or maybe he'd decided he didn't want to know the truth. *But she was tired of being along.* Her eyes blurred with hot tears and her constraints faded away.

"No, you need to know why I'm in Mindalby." In a low voice, she gave a brief account of Uncle Isaac's arrest and ultimate conviction. She then included what little information the family's private investigator had unearthed. She told Cole of the overheard conversation between Yasmin and Don Carter. But she made no mention of how Don had wined and dined her before offering her the job.

She paused when Mrs Nguyen returned with their wine.

"Thank you, Kim. Perfect." A faint frown creasing his forehead, Cole released her hands to pour the wine into their wine glasses. "Let me get this straight. You came to Mindalby to find evidence on Yasmin Carter in the hope of clearing your uncle's name."

"Or at least provide grounds for a mistrial."

"Are you certain you have the right woman?"

"Yes, the PI we hired was very thorough."

He leaned back, shaking his head. "It all sounds very thin."

She grimaced. "I know but we're desperate and Mum is so worried about my uncle. We all are."

"Did you find anything?"

Sasha closed her eyes and pressed her fingers to her lids for a few seconds. When she opened them, she read genuine concern. "No … Well, that is … Really, it's probably nothing. I could well be over-reacting but I'm beginning to have doubts about the real reason I was hired."

"I did wonder." Cole lowered his eyelids; his lips thinned.

That blasted Jo Johnson and her talk show. "You heard Chat Hour last Friday."

"No, but I've been told about it."

"Unsubstantiated gossip. There is nothing between me and Don Carter." Her voice was firm, while her heart cringed from the half-truth. "Our only link is his wife." She rushed on when he didn't respond, instead taking a long moment to sip his wine, like he was considering her words. "I believe that my inexperience in accounts was the clincher for me to get the job. From several comments Felicity Robinson has made, I could well be on the way to being the scapegoat for the company folding."

"Sasha, that's not a good position to be in." He sounded genuinely concerned.

"Tell me about it," she quipped. *So he had no intention of dissecting her assertion about Don.* Wise move, because she had no intention of admitting her questionable actions. Not with this sizzling chemistry simmering between them.

He leaned forward and captured her gaze. "Have you sought legal advice?"

"Not yet, although Felicity suggested I should." She huffed out a small sigh. "If I contact our family solicitor, Mum will get wind of it. The last thing she needs is to worry about me."

He reached over and rubbed his thumb gently over her scarred hand. "You must love your uncle very much to put your career on hold for him."

"I do love him dearly but I actually had little choice where my career is concerned." This was it, the moment she dreaded. Normally the very idea of talking about what had happened sent her rushing to the bathroom to throw up, followed by a meltdown.

Instead, a feeling of calm stole over her. Raising her chin, she met his eyes. "My last post was a refugee camp in the Middle East. Eleven months ago, we had to move due to the advancing conflict. The convoy I was travelling in got caught in cross-fire and our truck was hit by a submunition bomb. I was injured, evacuated home and spent months in intensive care in a Sydney hospital.

"When the connection was made between Don's wife and Uncle Isaac, I thought Mindably would be the perfect place for me to complete my recovery and help my uncle."

"It sounds like you were seriously hurt. Your hands are badly scarred." His jaw worked, like he held back strong emotions. Like he cared.

Her pulse tripping like a giddy dancer, she hesitated. Would he be repulsed? Would he back off and this toe-curling heat between them turn tepid? "I was badly burned. The rest of my arm and upper back … It's not a pretty sight."

"Nothing could ever take away your inner beauty." He winked. "Of course, what I can see of your outside isn't that bad either."

Flopping back in her chair, she laughed, enjoying his teasing. And oh so delighted that the ardent fire in his eyes hadn't died.

"Have you made a full recovery?"

"Physically—well, almost, I have physio once a week. I've got to pass a full fitness assessment before I can resume my nursing career and that includes my mental state."

"It must have been terrifying."

"Yeah." Swallowing, she looked away for a few seconds. "It haunts me."

He hesitated before saying quietly, "Were others injured?"

"Yes," she whispered. "Some of my colleagues didn't make it. Then there was Saad, my patient." She forced back the grief clutching at her throat.

"I'm sorry, Sasha, love. It's hard losing people you know in such tragic circumstances. I can't imagine the pain you've suffered." He cleared his throat. "I didn't mean to rake up unpleasant memories."

She wasn't the only one who had lost someone.

"No, the grief is always there. But this is the first time, I've spoken about it without feeling an overwhelming sense of guilt." She looked at him wonderingly as the realisation settled deep in her soul. A sense of peace softened the sharpness of her memories.

"Guilt is a hard cross to carry. When a mate died three years ago, I kept thinking I should have been there for him." Cole shook his head, the corners of his mouth turning down as his jaw tightened. "Al had been in a bad place for a long time, and I failed to see he needed help."

His steady gaze met hers, understanding, and so warm that all the cold shadows in her heart slipped away.

She turned his hands over, encasing them in hers, her hold gentle but strong. Did he also feel guilt over his wife's death? "That must have been very hard for you."

He glanced down at their clasped hands then nodded. After a few seconds he said, "Being injured so badly certainly explains your father's over-protective behaviour. I'm surprised he hasn't insisted on coming with you tonight." His tone was light and she followed his lead onto a less confronting topic.

"He's attending a meditation session at the commune. But I have a feeling I'll be on the receiving end of quite a few arguments once I'm cleared for duty again."

When I'll leave here. The image of the garden

outside her kitchen window sprang to mind. Gently retrieving her hand, she lifted her wine glass and sipped. Suddenly, she wanted to tell him everything. She wanted no secrets or barriers between them.

"There's more. I cycle because I just can *not* get inside a vehicle. I have a moped I use for long distances but I prefer to bike most places."

"PTSS? Post traumatic stress syndrome?"

She nodded.

"Understandable, given what you've experienced. After Al, I read up on it so I have a basic understanding." Frowning, he took a deep breath that caused his navy-blue shirt to tighten across his well-formed pectorals.

She sighed inwardly, imagining gliding her hands over those firm muscles.

"Sasha, about the camp. The last thing I want is to interfere with your recovery or cause you more suffering. It's okay if you want to change your mind. We can find someone else."

"Oh but I want to come!"

Cole's lips compressed. "You won't be able to get in the bus."

"No biggie. I'll ride my moped and meet you there." She lifted an eyebrow.

"You did say you're still attending physio, meaning you're not one hundred per cent recovered. There'll be hiking and climbing involved."

Her voice sharpened. "I'm no hothouse flower. I can deal with it."

They glared at each other.

Giving a rueful laugh, Cole raised a hand. "Look at us. Fighting already. It's as if we've known each other for years. I just want what's best for you."

"Cole, I value my independence. I've looked after myself for a long time. I don't need a sexy guy wanting to wrap me in cotton wool."

"Now that's telling me where to go." Picking up his glass, he saluted her, his gaze steady and intense. "I apologise if I slighted you. But I warn you, Sasha, it's my nature to protect those I care about. And that is something for which I won't apologise."

Her fingers shaking, heart stuttering, she clinked glasses with Cole. "That's … heavy."

"I know. Scared?" Grinning, he rolled his eyes in an exaggerated manner. "I am."

She laughed. "We can be scared together."

"I'd like that," Cole said in his deep voice.

The waitress walked over and laid down several steaming bowls.

Sniffing appreciatively, Sasha smiled. "Smells delicious. I'm starving."

"Good. So am I. It's been a long day."

She lifted the lid off a ceramic bowl and helped herself to fragrant jasmine rice. "Is the harvester fixed?"

"Yeah, the part arrived today. Another week and we should have the remainder of the cotton harvested."

Cole spooned a generous serving of stir-fried beef and broccoli in special sauce onto Sasha's plate before placing some on his own.

"What happens then?"

"We'll let the cotton fields rest while we plant a summer crop of vegetables in the other field. In a couple of months' time, we'll plant more cotton seed. If we have the money."

"Now that the creditor committee approved Felicity to continue as voluntary administrator, you might get access to your cotton in Carter's yard."

Cole finished chewing a mouthful of beef before saying, "I hope so. But I reckon we'll be pushed to pay our gin processing charges before they'll release our bales."

"That makes sense. But you also have unprocessed cotton at the mill which you can send elsewhere. And you may yet end up getting paid for your contracting work."

"Sounds good but I'm not holding my breath. Who knows when they'll release our bales? I've placed an application in with proof of ownership and all we can do now is wait. I really could so with that welding payment though. I've got plans already underway for the money."

"Like putting in a swimming pool for summer?" she joked as she wielded her chopsticks with expert precision and picked up a piece of succulent broccoli.

His answering smile was brief and fierce. "I'm using

that money to help fund a charity horse-ride. My goal is to raise public awareness of rural mental health issues."

His declaration rang with resolve. It sounded personal and she thought of what he'd said about his mate. "That's wonderful. Do you have a name for the ride?"

"I thought, *Ride for Outback Health*. Going all the way from Mindalby to Darwin."

"I like it. Short and says everything. My stay here has definitely given me a new perspective on living so far from suburbia and all the mod cons. I didn't understand the challenges isolated towns like Mindalby face." She placed her chopsticks onto the table, her gaze fixed on his serious face, every atom of her body humming with a mixture of curiosity and awareness of the man opposite.

He grimaced. "Mental health is a huge issue for farmers and remote regions like ours. Even everyday health problems are an issue. Our hospital can only cater for general stuff like broken bones, minor surgery, childbirth."

Cole picked up a bowl of gong bao chicken and offered it to her. "Most serious cases are airlifted to Dubbo or Newcastle which adds to the danger of losing a patient en route. We've got a small clinic attached to the hospital which is manned once a month for a few hours by a psychologist from Dubbo. And they're on a rotating roster system."

She nodded. "Hard for a patient to build a rapport if their counsellor keeps changing."

"Exactly." Cole abandoned his food and leaned forward. Passion for his cause blazed like brilliant blue diamonds in his eyes. "You get it. Not many people do. What I'd really love is for a permanent clinic to be established in Mindalby with a resident psychologist. We could service the outlying smaller towns and villages. People could get the help they needed before it's too late. And it's not only mental health issues. Alcohol is a big problem in the district."

"Go on." She closed her hand gently over his fist.

"The mate I mentioned earlier was Al Schumacher. He died in a car accident that I suspect was intentional. He'd lost the family farm to the bank months before and wasn't dealing well with consequent family pressures." He paused for a second, glancing away and blinking rapidly. When he turned back, his dark eyelashes were damp and her heart wrenched. "I got talking to Paul Carey on the anniversary of Al's death. I came up with the idea of the charity horse-ride and since both of us were on the same page, we nutted out a plan of action."

"The ride you mentioned?"

Cole nodded. "Pop and my kids are coming too. Some locals. Paul's on board. With his skills as a saddler he'll be able to deal with any repairs needed on the trip. If we can get enough numbers, we may make the news."

His voice was glum as he picked up his chopsticks and poked about in his bowl. "But, like I said, what we need are mental health workers who will either live in town or can visit regularly."

"Who else is helping you organise this event?"

"Apart from Pop and Paul Carey, Mum has done a couple of fundraisers but this is a small community. Although we pull together, most of us are short of spare cash. A splashy media campaign would help big time but that costs money. Government assistance wouldn't go amiss either."

She picked up her wineglass. "What you need is an experienced major donor fundraiser expert. Or two."

'You sound like you know someone." Cole quirked his eyebrows, his dark mood evaporating.

"I can't promise anything but I'll run your event past Mum and Raphael. That's my latest stepfather, and a whole other story! But they're both well-known in social circles for obtaining fantastic results with charity fundraising." She smiled.

"Thanks, I appreciate it." He indicated another bowl. "Try the Buddha's Delight. It's the best braised vegetables and mushrooms you'll ever eat."

"I need to be able to fit through the door when we leave."

Cole laughed as he dished a serving into her bowl. "Never fear. At one time this was a butcher shop and the rear entrance has a single roller door. I'm sure I'll be able to push you through it—in a wheelbarrow if necessary."

"My hero."

"Seriously, though, if you need help clearing your uncle, I'm here. But no more breaking and entering."

"Thank you, Cole. You haven't questioned his innocence. You've just accepted my word for it."

"I know integrity when I see it. Tell me, why nursing? And why the hot zones?"

Her face flamed. If he ever discovered she hadn't told the whole truth about herself and Don Carter, it would be the end of her so-called integrity. Fingers shaking, she sampled the Buddha's Delight then muttered, "This is wonderful."

"Isn't it, just? Don't try to change the subject. I want to know everything about you."

Like I want to discover everything about you. "There really isn't a lot to tell."

"What about children, any plans for some of your own? What about a significant other?"

For some weird reason, an image of Summer and Toby popped into her mind. She pushed back her hair, impatiently. "I did that once—the significant other thing. I dated a guy through university and for two years afterwards while I completed my training. The moment he offered me a ring, I told him I'd accepted a post in London."

"That's ..." He dropped his gaze to the table.

She tapped the tip of her chopstick thoughtfully

against her lower lip. "Cruel? Harsh? I know Gerald was hurt at the time, but six months later he was engaged to a paralegal in his law firm. Looking back, I believe I did the right thing for both of us. We weren't meant to be a forever couple and I … well, I wanted more than he could give me."

He looked up and for a split second, she saw that wary shadow lurking in his dark eyes. "Not monetary, I take it? Sorry, but you don't give the impression money is a problem for you or your family."

"It's not," she said frankly. "Mum is an astute businesswoman in her own right and came from a well-off family. Dad has a successful practice and even though he's always off travelling, he's comfortable financially. I have a small studio flat in Sydney which I rent out when I'm overseas working."

"Then what was it? What couldn't your boyfriend give you?" His gaze bored into her eyes, searching her soul.

"Fulfilment." She raised her eyebrows at his swift frown.

"These days women juggle both careers and family."

"I know. Maybe when it comes right down to it, Gerald wasn't my forever guy." She recalled Cole's words about his grandparents' marriage and his own. He'd given the impression he hadn't found his forever woman in his deceased wife. But was he still looking?

Cole dabbed the napkin over his lips then crumpled

it into a ball. Was he remembering Denise? Did he feel guilty for being here with another woman?

Sasha rubbed her brow where tension was brewing. She didn't know which was the strongest urge. To rush out and wrap her arms around his motherless children. Or to fling herself into Cole's arms and kiss away his pain.

She rushed to fill the expanding silence. "I've tried to explain my passion for nursing to Mum to no avail. Dad understood to a certain extent, but he's no longer comfortable with me returning to a refugee camp. All I can say is that it satisfies a need inside me to try and make a difference. Mum thinks it has something to do with my baby sister dying of SIDs."

"But you don't have to go to the other side of the world to a country at war to make a difference," Cole pointed out, sharply. "There's plenty to do here."

"My country needs me and that sort of thing?" she joked, hoping for a return of their earlier camaraderie.

He placed his chopsticks into his bowl with an air of finality. A dimple appeared in the crease of his left cheek as his sudden smile widened. "Just saying. Mindalby could use a nurse with your experience. And if you hung around, I'd get to see more of you."

"Is that what you want?" Her nails bit into her palms.

"Sasha, you have no idea how much I want to see all of you." His voice deepened, rolling over her senses like a juggernaut, obliterating her doubts over the wisdom of becoming involved with this charismatic man.

A man who, once she returned to her old life, she would never see again.

A man who thought she had integrity.

He picked up her hand and tenderly kissed her fingertips, one at a time.

Forget her deliberate omission about Don Carter. It was only a half-lie after all. A couple of dinners that had led nowhere. Once she explained, Cole would understand.

The tip of his tongue licked the sensitive pad of her palm. Heat flashed through her body, igniting a blazing fire. But this was nothing like that other agonising experience; this was all tingling nerves and prickling flesh—and sizzling anticipation.

Her thoughts became chaotic. She *could* stay. She could extend the lease on her flat, work on the garden in her backyard, get a job at the hospital or work in the clinic if Cole's dream came to fruition. She'd go on picnics with Cole and his lovely children, learn to ride a horse, dance under the moonlight with his aunt—and spend her nights wrapped in Cole's arms.

Her heart raced, adrenaline flooding her system. This small town was crying out for help. Why, she could go back to university and study psychology! Excitement sparked.

A silly day dream, but …? Could she make it work? *I don't know if it's possible for me to stay in the one place.*

And if she attempted to do so, if or when she gave into her restlessness and took flight, not only Cole would be affected.

His children.

His family.

She'd leave them behind. The thought was painful, slamming her back to Earth with a rude thud. She rubbed her aching chest, muttering, "I've been a bit of a nomad most of my life."

Cole raised his eyebrows.

Her cheeks flushed. As well he might look surprised seeing how she had just dropped that little gem out of nowhere. "Sorry, I was thinking out loud."

He opened his sensual lips as if about to question her, then closed them, a frown forming on his forehead.

She blurted, "What I really want to know is if you'll walk me home after dinner?'

"I'd love to." His answer was satisfyingly prompt.

"And come in for coffee?" she asked in a soft voice. If she'd been a piece of tinder she'd burst into flames at the naked hunger in his eyes.

"I'd like nothing better."

An hour later was Sasha walking along the footpath, hand-in-hand with Cole. He'd left his Land Rover at the restaurant, saying that jogging back to retrieve it would help burn off the dessert he'd consumed.

The night sky was ablaze with crystal-white stars. There was an icy hint of frost in the air that mingled wonderfully with the scents of wood smoke and the outback. *I like it here.* The thought lodged deep in her mind and she cuddled in to Cole's hard, warm body. Her career, the path she'd mapped for herself—it all seemed far away, like an old memory. Fuzzy around the edges, its power lessened by time and distance. And something else she wasn't prepared to give a name to.

Tonight wasn't about tomorrow or the days that would follow.

Tonight would be about a man and a woman and a need as old as the Earth.

Tonight was about her and him.

She couldn't wait to feel his hands on her naked skin for real. Her knees trembled as she imagined his slow glide over her sensitive inner thighs, the way he'd take care to explore and give pleasure. And she couldn't wait to give that same pleasure back to him.

A car approached, its headlights bright. She shaded her eyes, unable to make out the model as the vehicle slowed as if the driver was checking them out. Then it was past, picking up speed and disappearing down the road. For some reason, she thought of her earlier feeling of being followed. Frowning, she shook off her unease and cuddled closer.

His masculine scent was subtle and fresh, reminding her of the sea. She wondered whether he'd taste just as salty and couldn't wait to find out.

When they reached her flat, she paused, key in the lock, and looked into Cole's intent face. "Are you still game?"

His teeth gleamed in the darkness, as he smiled. "Love, I'm up for anything where you're concerned."

Oh, if only that was true. Her pulse sky-rocketed. She fumbled with the key for a few seconds before the lock caught and she was able to push open the door.

Cole moved, barely waiting for the lock to engage behind her before cupping her face in his cool hands. "I feel like I've waited my entire life for you. I know I damn well can't wait any longer."

Tears burned. She couldn't speak past her clogged throat. Instead she raised her lips to meet his.

They came down, hot and hungry, in a searing kiss that shot to the tips of her fingers and toes. Flinging her arms around his neck, she held on like nothing else mattered but the here and now and the magic surrounding them.

Sensation cascaded through her. Desire pooled and she fell deeper into the sexual haze sizzling like firecrackers between them. The desperate need to feel his skin against hers imploded in her brain.

"I can't wait either." Sliding her shaking hands from under his shirt, she yanked at his jacket.

He laughed huskily and slipped his arms beneath her, lifting her off her feet. "Which way to your bedroom? I'll be damned if I'll make love to you on a hard, cold floor."

PROPPED UP ON HIS ELBOW, Cole gazed down at Sasha as she slept. The moonlight from the uncurtained window revealed the thickness of her eyelashes, dark shadows against her pale skin.

What had happened with keeping his distance? One look at her and he was putty in her hands. What was it about this woman that swept aside all common sense, his reservations?

And he sure had more than one.

She was different from his wife, Denise, who'd been his best friend since childhood. Denise had seemed so content with a simple life, had never wanted a job outside the home and had hated the idea of travelling any further than Bourke. She'd never held any surprises for him, so well did he know her. But she'd been a good friend and wife, a loving mother and—the problem was, he could also imagine Sasha in the same role.

The fascinating woman so innocently sleeping beside him was fast filling the lonely void Denise's death had left behind.

She worked for a business that had shut its doors and hurt his town; an action that could well have put paid to his dreams of honouring Al's memory, not to mention placing additional strain on what was already a tight farm budget.

She crept around locked yards at the dead of night and in the middle of a thunderstorm, supposedly looking for a stranger's phone.

She appeared fearless and utterly resolved in her determination to help others; no matter the cost.

She was fiercely independent, disdaining any offer of assistance, and had so far lived an adventurous and somewhat dangerous life.

She was rumoured to be Don Carter's discarded lover but she'd denied that.

She was kind and caring towards her father and Cole's own kids, generous with her time searching for ways to help those who'd lost their jobs, diligent with looking for evidence to free her uncle.

And she was lovely; more than physically beautiful, even despite the scarring on her upper arms and back. It was the warmth that filled her face when she looked at her father, the joy that sparkled in her eyes when she laughed, and the honesty with which she steadily regarded the world around her.

And she was a woman who slept with a knife beneath her pillow.

He could hardly have missed it, especially since their energetic love-making had sent it thudding to the floor. Nor had he missed how she had tensed and leaned over, as if checking the knife's location, before she'd relaxed.

Tenderly, he brushed strands of her soft hair from her face.

She stirred, shifted then opened her eyes. "Hey there. You look … serious."

Cole smiled. Leaning down, he pressed a gentle kiss to her lips. "I was thinking about where we go from here."

The instant the words left his mouth, he regretted them as Sasha narrowed her sexy slanted eyes.

"Home for you. We both have to get up for work in the morning."

"So conscientious. I'm impressed," he teased, hoping for a return of their earlier rapport.

"I'm merely pointing out the obvious." Her smile seemed forced and his heart sank.

He pushed back the doona, then swung his bare feet to the floor. "Fair enough."

"Cole …"

When he glanced back, she was biting her lip.

Taking a deep breath and gathering the blanket closer, Sasha sighed. "I honestly don't know what happens next. I've never felt so adrift."

In an instant, he was leaning close, his fingers stroking the sides of her face. What he wouldn't give to stay the entire night with her. She felt soft and warm beneath his touch. Her cheeks were flushed and he recalled how glazed her eyes had been after they'd made love. An expression he was determined to see again. Unfortunately duty called. But he'd be damned if this would be his one and only taste of her. Because one taste of Sasha could never be enough. "Love, so am I, but I don't want it to end here."

He kissed the tip of her nose then brushed his knuckles against the side of her face. Her eyelashes fluttered in a very satisfying manner. Reluctantly, he pushed off the bed and began to pick up his scattered clothes. "Toby is counting on your presence at his school camp."

"I haven't forgotten. I'll be at the national park around eleven am."

Grinning, Cole hopped into his trousers then did up his zipper. "Mum said to tell you that if you're after quilt supplies, to drop into the CWA hall on Saturday. There usually is one or more of her hens around and they'll be able to give you some stuff."

Sasha giggled. "Hens!"

"What can I say? When they're all in a room together, it's like a cackling hen-house."

She smiled. "That's kind of your mother. Thanks. I was wondering where I'd find the material for Summer's quilt."

"She's really looking forward to it."

"I am too," she said simply, hugging the doona to her chest.

Cole laughed and found his boots. "It's all Summer's talked about these past few days. Between her chattering over the quilt and Toby raving about how you're coming to the camp, my kids are just about driving us all crazy with their excitement. You'll like the national park."

"It sounds like it's going to be lots of fun."

"With you there, love, what else could it be?" He placed his hand over his heart and emitted a mournful sigh.

"Idiot!" Grinning, she threw a pillow at him.

Cole buttoned up his shirt and found his socks. "Never fear when I am near."

She burst out laughing and threw the other pillow. "I can see where Summer gets her love of drama from."

Grinning, he held up her dressing gown. "Up you get and send me on my way, before I turn into a pumpkin."

They exchanged another long kiss on the front doorstep, which sorely tempted her to invite him back into her bed. Then he left. She remained standing there long after he disappeared from sight, waving and smiling like a loon, before heading back inside and securing the bolts. Yawning through a wide grin stretching her face, she wandered along the hall then stopped.

A scratching sound came from the back of the house.

She grimaced. Switching on the kitchen light, she began flinging open cupboard doors. Nothing. No tell-tale tiny dark droppings.

She sniffed. No dusty smell that caught in the back of her throat.

Frowning, she stopped her rummaging and listened.

Timber creaked as if some heavy force pushed it. Leaves rustled. The side fence? Could someone have just climbed over it?

She snatched up her wooden rolling pin from its cradle on the counter and tip-toed to the rear door. She waited for a couple of minutes but heard no more noises. After repositioning her grip on the rolling pin, she eased back the bolt and opened the door.

Nothing but the gloom of pre-dawn met her eyes.

No one rushed forward to attack.

No movement in the yard beyond.

Her tension eased. Then she stiffened. Her nose twitched as an acrid, familiar stench hit.

Decay.

Her gaze followed the smell and there, on the cement, lay a dead mouse. Its little head had been smashed.

Someone had left her a message.

WEDNESDAY DRAGGED BY, cold and with a stiff breeze that swept leaves over the footpaths in an untidy fashion and tangled wet sheets around clotheslines.

Inside the community centre, the oil heater beneath the window made the temperature in the office bearable—just. As she examined yet another debtor's folder, Sasha caught herself checking her mobile, again. No missed calls. No text messages.

And that was a good thing. She didn't want a needy guy nor did she want to come over as needy either. But she couldn't deny she would have liked to hear the sound of Cole's warm voice.

Problem was, she didn't know what she wanted anymore. Biting her lip, she paused and gazed out the small window and into the courtyard. Leaves and grass still wet from the early morning fog, glistened in the thin sunlight. A huge cobweb adorning a bush rosemary sparkled as if woven from diamond dust. And from a tree close by, a kookaburra burst into his signature cackle.

She was falling for him. No restless urge to pack her bags and run assailed her. She liked this life. So where does that leave her? What if he didn't feel the same? She doubted Cole wouldn't be looking for a serious relationship with her. Sure he was lonely but he'd hardly be eager to jump headlong into another with a woman he'd known for a few days.

And it sounded like his wife had left big shoes to fill.

If that was the way he felt, she should be glad. Settling down, a family—that was never her life plan. And yet, here she was, reluctant to schedule the health appointment that could clear her for work.

With a start, she realised since she'd met Cole she'd also stopped browsing the net for nursing jobs. That dumb idea of sleeping with him, hoping it would sate her needs, had been a mistake. All it had done was feed her desire for more: more Cole, more love, more … everything about him.

The idea of sharing with him all of life's joys and challenges was taking root—so tempting, so very tempting.

Deep in thought, she reached for her coffee mug

and downed the last drop of tepid liquid. If she couldn't find any evidence to assist Uncle Isaac soon, there would be no need to stay in Mindalby.

She wasn't certain she wanted to leave anymore, but could she stay here forever? Her passion, her life, had always been tuned towards helping others. And there was a hidden part of her that thrived in the challenge of being close to danger.

After a few years, would she become restless? Would she leave, desert everyone who loved her?

Hurting them, disappointing them—that was the last thing she wanted to do.

The prudent action would be to leave before she became any more involved with Cole and his children. But the thought of doing so wrenched her heart so painfully, she caught her breath.

Well, she had promised to go on that camp with Toby and make a quilt with Summer.

And she was a woman who always kept her promise. She pushed aside the archive box she'd been working on and opened the next.

At first, her eyes were too blurry for her to focus. She blinked. Sighed. Re-read the top piece of paper— then froze before grabbing her mobile and snapping a shot of the invoice. Heart drumming, she performed a quick search on the internet, carefully absorbing the little information she found.

After poking her head out the door and ensuring

that neither Felicity nor Dave were within earshot, she tried the phone number.

Breathless, she waited until a tired voice barked into the other end. "Yeah? Taylor's Repairs."

"Um, I'm phoning from Mindalby Cotton Company in relation to an invoice for repairs on the *Last Chance*."

"What about it? Is the lady still having problems with her engine?"

"No, no, the engine's fine. I wanted to know if you could give me more details regarding the exact nature of the repairs and email it to me? We need it for warranty purposes," she improvised.

"That doesn't surprise me," came the disgruntled voice. "That engine should never have failed seeing how Mrs Carter only bought the bloody yacht a coupla months before the thing clapped out. Previous owner reckoned the engine was brand new. She was lucky it happened in the harbour and not on that trip she had planned."

"Trip?" Sasha re-positioned her sweaty grip on the phone. "I work in the office and wasn't aware she's going away."

"This was some time ago, lady. She's probably been and gone. Let's see now. Give me a sec while I check me files."

She heard the clatter as the phone was placed down, the squeak of a cabinet drawer being opened, then the rustle of paper.

"Yep. Here it is. We did more than fix the main

Cummins engine. Did a complete check-up on the other two smaller wing engines as well and all the winches. She sure was a bloody pearler. We're a small business. We don't often get the opportunity to work on an expedition yacht."

"Expedition yacht?"

"Yeah, that's her classification. She's built to cruise around the world and with her low aspect sails and push-button winches, doesn't need a lot of crew."

Cruising the world! Perhaps Yasmin had it in mind to use the yacht to slip the country ostensibly on a cruise up the coast. "Could you sail her single-handed?"

"Look lady, I'm a mechanic. I don't sail myself but with this beauty, I guess it's possible. Hey listen, I thought you said you worked for that woman's company? Why all the questions?"

"Oh, I do, it's just that I know very little about boats."

"More than a boat, lady. She's a real little ripper."

"And that trip you mentioned, that was when she went to …?" If Yasmin had already gone on the voyage, then maybe she wasn't planning a runner and Sasha's imagination was the one doing all the running. Maybe she was making a whole pile of something out of fairy floss. It was probable the trip had been something simple, like a sail to the Great Barrier Reef and back. But just on the off chance, she had to find out as much as possible.

"Dunno, I didn't pay that much attention. When she

was in our office, Mrs Carter was on the phone to someone yakking about the Cook Islands. Or was it the Bahamas? Lady, we're going back at least two years ago here."

She frowned wondering what he'd said that sounded familiar. "That's all right. You've been a big help. If you could send the additional information to my email address, that would be great." She rattled off the details and ended the call.

The minutes seemed like hours until her mobile pinged, signifying she'd received an email. She opened it and read the contents; then, not wanting to be seen to be withholding anything that could, even remotely, have a bearing on the current situation, forwarded the information onto Felicity. After checking Dave wasn't in the office, she phoned the investigator her mother had hired.

Five minutes later, the call was over, and he was in possession of both the invoice and the email from Taylor's Repairs while Sasha was left slumped in her chair. She wiped her damp forehead with the back of her sleeve and wondered whether she should update her mother or wait until she heard back. The investigator had given her hope that finally they may have caught a break in their quest to find something on Yasmin Carter.

He'd told Sasha that he'd do a search into the registration and ownership of the boat and a little digging into when the boat was acquired. If Yasmin was the owner, at the very least it could raise questions with the Taxation Office how she could have afforded the purchase of a yacht that usually sold for around one and a half million dollars.

The significance of the figure wasn't lost on Sasha.

It could well be a coincidence that the sum, give or take a couple of hundred dollars, matched the amount missing from Uncle Isaac's employer's account; but Sasha knew in her gut, the purchase was connected.

Frowning, she leaned back in the chair and stared at the ceiling while she considered. There'd been that dead silence for a good sixty seconds, when she'd relayed her conversation with the bloke from Taylor's Repairs. Had it been the mention of the Bahamas and Cook Islands that had caught the investigator's attention?

She thought about her own reaction to those words and gasped. Hands shaking, she rummaged amongst the folders and files on her desk until she found a single sheet of paper. Dave had given her these details, not long after she volunteered to assist him and Felicity. It was a list of businesses she had to keep an eye out for. She traced her finger down the page.

There it was—Cook Islands Trust Corporation Ltd. *Cook Islands!* She googled the name and discovered the business specialised, amongst other things, in asset protection and offshore accounts. She promptly fired off another email to the investigator.

Needing to share her news, she phoned her father and then sat for three slow minutes eyeing her mobile.

Cole had said he was interested in helping her. *Go on. Call him.* Rolling her eyes at the way she'd seized this flimsy excuse, she tapped in his number before she changed her mind.

"Cole speaking." His warm tones shivered right through to her bones.

She smiled, half-closing her eyes as delicious memories of the night before cascaded through her mind. "Cole, it's Sasha."

"How's it going?"

"Good. Actually, I think today could well prove to be better than good." Leaning forward, she cast a quick look along the corridor. No sign of either Felicity or Dave but she lowered her voice anyway. "I just came across an invoice paid by Mindalby Cotton Company about two and a half years ago which I thought rather strange. It was from a Sydney firm called Taylor's Repairs and they're not listed as one of our suppliers."

"Why is that strange? You've only been here since January and you wouldn't be familiar with every company the mill has done business with."

"True. But the invoice said *'work done Last Chance'* which was the odd part. I mean, I couldn't think what *'Last Chance'* referred to, then I discovered it was the name of a boat that Yasmin Carter owns."

"Have you checked it out with Ms Robinson?"

"Not yet. She said she didn't want to be disturbed then both she and Dave rushed out over an hour ago and haven't come back."

She sucked in a breath before regaling Cole with a summary of her conversation with the repair shop manager and her discovery of the connection with an offshore business.

"This sounds like fantastic news," Cole said.

"Yes, the investigator we hired believes that we have finally discovered a legitimate trail he can follow and, with luck, use to help Uncle Isaac."

"You could be leaving Mindalby soon." His voice sounded flat, devoid of both emotion and warmth.

"Not yet." Swallowing, she decided to say nothing about the murdered mouse left at her back door. She'd wrapped the little creature in newspaper before disposing of it in the garbage bin. There was the thin likelihood that it had been run over and a cat had found it. And if it *was* someone's idea of a joke, there was no way she could discover who was the perpetrator. "I better get back to it. I'll see you Thursday."

"I'm really glad about this invoice, Sasha. Let me know how it pans out. See you soon." He rung off.

After some deliberation, Sasha phoned her mother with the news of a possible breakthrough and spoke until her mother stopped crying. They ended their conversation, with her mum saying how she'd phone their solicitor immediately to pass on a message of hope to Uncle Isaac as visiting hours had closed for the day.

With newly-forged resolve, Sasha resumed her work. Who knew what else she might find?

19

Sasha left her flat a little after nine o'clock on Thursday morning for the drive out to Wooraroogan National Park. The school principal had argued long and loud via the phone about her refusal to travel in the bus. Sasha had stood her ground, knowing that having kids witness a full-blown panic attack would not be healthy for anyone. In the end, he'd agreed only if she signed a disclaimer absolving him and the school in the event she was hurt on her ride to or from the park.

Her packed overnight bag, she'd strapped to the back of her moped seat. Her father she'd left behind, despite his voracious protests.

The drive out to the park was glorious, with no traffic once she left the highway. She cruised along at a steady speed, enjoying the scenery, emptying her mind of her concerns. An emu darted out of the tall grasses growing close to the road and scampered on its long legs and wide-splayed toes across the red dirt in front of her. She grinned and swerved around the running bird. She loved how up close and personal a person could get with the native wildlife here.

Lengthening its stride, the emu brushed through the swaying grass before stopping close to a flock of five other emus, of varying ages judging by their sizes. The new arrival emitted a deep, drumming noise. Startled, she slowed.

What *was* that?

Twisting at the waist, she stopped to watch. An emu with dark plumage ruffled its neck feathers and made that long booming sound again. Another emu broke away from the group, grunting.

She smiled and continued on her way. A pair of emus courting. Now that was something you didn't see every day. She rode on, enjoying the rich unfolding landscape with its weathered red soil contrasting brilliantly with the stark blue cloudless sky. Perfect weather for camping, although she understood the nights would be cold. She was glad the campsite would be set up by the time she arrived and that bathroom amenities were available. Even if the loos were pit toilets and the showers cold tank water.

By the time she reached the campsite, she was ready for a hot cuppa and a chance to stretch her legs. She throttled down the gears and coasted around the bus to where a hotchpotch of tents were erected.

Toby yelled a "cooee, Sasha" at the top of his lungs and raced over the red sand to greet her.

"You made it. I was …" He stopped beside her and glanced quickly away. He gulped then added, "I thought you might have changed your mind."

"I don't make promises I won't keep, Toby." She hopped off the moped and pushed it under the shade of a stringy paperbark. After unclipping her straps, she hauled off her helmet and fluffed out her flattened hair. "How's that? Helmet hair all gone?"

When Toby looked at her the slow, sweet smile on his face and the warmth in his eyes nearly undid her. "You look great," he said gruffly. "Dad's wrestling with the tent pegs. The ground's so hard, he's having trouble driving them in."

"I think we'll leave that job to him and stay well away until he's finished."

They shared a conspiratorial grin.

"Where's the loo? I need a pit stop first."

"This way." Toby crooked his finger and after Sasha unstrapped a small holdall from her rear bag rack, they set off towards a group of green iron-sheeting buildings—the usual national park amenity blocks. "Three-minute showers only, though."

"That's fine. I'm used to conserving water."

"I told my mates all about you. They want to know about when you were in Alaska and the polar bear tore down your tent. Is that okay?"

She laughed. "No worries. I'll save it though for the campfire story time tonight."

"Awesome!"

Outside the amenity block, Toby scuffed the dirt with the toe of his boot. "I'm glad you came."

"I bet I'm gladder." She grinned when he stared at her before bursting into an infectious peal of laughter.

Being there was the right decision.

BUSY WITH THE tent pegs and maintaining his steely determination not to curse his frustration in front of the kids, Cole didn't realise Sasha had arrived until the uplifting sound of her laughter reached his ears. Mallet in hand, he paused and craned his neck to see where she was, and found her with his son.

The warmth in her expression as she gazed at Toby loosened another brick in the wall protecting his heart. There was no dismissal or impatience in her expression or posture. Rather, he read respect and genuine interest.

She was a treasure. If only he could keep her in their lives forever.

If only he didn't suspect she was keeping some vital piece of information from him.

If only he could get this blasted tent up!

Ten minutes later, he stretched his back to work out the kinks before closing his toolbox. Ben Doherty, the school principal, called him over to where he and a few other parents were getting ready to take the kids on a walk to nearby Traditional First Nation art sites.

A park ranger had arrived while Cole had been fooling about with the tent and was currently running her gaze down a clipboard she held.

He called out, "Hey, is that really you, Mrs Withers?"

The middle-aged ranger with short white-streaked curly black hair looked him up and down. "Are you Jasper Mitchell's grandson?"

"Yes, that I am. Cole Mitchell." Grinning, he held out his hand.

"Can't mistake those Mitchell eyes," she said drily and shook.

"I can't believe you're still working here. You were running educational tours when I was at school."

"Where else would I be?" she snorted. "Don't tell me you've got kids of your own now. It makes me feel way too old."

"My son, Toby, is nine."

"Struth. Time can really get away from you."

"I was sorry to hear about your husband, Mrs Withers."

She busied herself for a minute ticking some boxes on her board. "The old fool should have known better than to take a nap in the park on the coldest winter night on record. Was too much for his ticker."

Her dark eyes glistened with unshed tears when

she glanced back up. "Cause the drink didn't help. Got worse after he broke his back in the stockyard. Weren't no one gonna employ him then. A counsellor from Dubbo came to see him once or twice. But oh well … it was a while ago now. These days, I focus on my job and try not to remember." She clicked her pen as if signalling subject ended. "Hey, Principal Doherty, are you ready to get this show on the road?"

"Of course, Mrs Withers. We're waiting for two children and one adult to return from the amenities block."

The ranger raised her eyebrows and tapped the diver's watch she wore on her left wrist with a large brown finger.

Slowly.

The school principal sprang into action, ordering kids and parents into lines and yelling at someone to go get the others.

Mrs Withers leaned closer to Cole and winked. "Some days, I just love my job." Turning away, she bawled, "Come on, people, I don't have all day."

Sasha rushed to Cole's side, all sparkling cat eyes and flushed cheeks.

His palms itched to pull her into his arms and capture her smile with his kiss, so he shoved his hands into his pants pockets.

"Oh dear. We're late. I'm sorry, Cole. It was my fault, not Toby's. I wanted to freshen up."

"No problem," he said, feeling foolish as he felt his grin grow broader.

"Where are we going?" Sasha asked, shoving her towel into her holdall and zipping it up tight. She tossed the bag over near a tent then took the satchel Toby had carried for her. "Thank you, Toby."

She patted the side and shoved the straps over her head. "My first-aid kit."

"Hat?" He tipped the brim of his own hat in a suggestive fashion.

"Ugh. It's in my bag."

"I'll get it. Tell Mr Doherty I'll catch up. Aboriginal art is on the agenda first up."

"How fabulous. I love their paintings. I've got this lovely one hanging above my bed at home which describes the story of a First Nation girl, a snake and her lost love."

"I'd like to see it one day," he said, meaning her bed. Then enjoyed the blush that spread over her cheeks. Was that the flare of desire in her eyes? Or merely his wishful thinking?

"My flat in Sydney or the painting?"

He grinned. "Not bad evasive tactics. I like."

She chuckled.

"We could go to the zoo and the museum," Toby inserted.

Cole ruffled his son's hair.

Toby danced about attempting to dodge his touch. "Dad! My mates are here."

"Sorry, son."

"Let's go, Toby. We don't want to be left behind." Sasha waved Toby to precede her.

Cole strode off to fetch Sasha's hat while Ben Doherty did another roll call. She hadn't answered his son. Any references to a future had been neatly avoided. A potent reminder that her plans didn't include either the Mitchells or Mindalby.

By drawing Sasha into their lives, he gambled with not only his heart but his children's as well—a realisation that weighed down on him like drenched cotton bails.

Maybe he was being selfish by snatching at such transient happiness.

Maybe it would be safer for his family if he kept his distance—treated her like a friend instead of a lover and potential partner.

But he was beginning to realise that was just about the hardest thing he'd ever had to do.

"Wow. This view is amazing." Sasha unscrewed the lid from her water bottle and took a long drink. Finished, she swept her gaze over the vista laid out before her.

The warm mid-morning sun shone from a blue sky where only the smallest of fluffy white clouds obscured its brilliance. Being early winter, no heat haze shimmered in the distance to blur the view. Standing on the top of Mount Woobooka, she thought that she could surely see forever. Undulating countryside of stubby-treed woodlands bled into floodplains and red sand-hills. High above her head, a magnificent wedge-tailed eagle circled in lazy arcs.

They had reached the top fifteen minutes ago and the children had broken off into groups. Some were sitting on large rocks guzzling water or chatting. Others were using their phones to snap shots of the scenery. A couple were grumbling about sore feet and no internet reception. The supervising parents and principal were hunkered down on their haunches, munching sandwiches and drinking water and flasks of hot coffee, their heads on a swivel as they kept checking on their charges.

"How high are we?" She lifted a hand to shade her eyes from the sun and studied the view.

"About five hundred metres." Cole gestured to the rough track studded with boulders, and scrub through which they'd just climbed. "There's a man-made look out on the other side, if you want to take any photos close to the edge. The range has quite a few gorges to explore but we're only doing Bennett's Gorge today. What did you think of the rock paintings yesterday?"

"Lovely and very humbling when I think how old they are," she said. "It was fun wading about in the rock pools even if the water only came up to my ankles."

"You'll have to come back during October through to March, that's when the waterlilies flower if we get sufficient rain. How are you feeling after our three-kilometre climb?"

"I'm fine, Cole."

"That's good." He reached out and pushed a strand of hair from her face. "I like the hot, sweaty look."

"You!" Grinning, she punched his arm. Her smile faded as her thoughts returned like an old broken record to her uncle, his situation and what had happened over about the past weeks. "This isn't a good time for Mindalby."

"Yeah. Have you heard anything more about the boat repair invoice?"

"Nothing as yet. I imagine it may take some time to follow the paper trail and come up with concrete evidence we can use. Reception is spotty here too, so it's possible I may not know if there's any news until we return to town." She sighed.

Cole nudged her shoulder. "Let's not spoil our day worrying until we have to. How do you feel about abseiling down a cliff?"

Throwing off her sombre mood, she rolled her eyes. "Not my favourite pastime although I have done it once or twice."

"Come on, then. We've got a session planned. First up, I'll perform a demo. You can be my partner. There's a cliff that's about forty metres high around the other side we've used a few times."

"I could just watch, you know," she said.

"No way. I don't want you to miss out on any fun."

A scream rent the air and they both turned swiftly.

"Mr Doherty!" shrieked a young girl, pelting towards the principal who was packing water bottles into his backpack.

Ben dropped his bag and shot to his feet, his head swinging this way and that as he rapidly scanned the other kids. "Belinda, what's wrong?"

"It's Hugh and Toby. They've fallen! I think they're dead,z' her voice ended on a wail, as she burst into loud sobs.

Before Sasha could react, Cole was moving. 'Where? Show me."

"Leila, keep the other children here," Ben called to another teacher then gestured to one of the parents. "Tim, bring the climbing equipment."

Tim Lawkins, a slightly overweight guy in his late thirties who worked in the butcher shop, hurried to where he'd previously dumped a heavy-looking canvas duffle bag.

Still crying, the young girl led the way along a faint track that wove around several large rust-coloured boulders.

Sasha raced after Cole and Ben Doherty, registering the bunching of her calf muscles as she negotiated the track leading in a steady decline.

"Cole! There's a couple of slings and harnesses missing," cried Tim, as he hurried up behind her, breathing heavily through his mouth.

She spared him a quick glance, noting his red

perspiring face, and hoped he wasn't about to have a heart attack. That was the last thing they needed.

"They're down there." Belinda pointed at the ground.

"What? I thought you meant they fell off the cliff?" Cole said, taking one cautious step forward before stopping.

Sasha joined him, gasping at the sight of a long fissure that looked to be a mere two metres across at its widest point. If the boys were stuck down there …

"Stay back," Cole warned in a low voice.

Belinda raised her tear-stained face to Cole. "Hugh dared Toby to go exploring. He said I wouldn't dance with Toby at the festival because he's a chicken. Then they took the climbing equipment out of Mr Lawkins' bag when he wasn't looking. It's my fault."

"We'll discuss whose fault this is later, Belinda. Go back and join the other students." Ben joined Cole's side and together they examined where two slings with climbing anchors attached had been secured around a nearby boulder. "What do you think, Cole?"

"They've used abseiling gear with harnesses which is something. But I don't like the look of the crevasse edge. It's shale and not stable. Everyone keep back while I shimmy over and take a look." After taking a torch from his backpack, Cole handed the bag to Ben. Then he dropped to the ground and, stretching out on his belly, wriggled towards the narrow fissure.

"Hey, how you fellas doing down there?" Cole

called, peering over the edge and slowly moving the torchlight left to right. "Toby? Hugh? Can you hear me?"

"Dad! Is that you?" Toby's faint voice sounded strained.

Cole yelled back, "I'm here, son."

"I'm sorry, Dad."

"Let's worry about that later. Are you okay?"

Silence for thirty seconds.

Finally, Toby said thickly, as if battling tears, "My leg's really sore. It hurts when I move."

"All good, son. Everything's going to be fine." Cole looked over his shoulder and lowered his voice. "I can see Hugh. He's about fifteen metres down and clinging to the side of the rock wall. He didn't look up or respond when the light hit him. I think he's frozen. I can't see Toby. He must be further down and out of reach of the torch."

"Oh my …" Ben clamped his mouth shut over what must have been curse words. A heavy frown formed on his face and his Adam's apple bobbed up and down for a few seconds.

Sasha stood silent.

Shocked.

Terror tore at her heart, threatening her composure. She wiped her damp palms over her thighs. Now wasn't the time to give in to a panic attack. *Focus! Stay sharp! Children's lives are at stake. Oh God. Toby. Dear, sweet, mischievous Toby.*

Cole did another sweep of the gap with his torch. "Okay, Hugh and Toby. Listen, we're going to pull you up, one at a time."

Silence again.

"No can do. The ropes are broken." Toby voice cracked.

Cole tested the ropes dangling over the side for weight on the other end. "Hang in there, son." He wriggled backwards and pushed to his knees. His face was grim, his cheekbones stark, when his gaze met Sasha's. "Toby's right. There's definitely no weight on the end of these lines." He scooted back further and reached for his bag. "I'll abseil down on my own rope and jam some hexes into any cracks I can find."

"It sounds too risky, Cole," the principal said. "We should call in Dubbo Rescue Squad."

"Ben, it could be hours before they get here. As far as I can tell, the boys are hanging on with their hands. Once their strength fails, they'll fall further into the crevasse. I'm going down. I'm getting my son and the other boy. Now."

"Okay, Cole. But I'm still phoning the Squad."

Cole nodded. "Understood, we'll have to report the incident anyway. They'll probably want to check the equipment too. Tim, I'll need you and Ben on the ropes. Once I reach each boy, you'll have to pull us up."

"No worries, Cole," Tim said while Ben reached for his mobile.

Cole hauled out a bunch of ropes, a harness,

climbing anchors and a sling. "Here, Tim, wrap this sling with the climbing anchor attached around that boulder over there. I'll abseil down and secure Hugh to my harness."

Sasha licked her dry lips. "You look like you know what you're doing."

"I've done a few courses with the SES in vertical rescue along with Tim and a few other SES members."

She touched Cole's hand. "Be careful. I know you'll save them."

Cole swallowed. "I'm concerned about moving Toby. He's usually calm in a crisis. He knows to remain still and brace his body against something solid if a climb goes wrong. But if he's injured ..."

"Then I'll go down and assess him. And together we'll get him out."

They stared at each other.

Cole's eyes blazed with fiery determination and something that she thought might have been pride. Pride in her. After a long moment, he nodded. "Hold the torch for me?"

"Of course."

He swung into action, organising his equipment, running through what the other two blokes had to do, and pulling on a pair of belay gloves. One last glance at Sasha, then Cole disappeared over the side.

20

On her haunches, Sasha slipped to the edge and flicked the torch on, doing her best to light the way for Cole as he descended the narrow passage. She strained her eyes following his shadowy form's slow progress while the other two men fed him the rope.

No one spoke.

Even Belinda had ceased her wailing from where she watched with the other students. Long minutes passed before Cole reached Hugh who still clung to the rockface.

Sasha heard the quiet rumble of Cole's voice gently reassuring the boy and the chink of metal against metal as he hooked them together.

"Hey fellas! We're good. Haul us up. Toby, I'll be back to get you next."

She lit the way, while Tim and Ben hauled on the

ropes, grunting as, hand over hand, they pulled Cole and Hugh closer to the surface. As soon as they were within reach, Tim braced the line using his heavy body as counterweight, while Ben and Sasha gripped Hugh then dragged him up the last few centimetres, over the edge and onto solid ground. The boy was ashen, his eyes bulging, and shaking badly as Ben unstrapped his harness.

Sasha assisted Hugh into a sitting position and wrapped him in her parka, murmuring soothing words as she discreetly checked him for injuries.

"Shock and mild hypothermia," she eventually announced and gestured for a teacher to sit beside Hugh. "He should be checked out properly at the hospital."

"I'm going down again," Cole said, preparing to descend.

Sasha took her mini first-aid kit from her satchel and slipped it into the deep pocket of her cargo pants. She was ready. "I'm coming with you. I'll use the boy's harness and another set of gear."

"Sasha …"

"I've climbed before and you may need me. We're wasting time." She didn't remind Cole how it had been several minutes since Toby last spoke.

Not a good sign.

"Okay. Tim, check her equipment, will you?"

"Sure thing, Cole." Tim helped her into Hugh's harness. "Just as well you're only a slip of a thing." He attached the last remaining rope to her tackle and secured the sling around a boulder. "You're good to go."

Tim slapped her on the back and yelled over his shoulder, "Baz, you're needed here on the ropes."

"Rightio." Another parent bounded forward to assist Ben with Cole's rope.

Standing well back from the edge, Tim fed out Sasha's rope while she slipped her legs over the edge, took a deep breath, and let go. For twenty seconds, she forgot to breathe as the sensation of dangling in mid-air froze her thought process.

'Okay, Sasha, love?'

Cole's voice vibrating with concern quelled the panic crowding her mind. She breathed deeply and concentrated on everything her father had taught her on their abseiling adventures. "Don't worry about me. Find Toby."

She heard the swoosh of air and the creak of rope mingling with a jangle of harness as Cole dropped lower. Pebbles rattled down. Dust filled the aperture and she sneezed.

If it was cold on the surface, it was freezing in the narrow passage. She risked a glance upwards and could only see a strip of bright sky that didn't extend far.

Shivering, she used her hands and feet to jump down a metre at a time. The crevasse was so narrow she had to take care not to bounce off the opposite wall. Loose shale and pebbles rattled down every time she touched the sides.

Darkness embraced her, like the cold arms of death.

Another few metres and she was engulfed by blackness and stuffy air. She hesitated as her brain screamed to get out—escape—leave this place. Her blood roared in her ears; her heart pounded so hard her chest hurt. She squeezed her eyes shut, one hand gripping the rope, the other holding onto a rocky protrusion, her feet braced against the rock wall as she froze momentarily.

"I've found him. He's landed on a ledge." Cole's voice rang with relief. "Toby, son, I'm here. Sasha, I'm sure his leg is broken."

She forced open her eyes and exhaled, then used her sleeve to rub her upper lip where sweat beaded. Sinking her upper teeth into her lower lip, relishing the sting, she flexed her stiff fingers, drew in slow, deep breaths then resumed her descent. "I'm seconds away. Don't move him."

She landed beside Cole and Toby roughly thirty metres from the surface; if not for Cole's torch they would have been in total blackness. Cole still hung from his rope, obviously afraid his additional weight could cause the ledge to give way. But he'd added a safety precaution to reduce the rope's strain, by inserting a hex in a crack a little to the side of the ledge. He waved his torch over Toby who kept his eyes closed, his mouth twisted with pain, his right leg at an awkward angle.

"Dad. It hurts." His voice was a thin thread of sound,

as he opened his eyes a slit. "Sasha?" His expression of trust almost undid her.

There'd be time for hugs and comfort later.

"Lie still, Toby, that's a good boy. I need to check your injuries before your dad can take you home." Sliding down another half a metre, Sasha hovered above his prone body. With an agile twist at the waist, she flipped herself lengthways and rolled until she faced Cole's son. "Where does it hurt?"

"My leg. My wrists are aching too."

As gently as possible she ran her hands over Toby, paying particular attention to his limbs and skull.

"There's no open wound, no obvious bumps on your head and your knee is swollen. It's too hard to tell whether it's a fracture, dislocation or sprain so we won't take any chances." She raised herself a little to enable easier access to her pants pocket without tipping the contents into the crevasse. "Toby, I'm going to immobilise your legs using bandages and tie them together at the thighs and ankles. When we get topside, I'll give you a proper splint. This may hurt, honey, but I need you to be brave and don't move. Okay?"

"Okay."

"What can I do?" Cole asked.

"Nothing yet. Keep the light steady. I'll work as fast as I can and as soon as I'm finished, hook him up to your harness."

"No worries."

Using the bandages she'd taken from her first-aid

kit, she began to wrap Toby's leg in a figure-of-eight pattern, side-tracking him by asking questions on how to set up websites. Despite her efforts to be careful, his breath caught now and then. But he didn't cry.

"That's the best I can do for now. You've been a real trooper, Toby, but now we need to get you sitting up. Here, take my hand."

Cole handed the torch to her to hold, then fastened Toby's harness to his using a locking carabiner between their slings. "We're almost there, Toby. You're doing great. Sasha, I'll get them to pull you up first."

"No, I'll wait. As soon as Toby's topside, keep him as warm as possible."

Cole hesitated then inhaled sharply. "You're a stubborn woman." He glanced upwards. "Okay, boys, nice and slow."

Left alone, Sasha kept her gaze glued to their dark forms as they ascended and concentrated on calming her panic. Then it was her turn; by the time she arrived back on the surface, she was trembling and almost numb with cold. A minute of stamping her feet and swishing her arms about helped restore her circulation.

Code strode over and enveloped her in a bear hug then lifted her off the ground. The press of his body against hers was warm and strong. And oh so sweet.

"Thank you," he murmured into her hair. The steady beat of his heart was reassuring. She never wanted to let him go.

"Toby?" She leaned back and studied Cole's face, noting fresh lines bracketing his sensual mouth.

"Attempting to negotiate his way out of being grounded for the rest of his life."

She smiled. "Both boys need to go to hospital immediately. I'll see to Toby's leg and then he'll have to be carried to the camp."

"All organised. The carrying and hospital part, I mean." Cole hesitated. "I need to go with them. I doubt I'll be back to the camp but Ben would like you to stay on until tomorrow."

"Not a problem."

He sighed and rested his forehead on hers. "We make a good team. You and I." And then he strode to where his son was waiting, white faced and shivering, huddled beneath a space blanket.

SATURDAY LUNCHTIME, Sasha was back in Mindalby and had placed a load of washing on before deciding to walk to the supermarket. It had been another foggy morning, and the fresh parka she'd donned was soon damp from the dissipating mist.

True to her word, she'd stayed at the camp until they'd packed up and departed early that morning. The mood had been sombre since the accident, made even more so by the principal's lecturing over the consequences of disobeying rules and taking dangerous risks. All in all, Sasha was glad to ride home.

Cole had phoned her a few hours after he'd arrived at the hospital on Friday afternoon. Hugh was going to be fine and, as she'd suspected, Toby had suffered a fracture and would spend the next few weeks with his leg in plaster. She'd asked Cole to pass on her best wishes for a speedy recovery.

Tomorrow, she intended to visit Cotton Fields Glory and assist Cole's daughter with her doll's quilt.

But tonight … ahh, tonight she'd wallow in a deep, hot Radox bath until she was pink and wrinkled, then enjoy the comfort of a real bed.

As she strolled along the main road, she phoned Dave; bypassing the usual pleasantries, she asked, "Were you able to use the information I gave you about Yasmin's boat?"

"No … good morning … or lovely day, I see." Dave paused and in the background, Sasha heard the rustle of paper and the clack of a keyboard.

The guy must live for his job. "Sorry, I've had a busy couple of days."

He came back onto the line. "Yes, we heard a couple of kids were injured at the school camp. I hope they're doing okay. Now in relation to Mrs Carter's boat we have added the details to the report we're compiling."

"What? That's it?" Reining in her impatience, Sasha poked her hair behind her ear. "You're not going to divulge anything else, are you?"

"Sorry, Sasha. The only thing I can tell you is, if there is the slightest indication of malpractice, the matter will be placed in the hands of the relevant authorities."

He said 'authorities', so not just the company regulator, ASIC. He may also mean the Taxation Office but was it possible he was referring to the police as well? "I guess that's better than nothing. Thank you, Dave."

The shriek of sirens exploded in the muffled quiet and a police car raced past.

"What was that noise?"

"Police. Possibly after a speeding motorist," Sasha answered.

"And I thought a few weeks in the country would be nice and quiet." He rung off.

Shaking her head and wondering how long Felicity and Dave would take to unearth any further information in relation to Yasmin's yacht, she pushed open the door to the CWA hall.

Fifteen minutes later she was back out the door, a smile on her face and a bulging flower-covered, cotton carry-bag filled with several metres of yellow and gold material in varying patterns, cotton wadding and an easy-looking quilt template. The two elderly women who were the only members of the quilting club there at the time, had obviously been well-primed by Maisy Mitchell to give Sasha as much assistance as possible. It was a pity the selection was so limited—she'd learned that the club members usually ordered their supplies online or phoned through to a shop in Dubbo.

Still, she was certain that Summer would love the sunny colours once the quilt was finished. Her own sewing skills were limited but the pattern looked simple enough and a promise was a promise.

A pleasurable glow spread through her.

She was changing. Or had her maternal urge always been there—only voiceless and buried under her blinkered focus on her career?

WANDERING down the aisles of the local IGA supermarket, Sasha mentally ticked off her shopping list. Not that she had a great deal to buy, just a few essentials such as fruit, tea and milk. And perhaps a pastry or two from the bakery. Surreptitiously she rotated her shoulders, still feeling a bit stiff and sore after her abseiling act on Friday.

Tapping her lips, she stood in the tea section and debated whether to try the lemon and ginger teabags, her mind winging to that awesome green and ginger brew Amber had given her at the Commune.

"Sasha! I was hoping to bump into you."

She glanced around to find Cole's mother standing behind her. "Maisy, how are you?"

"I'm fine, pet. What are you looking at?" Maisy Mitchell peered past Sasha to the shelves. A peculiar expression settled on her face. She sniffed. "Oh, I see. That rubbishy hippie stuff that my sister is so fond of. Trust me, you can't go wrong with good old-fashioned Billy Tea, Sasha."

Mrs Mitchell picked up a box of the tea and placed it into Sasha's basket. "I wanted to thank you for your heroic efforts in rescuing my grandson."

A woman's voice came from behind Sasha. "That's her. The same one who's seeing Donald Carter on the sly."

Sasha looked around to see two women with their heads together and their eyes fixed on her. The second they caught her gaze both women sniffed and turned away.

Looking back at Mrs Mitchell, she mumbled, "Cole was the one who rescued Toby. I simply rendered medical assistance."

"Mindalby could use a nurse of your experience. And both Toby and Summer already love you." Maisy winked, obviously choosing to ignore the women.

Words tangled in Sasha's throat when Cole's mother threw her a look so ripe with expectation, she had no idea how to respond. Perspiration prickled around her hairline. And she thought her father could be intrusive!

"Cole told me you're going out to the farm tomorrow. I'd really appreciate it if you could stay a few days to keep an eye on Toby and look after Summer for me."

Maisy heaved a heavy sigh while pasting an innocent expression on her face. "Normally, I'd be there in a flash but Roger has a specialist appointment in Dubbo early Monday morning and I need to be with him. I've already told Cole that I'd ask you. Will you help him, dear?"

"Well …"

Maisy continued blithely, "Pop and Cole have the farm to run and no time to supervise an invalid and a little girl."

"What about Amber? Could she help?"

"Unfortunately not. She has other plans." Maisy smiled serenely, looking pleased with herself as she blithely eliminated every option.

Resisting the urge to fan her hot face, Sasha said, "When will you be back, Maisy?"

"Possibly next Wednesday but it will depend if Roger needs further tests. We may as well get everything done while we're there to save another trip. That's settled then, pet. Thank you. I knew we could depend on you." Maisy pecked Sasha on the cheek, enveloping her in the comforting scent of talc powder and lavender cologne.

Sasha blinked, shaking her head. She hadn't said yes but apparently it was a done deal.

Maisy adjusted the straps of the handbag she carried over one arm. "I can give you a lift to the farm. I'll be heading home in half an hour."

"No, it's fine. But thank you." Sasha smiled,

squelching her shudder at the thought of being encased inside a moving metal death-trap.

"Very well then. Give my grandchildren my love and tell them we'll see them as soon as we get back."

"I will. Goodbye, Maisy, and I hope everything goes well for Roger."

"I keep telling him, it's gout. But he will insist on drinking whiskey." With an airy wave of her hand, Maisy whisked herself away toward the front of the shop.

Walking to the end of the aisle, Sasha was just in time to see her march out the supermarket doors. Maisy had no grocery bags in her hands and it looked like she had entered the shop expressly to speak to her. Shrugging, Sasha removed the Billy Tea from her basket then strolled to the check-outs. After paying, she left the supermarket.

"I need more, I'm …"

The desperation in the raised voice caught Sasha's attention. She paused, basket in hand, and looked along the street. Several shop fronts away stood Lesley Thompson talking to, of all people, Yasmin Carter.

Suddenly Lesley pushed Yasmin, who staggered back a pace but regained her balance in her siren-red stilettoes.

Spying a wide concrete planter box a few metres from the couple, Sasha hurried closer then dropped down behind the box. She couldn't believe what she was about to do but she did it anyway, fishing out her mobile and pressing record.

Her thoughts went back to every time she'd encountered Lesley and the outcome. What if Yasmin was orchestrating Lesley's moves? Yasmin knew Sasha was Isaac Blake's niece. She could have put Lesley up to that denouncement at the pub. Lesley had lost her only source of income when the mill closed. She could well be still in her employers' pay and was perfectly placed to be their eyes and ears in town.

Whatever Yasmin was saying must have had the desired effect because all the belligerence evaporated from the other woman's posture. Her shoulders rounded and she nodded several times, then walked off to climb into her battered kombi van.

Yasmin, not a hair out of place, sashayed to her car and drove off.

Heart beating fast, Sasha scrambled to her feet then checked the recording. The voices were too low for anything to be heard clearly. It could still be evidence if she could find someone who had the technology to improve the sound. But evidence of what?

21

The wide verandahs, high sloped tin roof and large chunky brick house, situated beneath the sprawling branches of several old jacaranda trees and red-river gums, presented a welcoming appearance. Sasha slowed the moped, allowing the scene to sink into her senses.

The garden beds were overrun with weeds and grasses but she could still discern where a path of paving stones meandered around straggling flowering shrubs to end in what might be an old herb garden. The place was begging for a little tender care and attention.

A tyre swing hung motionless from a low-lying branch. A kid's bike lay abandoned on the rough-cut grass along with a discarded football and skipping rope.

This feels like home.

The thought settled deep in her heart, as solid as building foundations.

She killed the engine, then pushed the moped closer to the verandah before mounting the steps and knocking on the door. The sound of light, running feet pattered down the hallway. Through the fly-screen door, she saw Summer.

"Sasha! You're here! Toby's in the lounge room." Summer flung open the door and, darting forward, wrapped her arms around Sasha's legs.

Smiling, her heart squeezing tight in her chest, Sasha brushed her hand over the little girl's soft hair. "I've brought the material for your doll's quilt."

"Yay!" Summer scampered off, leaving Sasha to follow her along the wide, dim hallway.

Upon entering the living room, she paused while her eyes adjusted from the bright sunlight outside. The room was large with a stone fireplace taking up a great deal of the side wall. Toby sat on a squishy-looking chocolate-brown modular lounge, which was arranged in one corner. His plastered leg was propped up on a cushion.

She was charmed to see how carefully Summer pressed a glass of water into her brother's hand.

Although almost two days had passed, Toby's face remained pale, making the thin scattering of freckles across his nose appear darker. His hair was tousled as if he'd been pushing his hand through the mess, a gesture that reminded her of Cole.

After placing her bulging satchel onto a side-table, she crossed to greet Toby. "How are you feeling?"

"Better. It's hard to sleep though. I can't seem to get comfortable and my knee still aches." He made to move but she stopped him.

"No, don't get up."

He peered from under his flop of fringe, saying shyly, "I didn't get a chance on Friday but thanks for taking care of me, Sasha."

"Oh, Toby. I only did what I'm trained to do."

"Dad says you have problems with feeling trapped. He reckons you're the bravest lady he knows."

She glanced away from Toby's keen eyes for a moment, blinking rapidly to expel the moisture blurring her vision. "I don't know about that but I'm only glad I could help."

He grinned. "Dad said to tell you, he and Pop will be back around sunset. Is it true that you're gonna stay with us?"

"Yes, but only for a couple of days until your grandparents get back," she corrected.

Summer jumped up onto the lounge and emitted an almighty squeal of joy. "Sasha's gonna sleep in my room!"

"She'll probably sleep with Dad."

"Why?" Summer stopped her jumping to stare owl-eyed at her brother.

Gobsmacked, Sasha wished for a deep, dark hole in order to hide from the two pairs of Mitchell eyes now fixed disconcertingly on her hot face.

" 'Cause they're like boyfriend and girlfriend, dummy."

"Like a mummy and daddy?"

Sasha's throat closed up, tears pricking as she plucked the empty glass from Toby's hand to place onto a side-table.

"Almost." Toby smirked.

Cheeky little monkey. Just like his father.

"Hmmm." Summer's bottom lip poked out and she planted her hands on her narrow hips. "I want Sasha to sleep in my room."

"I'll be sleeping in the spare room." Ignoring Toby's snort, Sasha changed the subject. "Before we start on your doll's quilt, Summer, I thought we'd make a casserole for dinner tonight. Unless of course, it's already been taken care of?"

Toby brightened at the mention of food. "Naah, Sunday night is potluck night. We usually have leftovers or something easy, like baked beans on toast. I'm starving." He patted his stomach. "A casserole sounds great."

She laughed. "Leave dinner to me. Summer, would you like to help? Yell if you need anything, Toby."

Taking Summer's hand, she headed into the oak-timber kitchen to check the contents of the pantry and freezer. She'd been at Cotton Fields Glory for all of twenty minutes but it was if she'd walked into the rest of her life.

And it felt perfect.

COLE SCRUBBED his dirty hands under the tap in the outside shower. He wondered whether, after his shower, he'd be able to sneak into the house and change into clean clothes without Sasha spotting him wearing nothing but a towel around his waist and carrying a whole pile of hope in his heart.

"She's got under your skin, hasn't she, son?" Pop asked from where he was leaning against the half-wall of corrugated iron and chewing on a strand of grass.

It would be useless for Cole to pretend he had no idea what his grandfather was talking about, so he sighed and opened the half-door to the primitive bathroom. He began to peel off his dirty clothes. "Yep. But Sasha isn't the type to hang around a small outback town, Pop. She's a career woman through and through."

"The power of love is a wonderful thing."

"Not for me." He firmed his jaw and ducked under the shower-head, repressing a gasp as cold water trickled over his bare skin. At least the coolness alleviated some of the ardour of his overheated body. Thankfully, the iron fencing was sufficiently high enough to stop his grandfather from inadvertently seeing that ardour.

"Not every woman puts her life on the line for a kid she barely knows."

"You don't know Sasha. That's what she's all about —helping others in the most difficult of circumstances," Cole said wryly, as he scrubbed the red dirt from under his fingernails.

"I can see that, and I see a whole pile more. The way she looks at you, puts me in mind of your gran, like she's seeing the moon, the stars and the sun. My Mavis-Rose made me feel like I could move mountains. She looked at me, saw the man beneath and loved me despite my failings."

Cole worked over the constriction in his throat before saying gruffly, "Sasha needs to make a difference."

"Cole, you're not thinking straight, boy. Show her the difference she can make here—in your life—in Mindalby."

"Denise ..."

"Is no longer with us. Bless the girl, I loved her too but she wouldn't want either you or your kids to be lonely," Pop said firmly.

"It's not only me that'll be affected if or when Sasha moves on."

"I know, son. But you're doing the kids no favours by hiding from life. They need to learn that happiness *and* sadness are both part of living. The good and the bad or, as your Aunt Amber would say, the yin and the yang." Pop chuckled.

Cole turned off the tap and reached for a towel. "Hearing you say these words, Pop, reinforces what I've been thinking."

"Then, what's stopping you?"

Something inside Cole shifted; crumbled and disintegrated into dust. Pop was right. He'd risk it all—his heart and his kids'—on the chance Sasha could one day believe her life was here—with them. As he briskly rubbed his hair dry, then his body, confidence and hope powered through him, stomping all over a little voice that whispered, *Donald Carter.*

He tucked the ends of the towel around his middle and pushed open the door. His grandfather was staring off into the distance, remembering, his wrinkles smoothed away by love, a tender smile curling his lips. "Wish me luck, Pop."

"If she's the woman for you, you won't need luck, son. Just be yourself. Personally, I'm hoping she's a decent cook." Pop grinned as Cole stepped aside to allow him his turn under the cold shower.

Cole inhaled, catching the scent of steak and onions on the cool evening air. "Yep, I'm sure getting tired of your meat and two vegies offerings."

"Cheeky whelp." Pop latched the door shut while Cole rolled his dirty clothes into a ball.

"Catch you inside." Grinning, he headed for the laundry door and his bedroom.

After changing into a long-sleeved t-shirt and jeans, he went looking for his kids. They were with Sasha in the kitchen, sitting at the table looking fresh and bright-eyed with excitement. He knew exactly how they felt.

Sasha turned as he entered. The way her face lit up like there was a golden lantern glowing beneath her skin warmed him all the way to his soul. This woman was special and for a few precious moments, that look —the brilliance of her green eyes, the tender curve to her lips—made him think that maybe, just maybe, he was special to her.

"Sasha, thanks so much for helping us out while Mum and Dad are in Dubbo," he said, inwardly cursing his betrayingly gruff voice.

"Not a problem." She hesitated, her forehead puckering as if she'd hoped to hear something else instead of a polite platitude.

Hoping to ease the sudden tension swelling between them, he sniffed loudly. "Smells great."

His daughter giggled as he continued to sniff like a dog on the scent of truffles while he worked his way around the table. "Daddy, you're funny."

"We've got braised steak with onions and mashed sweet potatoes and greens," Toby said in awed tones, indicating the covered dish in the centre of the table. "And, she's made apple cobbler for desert."

Cole fetched up beside Sasha. Stone the crows, but she smelt even better than their dinner. Something fresh and citrusy. He gave into his need and brushed his knuckles down her right cheek, loving how her skin heated beneath his touch.

Her eyelashes fluttered. There was a tiny pulse beating rapidly in the base of her neck, visible above the low, scooped neckline of the soft-looking woollen dress she wore. He wanted to press his mouth to her throat and feel the pulse surge under his lips.

But she moved away.

"How's the leg, son?" Opening the fridge, Cole relished the wave of cool air on his hot body for a few seconds then retrieved a container of cold water, which he placed onto the table.

"Getting there."

"You're still grounded."

"*Awwww*, Dad ...."

"Don't tempt me to ground you for the next five years," he warned.

Rolling his eyes, Toby ducked his head.

"What have you two been doing? Not pestering Sasha too much, I hope."

"We made a doll's quilt. It's beautiful, Daddy. Do you want to see it?"

He smiled, delighted at the joy in his daughter's sweet face. "After we've eaten and cleared up, princess pea."

"It's not quite finished yet, Summer. We have to add on the border pieces which we'll do tomorrow," Sasha said.

"I did my homework," Toby piped up.

Cole raised an eyebrow.

Toby sighed. "Yeah, I got it. I'm still grounded."

Pop tramped into the kitchen, calling out greetings as he inspected the contents of the casserole dish. "Mmm, stew!"

Sasha opened the oven door and out rolled the heady scent of fresh bread. She placed the small rolls onto a plate and brought it over to the table. She sat next to Summer.

Well away from me. Cole picked up his fork.

"So, how was your day?" Sasha sent him a brief glance as she spooned out generous helpings of what Pop insisted on referring to as 'stew'.

"Digging the last stretch of the new canal," Cole replied, popping a roll onto his plate. "By the way, I got a phone call today from Ben Doherty. The blokes from the Dubbo Rescue Squad took away the abseiling equipment Hugh and Toby used. They reckon the ropes have been cut half-way through. Tension and weight would have done the rest."

Sasha gasped. "It was deliberate? Who would do something so stupid?" She stared at Cole. "Could it have been kids?"

"I don't see how a kid would get access. All the equipment is kept locked up at the SES building and only members have keys." Cole fiddled with his fork, his gut turning over at how close he'd come to losing his son.

"Dad?" Toby turned a white face towards him.

Cole made a monumental effort to mask the rage boiling inside him. "Don't worry, son, the police are looking into the matter. The SES has a good security system. Their tapes should reveal the idiot's identity." And then he'd make damn sure the yobbo would never do such a reckless thing again.

Sasha woke Thursday morning feeling sore in places she'd never known existed. Rolling over, she checked her mobile for the time and, with a gasp, sat up. She'd slept later than normal and now that she came to think about it, she'd slept the whole night through. No waking up and peering out the window; no pacing of the house and checking locks; no jumping at the slightest noise.

Was it because she was on the farm, several kilometres from other people? Or maybe it was because Cole had spent the night in her bed, wrapped securely in his arms.

Climbing from the bed, she performed a series of stretching exercises to work out the stiffness in her joints. Who would have thought riding a horse could make her so sore?

The last few days had passed like a dream, with

Cole sharing more about life on the land and his childhood years, Pop taking her on a tour of the farm and pointing out spots where he and his beloved wife would picnic, her helping Summer with homework and conversing with Toby. She'd spent hours pushing both children on the tyre swing, enjoying their laughter. Then there were the nights sitting around the fire, just chatting or playing board games until the kids went to bed.

And those precious golden hours spent with Cole afterwards rapidly reinforced what had been missing from her life. They'd kept up the pretence of sleeping in separate rooms at her insistence. She believed if his family knew they were sharing a room then it was tantamount to announcing they were in a permanent relationship. And that was a step she had no idea whether they would ever take.

Her father had phoned the day before and given her an update of what was happening in town. A few brawls had broken out in the pub, people taking out their frustrations on each other. He indicated that some people he'd spoken to had moved on from anger to depressed resignation.

Not a good sign: anger mixed with depression. She hoped people were taking advantage of the counselling sessions. But she knew not everyone was comfortable seeking help.

After a quick shower, she changed into a honey-coloured woollen jumper and beige cargo pants then brushed the tangles from her hair. With thick socks on her feet, she padded into the living room.

"At last!" Summer jumped to her feet, scattering dolls and tiny clothes in all directions, and raced to Sasha's side.

"No school today?"

"I was too sick to go to school." Summer's lower lip quivered but Sasha wasn't fooled.

"I see. If you're so sick, I think you should spend the day in bed."

"But I'm better now! I've been waiting forever. Daddy said we weren't to wake you."

Sasha gave a rueful smile. "I slept in. Good morning, Toby." She looked over where Toby was sprawled on the lounge, reading. "How did you sleep?"

He grinned. "Good thanks. My leg doesn't hurt so much now."

Welcome heat radiated from the fire in the hearth. Patches, Pop's aging border collie, was curled up in a large, well-padded dog bed with Summer's cocker spaniel, Princess. Neither opened their eyes at her arrival. In fact, Sasha was certain Patches was snoring. With the heavy, maroon curtains drawn partially across the big window and a couple of lamps glowing, the room was warm and inviting. "Is it cold outside?"

"Yeah, freezing. That's why we're in here," Toby answered. "There's porridge on the stove if you'd like some. Or scrambled eggs but they might be cold by now."

"I think I'll go with the porridge and a cup of tea. Where is everyone?" Meaning, where was Cole. She peered down the hallway, longing for a glimpse of his crinkly smile and solid form.

"Dad and Pop are fooling about with the tractor. The engine was cutting out yesterday." His gaze drifting back to his book, Toby turned a page.

With Summer skipping beside her, Sasha entered the kitchen then helped herself to some breakfast. The little girl perched on a chair and watched her every move.

Sasha was in the act of filling the teapot with hot water when Cole pushed open the back door. Cold air swirled into the room.

Their eyes met.

Heat bubbled over her skin. She returned the jug to the counter and gripped the edge of the table to stop herself from rushing into his arms.

"Daddy! Sasha's awake."

"About time, hey princess pea? Morning, Sasha love."

What she wouldn't give to indulge in a long, hard kiss. But with his children present, not to mention his grandfather, she knew this wasn't the place. She repressed her sigh at the thought of snuggling up with him in a warm, cosy bed and loving the day away wrapped in his arms. "I'm making a pot of tea. Would you like some?"

Eyes twinkling, Cole blew air onto his hands and

rubbed them briskly. "Yes, please, if there's enough. Pop's right behind me."

As if summoned by magic, his grandfather ambled in and closed the door on the bleak, wintry day.

Sasha noticed both men had entered sans boots and approved of their unwillingness to track mud, dirt and who-knew-what-else inside the house.

As if he'd read her earlier thoughts, Cole came around the table and pulled Sasha into his arms. "I can't say good morning without a kiss."

He pressed his cold lips against hers and even though the contact was brief, she shivered at the constrained hunger sizzling in the coiled strength of his hard body.

When he released her to reach for the tea cups, she dipped her head, knowing her face was flaming. She wanted much more than a single kiss. "Good morning."

"The only way to start the day."

She did her best to ignore his smug grin and brought the teapot to the table. Whistling, Cole set out cups and collected a container of his aunt's homemade cookies from the pantry.

Summer scooped up a handful of the cookies and skipped from the room. Seconds later her high-pitched giggle echoed down the hall. "Toby, Daddy kissed Sasha."

"Perfect." Pop poured a dash of milk into his tea then dunked a cookie, shooting Sasha a wicked grin that left her in no doubt he wasn't referring to the treat.

"Sleep well?" Cole asked, helping himself to a cookie.

Sasha frowned a little as she stirred her tea. "Surprisingly well."

"That's good." Cole took a swallow. Setting his cup down, he said, "Sergeant Johnson phoned earlier. He's looked into the SES security tapes leading up to the school camp. It seems one tape is missing. He says he could dust the entire station for prints but there've been so many people in and out of that building, there is no way of knowing who was responsible for sabotaging those ropes."

"What about dusting the locker where the equipment is kept?"

"Done. Only members' prints were found."

"Then whoever it was must have worn gloves." She met Cole's narrow gaze.

"There is another possibility. Johnson suggested it could be an SES member."

She inhaled a sharp breath. "But why? And who would do such a thing?"

Cole shrugged, his lips compressed.

"Oh, this is terrible. We may never know who was responsible."

"Johnson even asked if I had any enemies."

She shook her head. "That doesn't make sense.

Anyone could have used those ropes, which means whoever was responsible didn't care who was hurt."

"Maybe." Cole sighed then sipped his tea.

Out in the hall, the landline rang. Setting his cup down, Cole rose to answer it.

"Sasha! Your phone is ringing." Summer came running into the room with Sasha's mobile in her hands. "I got it for you."

"Thank you, sweetie." Smiling, she scanned the ID but the number wasn't familiar. "Hello, Sasha speaking."

"It's Constable Ross from Mindalby Police Station. I'm calling to advise you that a Mr Obadiah Bernstein has been arrested. I understand he's your father."

It was mid-afternoon before Sasha heard Cole's four-wheel-drive coming down the driveway. Leaving Pop and the kids curled up on the lounge while he read to them, she went out to the front verandah and watched as two unrepentant-looking passengers hopped out.

"Cuddlepie!" Her father bounded up the steps, arms outstretched, his smile almost as wide.

"Honestly, Dad." She returned his hug. "What were you thinking? Hello, Amber," she added as Cole's aunt mounted the steps to the verandah.

Her father stuck his nose in the air. "People have rights. I had no intention of watching those clodhoppers tramp through private property like the Gestapo."

His shoulders shaking, as if suppressing laughter, Cole tossed the car keys into the air. "How about we go inside? It's freezing out here."

"Good idea, Cole. The living room sounds just the ticket. Have you got the fire going?" his aunt demanded.

"Yep. Pop is under strict instructions not to let it go out." Cole strode past and opened the door, ushering everyone in out of the cold.

A bit of shuffling and clumps ensued as boots and shoes were toed off then they all trooped along the hall and into the living room.

"Aunty Amber!" squealed Summer.

"Hi, Aunt Amber," said Toby.

"Toby, Summer, my how you've both grown since I saw you last. What have you been eating? Magic beans?"

Summer giggled. "I want some magic beans. Guess what, Aunty Amber? Daddy kissed Sasha. Lots."

Lips compressed, Sasha pushed her father when he nudged her with his elbow and waggled his eyebrows.

"Is that so?" Smiling, Amber settled down next to her great nephew. "Jasper, you're looking well. Sasha, I'm happy to see you again .."

After the usual exchanges petered out, Sasha perched on the side of the armchair where her father sat. "Okay, Dad, what happened?"

"The good news is we weren't charged with obstruction. Johnson let us off with a warning."

"Right, so that's the good news out of the way," she said drily.

She refused to look at Cole, knowing if she did so she'd burst out laughing. And what kind of message would that send Cole's children? Both were sitting as still as possible, obviously hoping if they kept quiet they wouldn't be ordered from the room.

"A person can do whatever they like on their own land," pronounced Amber.

"Only if they don't break the law," Pop pointed out.

"Pwush." Her father folded his arms and leaned back with an air of righteousness.

"Dad."

He straightened, his eyes almost bugging out from his head. "There we were minding our own business, working on our quilts for the Cotton Festival competition when ... whumpa! Sirens, speeding cars! You would have thought we were in some high-action movie the way those blokes carried on. Did you know, Sasha, that one of those police cars rammed into the water trough?" Her father turned an outraged face towards her.

Quilts? My father is making quilts? She smothered her grin and tutted. "People have no respect."

"Exactly what I said to that red-nosed Johnson when he barrelled up to me. Demanded I refrain from barring his way and mind my own business. I mean, who does he think he is?"

"Well, he is the police, Dad." She bit down harder on her lip.

"Why were the police there, Aunt?" Cole asked from where he leaned against the wall.

"An anonymous phone call tipped them off that an illegal still was on the commune."

Cole rolled his eyes heavenward. "Harry, Chook and Max and their 'honeyshine'."

"I wonder who the caller was," mused Sasha.

Pop steepled his fingers. "It *is* a good brew, made from local honey, you know, Sasha. I think they add cinnamon and cloves. It packs quite a punch."

"I prefer my rosehip wine," Amber said.

"Both illegal," murmured Cole, wiping his hand over his face. No doubt to hide his amusement from his kids.

"As I don't sell mine, I'm not breaking any laws, Cole," Amber snapped.

"Of course Amber isn't breaking any laws. Fancy suggesting such a thing!" Obie sprang to his feet and began to pace the room. "As I was saying, without any evidence whatsoever, the police charge onto Amber's property and demand to search every building. Johnson waved some fool piece of paper at Amber. Reckoned it was a search warrant." He snorted.

"If those guys are running an illegal still, Dad, then

they're in the wrong." Sasha met her father's gaze. "What happened when you refused to leave?"

Her father stopped and winged a triumphant smile towards Amber. "We formed a human chain. No way were we going to allow the police to pass."

Sasha choked on a laugh. "Oh Dad."

"Johnson said he had no choice but to arrest all of us." Her father raised his head proudly as if he'd faced down the hordes of Genghis Khan. "It took them three separate trips to transport us into town. We had to spend the night crammed into cells. I'm certain there is some legal negligence here, Amber. Isn't there a limit to the number of people allowed in one cell?" Her father tapped his chin thoughtfully. "Let's see now, over-crowding, illegal arrest, manhandling … Why, I could sue the police department and the government."

Pop grinned, his blue eyes twinkling with mirth.

Cole gave a laugh, which he hastily turned into a cough when his aunt glared at him. Choking and spluttering he left the room and opened the front door.

Seconds later, Sasha heard him laughing out on the verandah. With a rueful sigh, she looked at her father. "If I were you, I'd be grateful you weren't charged." Sasha rose and took hold of her father's restless hands. "How about a hot cuppa and something to eat? I made pea and ham soup last night."

"Sounds great, Cuddlepie." Her father winked. "Ask your squeeze if he'll drive me back to town in half an hour. I'm going to see a solicitor."

WITH COLE'S aunt volunteering to stay a few days at Cotton Fields Glory, Sasha decided it was time to go home.

Cole had taken her overnight bag with him when he drove her father into town; after a prolonged goodbye with both Summer and Toby begging her to stay longer, she'd wrenched herself away. To her dismay, she found herself crying as she rode back to Mindalby. *Wake up, woman. You'll see them again.*

But she wondered how she was going to feel when it came time to leave Mindalby for good.

The journey into town seemed to take forever. By the time she reached Woodburn Bridge, the sun was setting. Shadows were long over the ground and she was tired, shivering and completely miserable. At the corner of Woodburn and Burton Park Road, she gazed towards the main entrance of Mindalby Cotton Company. A crowd of people huddled around fires burning in large metal drums.

The yards beyond the fence-line had a deserted air and the place reeked of despair.

Sighing, she slowed, taking a left onto Louth Road.

She heard a vehicle approach from behind. No one was coming in the opposite direction but she moved her moped closer to the edge of the road giving the vehicle room to over-take. But the car remained behind—tailgating her.

Her heartrate sped up. She risked a glance behind but with its headlights on it was hard to make out the make or model; she gained the impression of a work utility.

Why didn't it pass?

Anger swelled within her. She flicked on her indicator, and braking, steered off the road onto the verge. But when she turned around all she could see was a pair of tail-lights as the car swung onto Short Street and moved down the road.

She must be losing her mind. For a moment there, she had thought ...

Shaking her head and willing her paranoia to disappear, she moved back onto the road. At the next intersection, she took a right onto Edward Street then rode along the quiet back street. Smoke from the residences' woodfires drifted low in the icy air and gradually her pulse steadied.

A couple of lights glowed behind curtains in the other occupied flats of her building. She was grateful for the porch light next door when she stopped the moped and turned off the engine. Feeling tired, she pushed it along the path, intending to park the moped on her porch. The wide yellow beam from her headlight illuminated the front of her flat.

Bile burned up her throat.

For a few seconds, she stood and stared at the mangled creature with its broken neck and bulging blank eyes.

Feathers were sprinkled like shattered lives on the hard concrete.

Rage erupted.

Fingers shaking, she pulled out her phone and dialled the local police station. "It's Sasha Bernstein. I want to report a malicious act. Someone has strangled a chicken and left it on my doorstep."

The next day, after giving a statement to a constable who looked as if he was barely out of high school, Sasha fronted the community centre where she handed over her official resignation from Mindably Cotton Company.

Felicity pursed her lips and stared over the rim of her glasses. "Any particular reason?"

"The radio chat show last week has done me no favours with the townspeople. Many believe I'm involved either with Don Carter or the company closure." She shrugged and went on to tell the other woman about the dead *'messages'* left at her door.

"Have you reported this to the police?"

"Yes. But I got the impression they don't hold much hope of identifying the perpetrator. I feel that I need to distance myself from the company."

Felicity placed her glasses on the table then folded her hands. "I hope you have no plans to leave town."

Heart leaping to her throat, Sasha's gaze met and clashed with the administrator's. "You still believe I'm involved."

"I'm hedging my bets." Felicity sighed and rubbed her nose. "Personally, no. But I can't and I won't take any chances where work is concerned. I meant to tell you earlier that I appreciate your honesty in forwarding the information you discovered on Mrs Carter."

"Do you think it's got anything to do with the company closing?"

"Dave is looking into it and hasn't completed his report. At this point anything you haven't told us would help."

Sasha flicked her glance to the window where a willy-wagtail was hopping along the sill. With matters finally progressing where her uncle was concerned, perhaps it was time to reveal the real reason she was in Mindalby. Drawing out a chair, she sat in front of the desk, then gave a brief account of the events leading up to her arrival in town.

"I knew you'd have a logical reason for being here," said Dave in a satisfied tone.

She hadn't heard him enter the room.

Felicity nodded. "I can see why you'd be reluctant to share your background with us. And I hope your recent discovery will assist your uncle. What are your plans now?"

"I will stay in town a little longer," Sasha said slowly, her thoughts winging immediately to Cole.

"Good. I think that's a wise decision. Disappearing at this point in time will only cement local opinion. There's a lot of anger simmering in this town."

"I expected you to question me about Don again," Sasha pointed out.

Felicity grinned. "I've already guessed the rest. I like a woman who isn't afraid to get things done. If your PI comes up with any information we could use, I'd be grateful if you could pass it on."

"Not a problem. I'm happy to do so." Sasha drew a deep breath. "There's more." She told them about the night before the meeting and how she'd discovered Yasmin Carter in the admin building.

Excitement sparked in Felicity's eyes. Ignoring Sasha's admission about trespassing, she said, "What did she take?"

"I'm not certain but it was the size and shape of an external hard drive."

"This could be what we've been looking for—another set of company accounts," Felicity said fiercely. "Get the necessary paperwork done, Dave. I want that hard drive.'

"I'm on it."

"If you do find those missing accounts and there's something in there that could help my uncle …"

Felicity nodded. "Don't worry, Sasha. I'll ensure that it's passed onto you."

"Thank you." Smiling, Sasha rose, then held out her hand.

They shook, perfectly in accord with each other.

Feeling lighter than she had for several months, Sasha left the building and returned to her flat. For the remainder of the day, she worked on her mindfulness techniques and cognitive behavioural therapy exercises.

No matter where her path ended up, she had to complete the treatment mapped out for her if she wanted to live a life without fear or anxiety.

AFTER RECEIVING Cole's invitation late Friday afternoon, Sasha spent the weekend at Cotton Fields Glory again. Saturday afternoon, Cole and Pop disappeared into town to give free pony rides in the park. Before he left, Cole swept Sasha into his arms in full view of his children, and gave her a kiss so sizzling she thought her hair would ignite. He sure had a way of saying goodbye that had her hungry for his return.

On Sunday, along with Cole and Summer, she rode her pony to the commune. Pop drove Toby there in the farm ute. Both she and Summer participated in a yoga session while the men fished for yabbies down by the river.

It hadn't surprised Sasha to find her father already there, appearing to be quite at home in Amber's yurt. The commune had invited the townspeople to an open day and had provided free food and entertainment by way of games for the kids and music.

Not many attended, however. It was a reminder of how many remained suspicious of the commune and its members. Cole's parents turned up and spent the time wandering the grounds arm in arm, as if content not to mingle.

The day was glorious. Mild and sunny with a gentle, fresh breeze that rustled through the trees and sent windchimes tinkling.

Lunch was spent around an open fire, eating a scrumptious vegetarian meal and listening to a man called Ray strum his guitar and his partner Tai accompanying him on a violin. Summer snuggled into Sasha's side and Sasha hugged her close. Cole sat on Sasha's other side, his hand resting warm and heavy on her thigh. Across the circle, Toby and her father were busy whittling a whistle out of a piece of timber.

Late in the afternoon, the three rogues from the Ace in the Hole belted out an old Elton John song. Max Dooley played the spoons, Chook the accordion, and Harry … Harry sang the lyrics with an amazing baritone voice.

All in all, the weekend went by way too fast for Sasha. She could have stayed at Cotton Fields Glory, surrounded by the Mitchell clan, forever. They made her feel as if she was one of them. When she left late Sunday afternoon, the prospect of facing her cold, empty flat failed to spark any interest whatsoever.

But when she arrived home, it was to find the front window defaced by graffiti. Red paint depicted the words *'last chance'*. Was it a co-incidence the graffiti mirrored the name of Yasmin Carter's yacht? Or something more sinister?

Furious, her happiness with the weekend marred, she phoned the police.

Sounding just as irritated, Sergeant Johnson growled, "Not you again! What is it this time?"

After ending the call, she rang Cole and told him about the graffiti. His concern chased the jitters from her belly.

But after she'd hung up, she felt bereft.

She sighed, fatigue stealing over her. Before switching off the lights, she made certain there wasn't another delivery on her doorstep then checked the windows and doors, her mind replaying the weekend.

It had been a long time since she'd laughed so much her sides ached. A long time since she'd experienced such a sense of peace.

Normally, she relished living alone. She twitched the curtains closed with a fierce jerk and marched into the bathroom to clean her teeth.

The more time she spent in Cole's company, the more she questioned her choices. Could this yearning to be part of his life be a residue of her PTSS?

Cole gave her a sense of safety, of being protected, and his presence diminished her nightmares. So was this about feeling safe? Or had she fallen in love?

The sense that she stood at a crossroads grew stronger with every hour she spent in this town. The wrong turn could lead her down a path she might well regret.

If she left Mindalby, the fear could stay with her. She needed to know the answer, but the only way to find out was to leave.

The hours spent at the commune had reminded her that life didn't always have to be about responsibility and work—it could also be about sharing and community.

About family.

As she snuggled under her doona, she wondered whether she dared dream she could have it all.

THE INVIGORATING *Rocky* ringtone woke her from a deep sleep. She reached groggily for her mobile, dimly aware there was also a pounding noise close by. It took her a few seconds to realise someone was hammering on her front door.

"Morning, Dad," she croaked as she flung aside her covers.

"Cuddlepie," boomed her father in her ear. "Have you seen the papers this morning?"

"Huh?" She yawned and rubbed her gritty eyes, then reached for her robe.

"You sound like you're half asleep!"

"You woke me."

"Tsk, tsk. It's gone seven-thirty."

"God, Dad." She sighed as she pulled on her dressing gown. "Hang on. Someone is knocking on the door."

"Don't open it!" Her father fairly shrieked the words.

Her hand hovered centimetres above the knob. Frowning, she moved into the lounge room and twitched aside the curtains. There was quite a sizeable crowd out the front, stamping their feet in the cold. No smiling faces beneath the beanies and hoodies, only scowls and sneering mouths. A crumpled beer can clattered against the window; thankfully, it didn't break the glass.

She pulled back and pressed against the wall, out of eyesight. "What's going on?"

"You need to go online. I'll phone the family solicitor. Don't leave the flat and stay away from the windows." Her father ended the call.

She raced to her bedroom and booted up her laptop. It was only a matter of seconds and she found what had her father in a flap. Her spirits dive-bombed as she stared transfixed at a photo of Don Carter and her enjoying what looked to be a romantic candlelit dinner. In the background, fireworks exploded in the night sky illuminating the iconic Sydney Harbour Bridge.

A curse exploded from her mouth.

Hands shaking, she scrolled through the article which consisted of innuendoes and suppositions. The photo was damning enough.

Something hard and heavy smashed against her front door.

The crowd outside erupted into a barrage of shouted abuse.

Now what was happening?

She placed her laptop onto her bed and edged back to the lounge room to peer out the curtains, feeling like a thief sneaking about in her own home.

A ruby-red sports car was nosing its way through the throng then stopped. The driver's door swung open and out stepped Yasmin Carter. Under her glacial stare, the crowd fell back allowing her to pass.

Yasmin strode down the path as if the others didn't exist.

Muttering under her breath, Sasha raced to her room, throwing off her bulky dressing gown as she went.

Knocking sounded on the front door.

Sasha pulled an emerald-green jumper over her head, dragged off her sleep pants and tugged on a pair of jeans.

The knocks became thumps.

What a way to start the day.

Hurrying back down the short hallway, she finger-combed her hair. She took a deep breath, pinned a smile on her face and opened the door.

"There she is!" screamed some lout from the crowd who sounded just like Cody Nossiter, not that she was surprised. Any sign of trouble or any excuse to rail against the world and he was your man.

Yasmin thrust a newspaper toward her face. "Well? Care to explain yourself?" The words were harsh but there was a satisfied tone in Yasmin's voice that made Sasha pause.

Her previous suspicions swept through her mind. The ease with which she'd gained the job at Mindalby Cotton Company. How Don had almost fallen over his feet at their meetings in Sydney then how he'd blown her off once she arrived. How her uncle had been used as a patsy.

"I don't believe I need to. This is all your doing, isn't it, Yasmin?" she said coolly.

The other woman fell back, her hand dropping to her side. A watchful expression settled on her smoothly made-up face.

Sasha raised her voice. "I know a set-up when I see one. What I still don't understand though, is whether Don knows what you're up to or whether you orchestrated the mill folding all by your lonesome."

The crowd fell silent.

"I ..." Yasmin clutched the pearls at her throat.

Behind her, the crowd had grown still, all eyes and ears.

"Spare me your act of an outraged wife confronting her husband's girlfriend. It's all lies. You organised for me to be given the job, intending that I take the blame. But the truth is, Mindably Cotton Company has been trading insolvently before I ever arrived in town."

Mutterings swept through the crowd.

"And by the way, my solicitor, at the very least, will be seeking monetary damages for defamation," she added sweetly.

Closing the door in Yasmin's furious face, she leaned against the timber and grinned.

Now, that is how to start the day.

Cole swung out of his Land Rover, then reached for the folder tucked behind the driver's seat while his grandfather climbed from the passenger side. The main street was busy this morning, with plenty of townspeople about, shopping or standing in tight clusters, chatting.

A bunch of elderly ladies turned to look as he and his grandfather headed towards the bank. One of them was clutching a copy of the local rag and, elbowing her neighbour, nodded toward him. He distantly heard her mutter, "Poor boy. He has no idea."

Pop marched by his side, shoulders straight and only a slight limp when he leaned on his walking stick betraying he'd had another bad night with arthritis. No words of complaint passed his lips. Cole had to give Pop credit for being a soldier through and through. The past weeks had been especially hard on him. Cotton Fields Glory had been his and grand-mum's life.

Upon entering the building, they made their way over to the counter where they were asked to take a seat until the bank manager was off the phone.

Sighing, Cole settled into the hard chair and mulled over the past few days.

He wasn't certain what to make of the malicious tricks being played on Sasha. First a mouse, then a dead chicken and then graffiti on her window. Someone had it in for her and he hated the thought he lived so far from her. Despite Cole having several heated conversations with Sergeant Johnson, there was nothing the police could do without an eyewitness. Or unless the culprit was caught in the act.

And wasn't that the clincher—the idea this person intended to continue his or her harassment campaign.

The last thing Cole needed was Sasha so scared she'd leave town. He needed time to show her she didn't have to travel to another country in order to make a difference in others' lives.

A few minutes later they were ushered into a utilitarian office. Marshalling his thoughts, Cole took a seat and prayed for a positive outcome.

But the manager had little good news to deliver. Stunned, Cole and his grandfather left the building.

They stood on the pavement in heavy silence. There was a grim twist to Pop's mouth that churned Cole's gut. Pop was staring fish-eyed dead ahead, his hands curled into fists. The last time he'd seen that expression had been when his gran had died.

Cole dragged in a lungful of air. "It'll be okay, Pop. We'll work it out. If we can come up with more collateral Kiera reckons we'll get our loan extension approved."

"But there's nothing left to use."

"I've got the last of my inheritance."

"Out of the question. That's for your kids' future. I won't let you pour it down the drain on our farm."

"I think that's my decision to make, Pop." Cole raked a hand through his hair. "We've still got some time before the administrator hands down her report. It may not be as bad as what everyone is saying."

"And if it is?" Pop said quietly. "The buyers for the load we just delivered are bleating they can't pay us for another thirty. We've been issued with a notice to pay for the ginning of the bales in Carter's yard within ten days. Plus, we have the harvester to pay. This isn't good, son."

Cole patted one of his grandfather's wrinkled hands. "Something will come up."

"Your gran would have said, have faith and use your brains. But I can't see a way out. We may have to sell Cotton Fields Glory!"

"I won't let that happen."

Pop shook his head and leaned on his walking stick, a recent addition since he twisted his ankle the other day when jumping down off the tractor. "Let's face it, son. We may have no choice."

About to argue, Cole paused, aware that someone stood behind them. Turning, he saw Lesley Thompson. How much had she heard? They didn't need a rumour sweeping the town about Cotton Fields Glory going belly up.

"Cole! How are you? I was about to drive out to your farm." Her gaze shifted to his grandfather's face. 'You don't look well, Mr Mitchell. Maybe you should sit for a while?'

"No time for sitting. Or jawing. Let's head to the realtor."

"Pop, no! There's no need to make any hard decisions here and now. We still have some time before we have to decide."

"What's going on?" Lesley stared past them to the bank entrance. "It's your farm. You're in trouble. Will you have to sell?"

Feeling hunted, Cole snapped, "Look, there's a lot to consider and anyway, I don't feel it's any of your business."

"Too right it's not." Latching onto his arm with nails that dug into his skin, she said, "I take it you haven't seen today's paper. You should check it out. It shows just how well-acquainted Miss Snooty Sasha is with Don Carter."

She pointed toward where Sasha was pedalling

along the road in their direction. She gave a toss of her head, then darted into a nearby shop.

"Cole. Pop." Sounding breathless, Sasha hopped off her bike and wheeled it a tad closer. "I'm so glad I caught you. I tried phoning but your mobile must be switched off." Her throat worked, like she was swallowing something distasteful.

"Morning, Sasha." Pop attempted a smile but it came out as more of a grimace.

Sasha removed her bike helmet. Her face was pale, her eyes huge and stark. And shadowed.

"Sasha, love, it's great to see you." Cole jerked his head in the direction Lesley could be seen inside the shop with her face pressed close to the window. "Any idea what that was about?"

"I can guess." She squared her shoulders and his heart sank. "Heard the local news this morning? Or read the paper?"

"Not yet. We've been busy."

She glanced at the bank then back at him. "I see." Half-turning, she rummaged in her satchel for a moment before handing over a folded newspaper. She took a step backwards, like she was distancing herself. "Front page. You can't miss it."

He stared at the photo. At first, not believing his eyes. She'd lied to him all along. She *did* have a relationship with Don Carter that went further than boss and employee.

Fury welled, hot and red, blinding him for a few seconds until he rammed a lid on his emotions.

He showed the paper to Pop, who tutted and shook his head.

Raising his eyebrows, Cole waited for Sasha to speak. Because he sure couldn't. If he did, he knew all that would spew forth would be accusations and disappointment. And hurt—bone-deep, gut-wrenching hurt.

"I'd like to explain, if you're willing to listen," she offered in a quiet voice.

Cole nodded.

"We could go to the park and speak there."

Pop cleared his throat. "I'll just duck into the hardware store and look for some stuff."

But Sasha said, 'I'd like you to hear me too, please.'

Pop shot Cole a keen glance beneath his beetling white brows. 'Okay with you, son?'

The main street of Mindalby wasn't the place to have it out. Already, Cole felt like a hundred eyes and ears were tuned in their direction. But this couldn't wait.

"Why not here and how? Unless you have something else to hide," Cole grated then, seeing how badly her hands shook, regretted his harsh tone.

He firmed his jaw. She was the one who'd betrayed his trust.

Sasha averted her face, hiding her expression from him as she pushed a lock of hair behind her ear. "I haven't done anything to be ashamed of."

"Yeah, right," he exploded. But damn it all to hell and back. He hoped with every atom of his being, she had a bloody good explanation.

Otherwise, he'd cut her out of his and his kids' lives forever.

In halting tones, she said, "It was two dinners and one coffee meet. That was it but I won't deny I went there with the specific intention of doing whatever I could to help my uncle."

"You had a relationship with Carter. When did it stop? Or hasn't it?" His voice shook, so great was his anger. "Whenever I saw you with him at the mill, he was always touching you, laughing."

"He does that with every woman. It means nothing. I allowed it because I'd hoped to pry information from him." Raising her chin, she met his eyes. "I never lied, Cole. There was no relationship. I just didn't tell you the whole story."

"You mean, you didn't trust me sufficiently with the truth," he said flatly, turning away. "Friendship and trust is as important to me as love and great sex."

"Is that what you had with Denise?"

"Don't bring my wife into this—this is about you. You said you'd do anything to help your uncle. Define 'anything.'"

"I can't and I won't." Tears glistened in her eyes. "You told me once that you protect those you love. Well, I'm the same and I won't apologise for doing what I thought I had to do."

"I need to think. I can't talk to you right now."

Holding her head up high, she nodded. "Goodbye, Cole." And she wheeled her bike away.

His hands fisted. His heart was pounding like it would burst from his chest at any second. He'd be damned if he ran after her on the main street of Mindalby. He turned to look at his grandfather.

"You don't need me to tell you what a fool you are boy. Take a walk and think about what Sasha has told you." Pop shook his head. "I'll be in the hardware store."

So, Cole took that walk.

Hands in his jacket pockets, shoulders hunched, he strode off. His head whirled with so many thoughts and emotions he barely registered where his feet led him.

She'd explained. It hadn't been the explanation he'd hoped for but he knew in the depths of his soul, it had been an honest one.

Her words haunted him and the longer he walked the more they drowned out the image of Sasha in another man's arms. And not just any man—the man he believed responsible for bringing the town to its knees and Cotton Field Glory to the brink.

He stopped, oblivious to the group of teenagers scooting along the footpath on their skateboards. They shot around him and still he stood there, thinking, remembering.

She was right—he would do anything it took to protect those he loved. He could hardly stigmatise her for doing the same. Besides, it was in the past and now that his initial jealousy and disappointment had ebbed, he knew Sasha would never betray him. If she'd wanted out of a relationship, she'd say so; she wouldn't sneak about having an affair on the side.

Tipping his head back, he closed his eyes. The cold wind ruffled his hair and a couple of splatters of rain brought him to his senses.

The last of his hurt faded.

Pop was right—he'd been a fool. That newspaper article had been published with one purpose—to tarnish and humiliate Sasha. Make the town turn against her.

And he couldn't believe he'd come so close to doing exactly that.

He looked at the shop next to him. Then smiled and walked closer. There in the window was the sign he didn't even know he'd been looking for: a yellow sapphire engagement ring.

Perfect.

Now all he had to do was wait for the right moment. But first, he needed to mend some bridges.

Breaking into a jog, he took off down the main street of Mindalby, his mind fixed firmly on his quarry and the life he hoped they'd share.

AS DARKNESS FELL over Cotton Fields Glory, Cole counted his blessings. Beneath the thick canopy of a weeping myall tree he and Sasha swayed together, locked in each other's arms.

Thin wisps of cloud floated like veils drawn over the glittering stars. With the peaceful evening hush, Cole experienced a sense of rightfulness. The last of his reservations had been stripped away. Giving a satisfied sigh, he pressed a kiss to Sasha's soft hair.

"You believed me," she whispered in a wondering tone.

"I knew you were keeping something from me," he admitted. "At first, all I could think of was you in Carter's arms. It downright near killed me."

Leaning back, she gazed into his face and his gut clenched at the love shining in her eyes. "You were jealous!"

He snorted. "Of course, I was."

"But you do believe I never had an affair with him? I never even let him kiss me, although he did try it on once."

"Sasha, love. I wanted to beat him to a pulp. But in my heart, I knew you'd never hook up with a married man. I'm sorry I stormed off like that—I needed time to think things through. It didn't take me long to realise I was wrong. I behaved like an idiot."

"You're not the only one who's made mistakes. I should have trusted you sooner with the truth." She snuggled closer. "I've never seen you so angry. You were really mad."

"That I was." His smile died. "What bothers me is the notion that you were deliberately employed to be framed."

"It fits the pattern I believe Yasmin has used in the past. But I have a good solicitor, so don't stress. I'm sorry about you and Pop not getting an extension on the loan."

He rubbed his cheek against her silky hair. "I can use the last of my inheritance from my other grandfather. I know Pop will rant and rave, but I won't let Cotton Fields Glory be sold. It'll be tight though, and my plans for the charity ride will have to be put on hold."

"Maybe I can help?"

"We'll see. I'm glad you agreed to come and stay for a while, Sasha love. I need you. We all need you. And I'll sleep more easy now with you in my home and not alone in that flat." *And now that you've forgiven me for my lack of faith.* He had to admit, he'd experienced one hell of an anxious thirty minutes while he fumbled his way through his apology and waited for her verdict. He'd asked for another chance and she'd agreed. Proving for all time that Sasha had a heart the size of Australia.

She'd ridden out on her moped and arrived just as night fell. His kids had been ecstatic to see her again and Pop had welcomed her as if nothing had happened.

She fitted into his family as if she belonged; now all he had to do was convince her of that.

Those first days when he'd been leery about allowing her into their lives were long gone. Her determination to help her uncle had endorsed his belief in her integrity. Sasha was a stayer. But she was also a crusader.

He just had to convince her there were plenty of causes in Mindalby to keep her occupied for a lifetime.

"Are you certain the kids are asleep?" Sasha raised her head from where she'd been resting on his chest, to peer around him at the dark house.

"Probably watching us with a pair of night-vision goggles."

Sasha giggled then gasped. "I hope you're not serious."

"Nah, they haven't got any. Yet. They *are* on Toby's Christmas wish list."

"He's a great kid. They both are, Cole. You're a wonderful dad."

Face warm, he shrugged. "I've got a solid support team with Pop and my parents. Aunt Amber contributes the crazy the rest of us ordinary beings lack."

"I don't think any of you are the least bit ordinary."

His eyes met the intensity blazing in hers and he trembled, humbled by the respect in her gaze. He thought of what Pop had said about Gran and hope burned steady and bright. He slipped his right arm from her waist and traced the side of her face with the pad of his thumb, over skin softer than flower petals.

"Sleep with me, in my bed, tonight. All night—every night." His words were more command than question.

"But what about your kids? And your grandfather—they'll think we're … living together."

"So? They know we're an item. Think of it as a fresh beginning," he said, only half teasing.

The silence stretched on until broken by the soft thuds of one of his horses moving along the fence.

"There's that crossroads again," she mused.

"Sorry? I don't …"

Sasha shifted in his hold and placed her hands around his neck. "Something I've been thinking about a lot lately. I'd love to make a fresh start with you."

"Then stay with us—here in Mindalby." He tensed, holding his breath. His heart pounded while he waited. "I would love to show you what great things you could do for the town. Let me be honest. What I really want is you here with me and Summer and Toby forever."

Tears glistened in her eyes. Through the clothes separating them, he could feel the sudden rush of her heartbeats.

"I don't know what to say," she said.

"I'm not after an answer right now. But keep an open mind, hey?"

"I can do that," she whispered.

He exhaled, his hope of a moment ago slipping

away, leaving behind a desolation that was pure pain. "That's not a yes."

She placed her hands on his cheeks and stared into his eyes. "It's not a no either." Her lips touched his, her kiss tender and sweet, igniting into heady desire.

Hunger for the woman who had captured his wary heart licked a fire of passion through his veins. He rallied, searching for something to hold on to. Hope resurfaced. In the here and now, he had the most wonderful woman on earth snug in his arms. And who'd soon be snug in his bed, where he'd work on gaining that *yes*.

Some moments in a person's life were pure magic.

This was one of them.

He'd be crazy not to make the most of it.

HIS MOBILE RINGING woke Cole from a sound sleep. Grunting, he fumbled for the phone on his bedside table, automatically registering the time as four am. Beside him, Sasha muttered drowsily, snuggling deeper under the doona.

Still half-asleep he mumbled a 'hello'.

"Cole, is that you?" barked his father.

Cole yawned. "Yeah, Dad. What's up?"

"It's my studio. Some joker's broken in and trashed the joint."

Now fully awake, he sat up. "I'll get dressed and be there in about fifteen. Did you call the police?"

"Yes. Hang on, your mother's talking. What's that, Maise?"

Silence for a few minutes, while Cole groped in the dark for his clothes, phone clamped to his ear.

Then his father came back on the line. "Unbelievable. They've even smashed the family photos in my office and drawn a smiley face on the painting I did of your mother."

"Geez, Dad. I'm on my way." He hung up, shaking his head.

"What's going on?" Sasha sat up in bed and flicked on the lamp.

While pulling on his socks and shoes, he filled her in then said, "I'm not certain how long I'll be gone. I may even bring Mum and Dad back here. Can you let Pop know when he wakes up?"

"Sure. Take as long as you need to, Cole."

He leaned down for a kiss, drinking in the sweetness of her lips and the soft, warm press of her body as she wound her arms around his neck for one last hug. "I'll be back as soon as I can."

Then he grabbed his keys and headed out the door.

SASHA WAITED out the long day until finally, around four in the afternoon, she phoned the family investigator. He'd sent a brief text early in the morning advising he should have a report for her later. After exchanging brief pleasantries, he explained how a search into the registration of the yacht revealed the owner to be Trove Financials Pty Ltd.

A direct link to Yasmin Carter.

The boat had been purchased two years last December, five months after the embezzlement had been discovered when the business her uncle was involved in had folded. In Sasha's opinion, the timing dovetailed beautifully. Yasmin apparently waited only long enough for the media sensation to die down before buying the yacht. A nice Christmas present. Or a reward for a job well done?

Throat clogged, Sasha listened while the investigator explained how he'd unearthed the parent company of Trove Financials to be a limited liability company registered in the Cook Islands. Yasmin Carter was the sole director. In other words, Yasmin was hiding assets and, in all probability, dodging taxes.

All the information had been emailed to their solicitor.

Sasha thanked him and rang off, her head whirling.

This was all they needed to push for a fresh investigation into Uncle Isaac's case and, with luck, a re-trial or an acquittal. Hands trembling, she phoned her mother to relay the news and together they cried.

Cole returned home as she was serving dinner and detailed how he'd helped his parents clean up the mess left by vandals. He looked tired and rumpled and her heart wrenched at the sight. She'd tell him her news after he'd had something to eat and unwound.

Pop handed Cole a beer. "What did the police say?"

"They suspect it was the work of teenagers stirred up by the tension in the town with the mill closure."

"In other words, they haven't a clue," Pop declared, thumping the kitchen table with his fist and making the coffee mugs jump.

Cole leaned against the wall and took a sip of his beer. "They've been rather busy lately."

Pop snorted.

"How much did the thieves steal?" Sasha placed the evening meal of falafel balls and steamed broccoli in front of Cole. "Eat."

"Some loose change. The idiots smashed a couple of chairs by slamming them against some of Dad's paintings, totalling destroying five. One was a favourite of mine. You remember the painting of Bennett's Gorge, Pop?"

"That's a shame. I liked that painting too." Pop beetled his brows, looking fierce.

"Is Grandmum and Grandpa okay?" Summer asked, her eyes as big as saucers.

"They're fine, honey but very unhappy at the damage. They have insurance which will help monetary wise. At least I cheered them up a little." Cole met Sasha's eyes and a glint of mischief lightened his shadowed expression.

"What have you done?" she asked, her lips twitching.

"I told Mum that I've asked you to stay in Mindalby. No sooner did I tell her than she was on the phone to my sisters and then Aunt Amber. I bet half the town knows by now."

Both kids began to talk at once, excitement pitching their voices high.

Shaking her head, Sasha mouthed 'not fair' to Cole.

He grinned.

A smug expression settling on his face, Pop said, "You know what they say, Sasha, about all being fair in love."

"And war," she reminded him with a touch of exasperation.

"Hey." Cole lifted his hands in the air. "Mum needed a distraction to take her mind off the break-in."

Sasha picked up a wooden spoon. "So the big bad wolf sacrificed me."

"A very hungry wolf," Cole said then burst into laughter as, spoon in hand, she chased him around the table.

25

Sasha returned to her flat Thursday afternoon and booked her health assessment in Sydney for two weeks' time. The following morning, she jogged with her father through the heavy dawn fog towards Woodburn Bridge. The pale, yellow beam from her torchlight was barely sufficient to see the road ahead through the swirls of grey mist.

Her dad jabbed at the space in front of him with his gloved fists, his breath puffs of white steam in the icy cold air.

She smiled, content with the moment and hopeful for what the day might bring. She'd woken fresh and alert this morning, after a night where she hadn't been restless and constantly in and out of bed checking the doors and the windows.

Maybe a sign she was finally healing. The future shimmered as colourful as Christmas.

Her fingertips tingled—life was on the up—she knew it. If she was cleared for duty at her forthcoming health assessment then it would be life-defining decision time.

If she decided to move on—then Mindalby could soon be nothing but another memory in her life album.

Cole's face swam before her eyes. His crinkled smile, the brilliance of his blue eyes and the generosity of his heart. How could she leave him? Especially when he was facing the ruination of his life's dream—Cotton Fields Glory.

His decision to believe in her explanation and not in the evidence of a damning photo had humbled her. He was a man any woman would be crazy to walk away from. And with every minute that passed, she knew she wanted nothing more than to be with him.

But how to help him? There was still Cotton Fields Glory and a town that could well plunge into economic ruin.

The impact the winding up of Mindably Cotton would have on Cole, Pop and the town was horrifying.

If Cole and Pop were forced to sell Cotton Fields Glory, Pop would be devastated; the land and home held more than memories—it held his history and the shadow of his deceased wife's love. At his age, the emotional loss would be crushing.

Cole could always get a welding job, she supposed. But if he had to move away for work, his children would have to leave their friends, school and grandparents behind.

She could offer him money, a loan even, but she doubted he'd accept even if their budding relationship turned lasting.

Her happiness of a moment ago dissipated as fleeting and whimsical as a will-o'-the-wisp. There had to be something—a solution to all their problems. Her instinct told her it was out there, waiting for her to stumble over it. All she had to do was sniff it out.

"Let's run along the riverbank, Cuddlepie," her father said.

"Great idea."

She followed her father off Woodburn Road and onto a gravel road that wasn't much more than a track.

She slowed as she passed shrubs and straggly bushes growing by the side of the road. The fog was thicker here, giving her a creepy sensation, making her scalp prickle under the thick beanie she wore. Already her father had disappeared into the mist ahead of her. The only way she knew he was still there was the crunching of his joggers over the loose stones until even that faded.

To her right, leaves crackled. A twig snapped.

She jumped, heart pounding.

Was that an animal or a human?

Her throat closed, snatching away the option of calling to her father. Her pulse was like thunder in her ears. The memory of lying trapped beneath the broken truck roof, as the rat-tat-tat of gunfire crept closer, sent adrenaline flooding her system, launching her into action.

If someone was lurking, she wasn't waiting for a surprise attack. She'd meet it head-on and on her terms.

She leapt off the road and plunged through the bushes with such force she snapped off twigs and leaves.

"Sasha! Where are you?" Her father's frantic voice cut eerily through the fog.

Panting, she halted her headlong rush to listen.

Footsteps pounded ahead of her, fading rapidly. The wrong direction to be her father.

She pushed on until she was faced with a thicket of brambles. It was pointless to continue. She could hear nothing but her own breathing and her father's distant shouts.

Whoever had been out here was gone.

"I'm over here, Dad!" she called and turned back.

She emerged onto the road to find her father pacing up and down, throwing his hands in the air.

He rushed towards her. "What happened? Are you hurt?"

"I'm fine. I thought I heard someone in the bushes, so I gave chase."

"*What?*" His piercing cry made her wince. "And you decided to check for yourself? Alone?"

"Honestly, Dad, I could have been mistaken. Maybe it was a kangaroo." She shrugged.

"I don't believe it. You've never been one to jump at shadows, but …" He hesitated and in the growing light she saw him bite his lip.

She patted his arm. "I know the accident has changed me."

"Cuddlepie, I didn't mean you're not the same, courageous girl you've always been." His voice was so warm and loving, Sasha's heart swelled.

"Oh Dad." She kissed his cheek. "I'll race you when we get to the river."

"You're on."

They fell into step. The fog was lifting and as they came upon the bridge, the mist drifting over the river looked like silver droplets glistening in the thin early morning sunshine.

A truly mystical moment.

"Looks like we've got company. There's a car beside the bank." Her father broke into a jog.

"Dad! Wait." She raced after him.

His voice floated towards her. "Woowee! What a beauty! This is a late model F-Type sports Jag. I bet she flies along the open road."

She arrived at his side where he had cupped his hands around his face and was peering through the rear windows, his nose close enough to squish against the glass. "Dad, what are you doing?"

"Taking a sticky. The car's full of luggage but I can't see any sign of the driver."

"I recognise this car. Yasmin Carter was driving it when she came to my flat the other day." Frowning, she examined the area. Now that the fog had thinned, the road and most of the jetty was visible, as were a decent stretch of fields on her right and the river on her left. What could she be doing here?

"I can't see any anyone around."

"Same." Her father planted his hands on his hips and gazed up and down the road.

"Let's forget about it." She performed a few stretches then grinned. "Ready to race, Dad?"

Her father touched his toes then sprang forward. He took off shouting over his shoulder, "See? Your old man still has some moves."

Grinning and shaking her head, she sprinted after him. She settled into an easy rhythm, not too fast, pacing herself as they ran along a rough track close to the water's edge. Out in the middle of the river, a flock of waterfowl paddled through fog tendrils. A heron waded near the shallows, moving amongst the reeds then stopping in mid-step.

What had made the bird freeze like that? Curious, she slowed her pace; her father powered on, whooping as he passed her. Her eyes tracked the direction of the bird's beak.

A dark bundle lay on the ground. A bundle from

which protruded a pair of feet clad in spiky nude stilettoes.

The bundle wasn't tossed-out garbage.

A body.

She leapt over the ground to halt panting near the body which was covered by a man's bulky overcoat obscuring the face.

"What's wrong? What is it …?" Her father arrived beside her and went to move forward. "Oh my goodness! The poor woman has tripped and fallen."

"Hold on, Dad." She pointed to the ground. "I'm certain there's blood on that rock. She could have been assaulted. Remember those footsteps I heard?"

Gesturing for her father to remain where he was, she took a step forward, taking care not to walk where the springy grass was flattened. It was possible a footprint had been left and she didn't want to disturb any evidence.

He whipped out his mobile. "I'll phone for an ambulance and the police. If you're right, whoever did this may still be here."

Her father's quiet voice floated towards her as he spoke to an emergency operator while she took another careful look around before crouching beside the figure. Lifting the overcoat with her gloved fingers, she peered beneath. Her breath hitched in surprise. "Dad, it's Yasmin Carter."

"Are you sure?"

"Yes." She leaned closer and pulled off her right

glove to check the woman's pulse. Next, she gently lifted the closed eyelids to examine the irises and listened for a few seconds. "Yes. It's her. She's breathing but I don't like the sound of it. It's too stertorous. Her pulse is erratic and her pupils dilated. There's a pool of dark blood beside her. The wound must be on the back of her head. I don't want to move her in case she has a serious skull fracture. All we can do for now is keep her warm."

Being extra careful, Sasha re-arranged the coat so Yasmin's face was uncovered giving her access to fresh air, then tucked the edges around her neck. "This coat is all that's stopped her from getting hypothermia. As it is, her skin is icy. She needs help fast, Dad." She gently rubbed the other woman's cold hands.

"This is terrible. A woman attacked and left for dead.' He tutted. 'I wonder what she was doing out here alone."

Sasha rocked back on her haunches, and glanced at her father. "Her car held a lot of luggage."

Her father frowned. "Hoping to make a run for it, do you think? In case she's dragged into her husband's messy business dealings?"

"Could Don have been with her? They could have had an argument; perhaps began to blame each other."

"Then Carter loses his temper and assaults her? It's possible, Cuddlepie."

Sasha checked the woman's pulse again. "I'm not convinced. Don doesn't strike me as the violent type.

He's more bluster and bluff. She could have been on her own and for some unknown reason, stopped here, got out of her car and in the fog, lost her footing. The ground is very uneven."

"It's a weird place to stop."

"Yeah, you're right. That part only makes sense if she intended to meet someone here. I wonder where she was going?" Sasha stiffened with a sudden thought, lost her balance and plopped onto her butt in the damp mud.

"The boat. I bet she was heading for her boat! She may have thought it would be easier to leave the country by sea rather than to fly out. Dad, can you remember whether you noticed a handbag in the car?"

"I don't think so. Want me to go back and take a look?"

"Yes, please." She looked at the unconscious woman. "I can hear sirens. The ambulance mustn't be far off."

The sound of wheels rolling over gravel announced the arrival of the ambulance. She left off her search and hurried to greet the paramedics as they climbed out of the cabin, quickly giving them a succinct report.

The senior paramedic frowned. "Are you saying this is a crime scene?"

"I'm saying it's possible she was pushed rather than fell. Might be a good idea to take precautions, just in case."

"Fair enough. Come on, Jake, be careful where you

step. Don't go far, ma'am, the cops will want to talk to you." Gear in hand, they hurried to Yasmin.

After watching them for a couple of minutes, Sasha moved off, ensuring she retraced the same steps she'd taken to approach Yasmin while her father jogged back towards the jetty. Picking up a stick she began shifting leaves and poking under bushes. What she was looking for, she wasn't certain, but she didn't find anything.

While the paramedics were busy stablising Yasman she decided to check along the river's edge where marshes grew thick and dense on both sides of the old jetty where her father was poking about.

Intent on her search, she was only vaguely aware of another vehicle pulling up. Her father's excited voice was answered by Sergeant Johnson then the dim thud of footsteps as they moved to where Yasmin was being loaded onto a stretcher.

Their voices carried clearly above the dawn bird-song. Johnson ordered his constable to take a barrage of photos of anything and everything.

Sasha spied an object near the stumps of the jetty. A large beige handbag with a gold clasp, open with the contents spilling out. A couple of receipts floated in the shallows. Bending down, she saw the edge of a passport and, joy of joys, the blue gleam of an active mobile phone.

Straightening, she shouted and waved her hands above her head.

When Johnson and his young constable, Meredith

Ross, came within hearing distance, she pointed to what she'd found.

"You should never have touched the body. This isn't a TV cop show, Ms Bernstein and you're no detective," snapped Johnson.

"I'm a registered nurse, Sergeant, and I've got eyes in my head. Although I could be wrong, I thought it best to be careful just in case."

Her nose wrinkled when a waft of sweetly sour breath reached her nostrils. She noted Johnson's blood-shot eyes and the faint red tinge to the tip of his nose. He looked like he'd had a big night on the turps. But he remained professional, wearing blue disposable plastic gloves. The bloody rock he held in his hand had been wrapped in plastic. Not a man to take chances even if he enjoyed the bottle too much. "My father and I can call into the station later today and make our statements."

"Make sure you do that." Johnson glared at the offending handbag. "Remember, Ross, I want photos in situ, before sealing everything in individual evidence bags. And don't take your gloves off."

"Yes, sir."

Johnson scratched his head. "I don't know what this town is coming to, what with the mill closing, dead animals left on doorsteps and fights almost every night at the pub."

"You failed to mention the illegal still which you have yet to find," Obie pointed out as he joined them.

"And the rough treatment meted out to innocent people protecting their property."

"Innocent?" spluttered Johnson, his face turning as red as beetroot. "I'll give you innocent. You and that … that woman incited a mob."

"Hardly a mob," her father scoffed, looking down his nose. "Illegal entry, hauling people off in paddy wagons as if we were criminals, and then throwing us in jail!"

"I should have charged you with aiding and abetting while I was at it." Johnson hooked his hands over his utility belt. "I won't forget, Mr Bernstein, this is the second time I've found you at a crime scene."

"Pwush!"

Smothering her grin, Sasha stepped forward before her father was hauled off to jail. Again. "Yasmin's phone is in that handbag. I'd like to make a formal request that if there is any reference to Isaac Blake's case, that our family solicitor and the investigator we've hired be informed immediately."

"I'll bear it in mind." Johnson's voice was dry. He made shooing motions with his hands and, not wanting to rile the man further, Sasha propelled her father to where the ambulance was parked.

As soon as she was out of earshot, she'd phone and update both their solicitor and the investigator.

She shivered when a gust of wind rose. Her adrenaline was draining fast, leaving her feeling the pinch of the chilly morning. Pulling her glove back on, she and her father watched the paramedics load Yasmin into the ambulance. A few seconds later, the vehicle roared into life and sped towards Mindalby, lights flashing, siren blaring.

"Think she'll make it, Cuddlepie?"

"Head injuries are difficult to predict, Dad. It will depend on the force of the impact and the density of Yasmin's skull. She may suffer nothing but mild concussion. On the other hand, she could end up with a brain injury."

"Tough. Whatever she's guilty of, she didn't deserve to have her head bashed in."

"I agree, Dad." She met her father's concerned gaze. "If it wasn't an accident, then someone in this town attacked her and may well have meant to kill her."

Sasha's mobile buzzed as she jogged to her flat, having waved her father goodbye at the intersection. They planned to meet at the police station before she went to the hospital. She wanted to check Yasmin's progress for herself, although she'd already rung through to the doctor on duty and given a report.

Nearing her front fence, she pulled her phone out and smiled when she recognised the number. "Hi, Cole."

"Sasha love. I know it's early but I had the strangest urge to hear your voice."

Her hand tightened on the phone. Was their connection that strong, he'd discerned her stress? She related the events of the morning, winding up with, "I'm off to the hospital in a minute."

Cole's voice sharpened. "What a terrible shock for you and Obie. Are you all right?"

"It was a little intense but the worst part is, I think someone was in the scrub when we first arrived."

"The attacker could have been hanging around. Sasha, you may have been hurt!"

"They ran off. Anyway, I had Dad with me." She fished out her keys and unlocked the door. "You'd be surprised what my father can do. He once fought off bandits when trekking alone through Peru."

"Nothing your father does surprises me. Nor you for that matter. You're the most competent person I've ever met."

She sighed, her thoughts winging back to the Middle East. "Not always."

"Yes. Always. What happened in Syria was beyond your control."

'Oh, Cole, you're so sweet." She blinked away a flurry of tears. How had he known what she was thinking?

"It's only what you deserve. Sasha love, could the attacker have been Carter? I heard the cops were knocking on his door yesterday, looking for missing documents, I think."

"Then perhaps the police turning up spurred Yasmin to leave town. Although, why she'd stop at the jetty is beyond me."

"Flagged down by someone? Or she could have been meeting someone she didn't want near the house."

"That's what Dad and I were thinking. She'd arranged to meet this person and they had an argument. Still, it's hard to say for certain whether or not she fell of her own accord or was pushed. Oh, I didn't tell you but she had an iPhone in her handbag."

"The one that went missing?"

"I've no idea but it's possible. Damn, I should have tried to access her contacts and messages while I had the chance."

"What? With the police crawling all over the crime scene?' Cole scoffed. 'That would not have been a good idea, Sasha love."

"I guess. Not that it matters now. The phone is in the police's possession." She paused, tossing her keys onto the couch before locking the door behind her. "I wonder whether I'll be able to sneak a few minutes alone with Yasmin at the hospital? If she was attacked, she may be more forthcoming about how she framed Uncle Isaac. She'd be scared, maybe more willing to do a deal. That is, of course, that she's stable and conscious."

"You sound exactly like a detective in one of those crime shows my mother watches." She could hear the smile in his voice. "I doubt you'd be granted time alone with her. Have you called your solicitor?"

"Yes, and the investigator. Our solicitor is firing on all cylinders now. He'll lodge a notice of interest in any evidence the police discover. He also mentioned contacting the detectives who were involved with Uncle Isaac's prosecution."

"I'm really glad that things are moving for you and your uncle." His warm voice thrilled her.

"Thanks, Cole."

He cleared his throat. "I'd like you to pack your bag and stay at the farm. If Yasmin was attacked I don't like the implications given that some idiot has been threatening you as well. It'll give us a chance to work on your riding lessons."

She smiled, walking and talking as she entered the kitchen. "Sounds tempting. Apart from the horse-riding. My butt is still aching."

He laughed. "I'll kiss it better."

"More tempting." She opened the fridge and scanned the contents, while thinking how wonderful it felt talking and sharing with him.

"Pop told me to stop hiding from life."

"Is that what you think I'm doing?" She frowned.

"No. You embrace life. I better get moving. I'll talk to you later, Sasha love. Think about what I've said."

"I will. Bye, Cole."

Since the thought of eating made her feel queasy, she settled for a strong cuppa with three teaspoons of sugar then ate a banana. She showered and changed then rode to the community centre where she updated Felicity and Dave about Yasmin.

They expressed shock but when Sasha mentioned Yasmin's car was stuffed with luggage, they exchanged a quick look of satisfaction. It was as if Yasmin's actions had merely confirmed what they already suspected. And neither appeared surprised at the woman's possible attempt to do a runner.

Afterwards, Sasha continued on to the police station where she met her father and they made their statements. Her father wanted her to have a coffee with him at Joe's Café but she declined.

By the time she reached Mindalby District Hospital it was well after midday. She asked if she could speak with the doctor treating Yasmin. As she wasn't family, she had no right to request any medical information; however, she was hoping professional courtesy might make him a little forthcoming. And give her a few minutes with Yasmin, if she was up to it.

After rolling her eyes, the nurse trotted off.

Sasha was waiting outside the small ER ward for the nurse to return when Don stormed through the entrance doors then charged past her without a second glance. Reaching the ER reception window, he jammed his finger on the bell and held it down.

This was the first time Sasha had set eyes on him since going to his house and his haggard face shocked her. The past few weeks had obviously taken its toll. He even appeared to have lost weight as his favourite coat seemed to hang formless from his shoulders.

A nurse pushed through the swing doors, a ferocious frown on her face which disappeared when she spotted Don. "Mr Carter! We've been trying to reach you."

"I've been busy. The police said my wife was attacked."

"As far as I'm aware, your wife has had a serious fall. If you wouldn't mind waiting here, I'll get the doctor. I know he wants to speak with you."

Don waved away the doctor with a flick of his hand. "You'll do. What's wrong with her? Is she awake? What's she been saying?"

The nurse recoiled and her sympathetic tone vanished. "Your wife is in a coma, Mr Carter. We're very concerned about her head injury and arrangements are being made for her to be flown to Newcastle for further tests and scans. If you will wait …"

"I don't have time to hang around. I need to know when she'll wake up."

"Brain injuries are difficult to predict and we're unable to give any indication until the tests have been completed."

"In other words, you know nothing apart from the fact she's in a coma." Don pushed up his coat sleeve and checked his watch. "If there's any change in her condition, I expect to be notified immediately."

He turned away.

The nurse said, "The doctor really wishes to speak to you, Mr Carter."

"You have my mobile. Get him to call me."

"Mr Carter!"

Don stalked towards the doors only to pull up short as the police entered.

Sergeant Johnson thinned his lips when his gaze fell on Sasha, hiding behind a magazine. Ducking her head, she quickly pretended to be absorbed in its contents, while straining her ears so she didn't miss anything that could be important. The fact that Yasmin wasn't conscious and about to be transferred was a bit of a blow. No way would she be able to get to Newcastle to ask her any more questions but perhaps her solicitor could do that? She made a mental note, turning her attention to the police sergeant as he approached Don with Constable Ross at his side.

"Mr Carter, we need to speak to you about your wife's movements."

'I'm a busy man, Johnson.' Don checked his watch again and went to brush past.

'We won't keep you long.' He nodded to Ross who pulled out a notebook and pen. 'I would have thought as a concerned husband your first priority would be staying by her side.'

Don flashed a toothy smile. "I've just been advised my wife is being moved to another hospital, Sergeant. I need to be with her when she wakes up and I'm keen to arrange for a charter plane as soon as possible rather than waiting for the Royal Flying Doctor service to be available."

"Before you leave, sir, you'll need to give us details about where you'll be staying. A few minutes are all we require. For the moment." Johnson's stern tone brooked no other option.

"Very well. Be quick about it."

"When was the last time you saw your wife?"

"Last night, around eight-thirty."

"You never spoke to her this morning?"

"I said, last night."

"You said, last night was the last time you saw her. However, I asked if you'd spoken to her since then."

"No," snapped Don, shifting his weight from foot to foot.

"Do you have any idea whether she left the house during the night or this morning?"

"Couldn't tell you." Don fixed an icy glare on the police officer.

"What was she doing at the jetty? Was she meeting someone?"

"How would I know?"

"Mr Carter, your co-operation would be appreciated. This is an official investigation into a possible attempted assault, possibly even attempted murder."

"Murder!" Don goggled at the senior policeman. He was obviously shaken at this news, the first time he'd evinced any kind of emotion apart from repressed anger or irritation since he'd marched through the doors.

"I repeat, what was she doing at the jetty?"

"I have no idea." Don's gaze darted to the door.

"There was luggage in her car. Was she taking a trip and if so, where?"

Sasha sat as still as possible, lapping up every detail and hoping they wouldn't move out of hearing distance. She risked a peak over the top of the magazine, noting Don's tense expression.

Sweat sheened on his forehead. "Look, Johnson, Yasmin runs her own company and has clients she has to deal with. She was probably off to some meeting."

"With a car full of luggage?"

"She never travels light." Don clamped his mouth shut.

"You're saying, you haven't seen or spoken to your wife since eight-thirty last night and have no idea what she was doing at the jetty nor where she was heading. Is that correct, sir?"

"Yes, damn you," he said through his teeth.

"And what about your movements last night, sir? Where were you between the hours of eight-thirty when you last saw your wife and five am this morning?"

"*What?* I was working in my office until ten or eleven and then I went to bed until I was woken at seven-thirty this morning by a phone call from some wet-behind-the-ears constable."

"You didn't notice your wife come to bed?"

"I sleep in another room when I've been working late so I don't disturb her. I've been patient, Sergeant, and I've told you everything I know. Now if you don't mind, I have arrangements to make concerning my wife. If you have any further questions, contact my solicitor." After tossing off that final remark, Don stormed out of the hospital.

Sasha tossed down the magazine and paced across the waiting area. "Sergeant?"

"Yes, Ms Bernstein?" Johnson sounded weary as he transferred his glare from the exit to her.

"Have you had a chance to examine Yasmin's iPhone?"

"I have someone working on it. May take some time as its password protected and her husband was unable to assist when he was contacted earlier." He held up a hand when she would have surged into speech again. "I haven't forgotten your request."

"Thank you," she said simply.

Johnson frowned, looking towards the closed doors leading to ER. "Any change in Mrs Carter's condition? The hospital said they'd notify me, but I know they're short-staffed."

"I heard the nurse say Yasmin is still in a coma."

"Poor woman. Good afternoon, Ms Bernstein." He nodded, then stalked off with Constable Ross, leaving Sasha staring after them and pondering all she'd overheard.

From their line of questioning, it appeared the police thought Yasmin could have been assaulted and not fallen of her own accord. Yasmin was too savvy a woman to ever meet a stranger in a lonely location. She must have known whoever assaulted her.

Did they suspect Don or were they merely covering all bases? But if it wasn't Don, then someone else was involved.

Maybe someone venting their rage and frustration over the closure of Mindalby Cotton Company. But if so, why target Yasmin? Surely Don should have been the one with a big red circle on his back?

Unless ... the reason behind the attack was something else entirely. Nossiter was always sneaking around the Carters' business and house. It wouldn't hurt to track Cody down and ask a few questions.

She thought about the 'gifts' left for her and shuddered. It made her skin crawl at the possibility the events were connected.

The odds were, whoever attacked Yasmin was someone she knew, that they all knew, someone who lived in the town. When she reached her bike, Sasha gazed around the small carpark, checking for anything unusual.

Anyone acting furtive.

Suspicious.

But she was alone.

Later that afternoon, Sasha phoned Cole and accepted his invitation, then rode her moped out to Cotton Fields Glory. Her heart soared as the homestead came into view.

Summer was pushing Toby on the tyre swing, his plastered leg stuck out in front. They caught sight of her and in unison hollered "Sasha's here!" Leaving her brother struggling to get off the swing, Summer, her smile as wide as sunshine, raced over the grass, her dog yapping at her heels.

The front door swung open and Cole appeared on the verandah. He bounded down the steps, just as Sasha turned off the engine. The glow in his eyes slammed into her like she was a missile target. She stepped off the moped and into his arms.

He cupped her chin with one hand and leaned in close. His kiss was hot and fierce, his body hard and tense, showing her without words how much he'd missed her. How much he wanted her.

"Sasha! Sasha!" A little hand tugged at her parka.

She emerged from Cole's warm embrace and glanced at his daughter who had her arms held out.

She swooped down and hugged Summer, the little girl squealing in delight.

Toby hobbled towards her on his crutches, calling, "Great to see you, Sasha."

She walked to meet him with Summer clinging to her hand while Cole parked her moped beside the verandah. "How's the leg, Toby?"

"It's not sore anymore. Just itchy."

"That's a good sign." She smiled and lifted her hand in greeting as Pop limped around the side of the house, an oil rag in his hand and a smile on his face.

This is what home feels like. She could feel her grin growing wider and wider in tandem with the fullness swelling her heart.

"You look like you've just won the lottery," Cole said as he unstrapped her holdall.

Warmth washed over her face when Pop gave her a nod of approval, of encouragement.

Could she do it?

His deep blue eyes glowing, Cole hoisted her bag onto his shoulder, strode toward her and captured her free hand.

His grip was loose, gentle, as if giving her permission to tug away. To run. But she was done with running.

Intertwining her fingers firmly with his, she smiled and cleared her throat. "I think that maybe I have."

COLE'S MOBILE went off early the next morning at five am. "What the …?"

Sasha rubbed her gritty eyes and rolled from the bed. This was the second time they'd been woken so early and fear knotted her stomach. No one rang with good news at that time of the morning.

While Cole spoke to whoever was on the other end, she pulled on one of his large shirts, catching bits and pieces of the conversation. Her lungs seized when she heard the word *'fire'*.

Cole was already rushing about, reaching for his jeans and shirt.

"What's wrong?" she asked.

"Grass fire on our boundary fence. Aunt Amber has contacted the brigade and I'm on my way. Sorry about this, Sasha love."

"It can't be helped. But, Cole, do you think all these incidents may be connected?"

"Incidents?" Buttoning up his shirt, he paused to look at her.

"The dead animals, graffiti to my flat, the damage to

your parents' place and now a fire?" But how did Yasmin's assault fit in?

An expletive exploded from him. "I never thought to connect the dots."

"It could be there are no dots, only my imagination."

"I dunno, love. I'm not one for believing in too many coincidences." He sighed and finished dressing.

"I could come with you."

"No, I need you here with the kids. Besides …" He snuck her a careful glance. "You can't get in a car."

Her belly jolted sickeningly. He was right. Her hands fisted at the unfairness. *I'm over this; tired of letting my fear rule me.* But the panic swam below the surface, a savage shark ready to drag her under.

"I'll phone and keep you updated."

One belly-quivering kiss and he was gone.

Alone, Sasha curled up on Cole's side of the bed and hugged his pillow, breathing in his scent. She tried not to let panic overwhelm her. He was a grown man and could take care of himself. Eventually, she rose and tidied the bedroom before taking a shower and dressing.

Two hours later, she still hadn't heard from Cole. Breakfast was a quiet affair with the kids still asleep and only Pop and herself at the table. Every so often, Pop walked out onto the verandah, to sniff the air.

"I don't like this, Sasha. The wind is picking up and it's turned," he said, as he came back inside the house. "Any word from Cole?"

She checked her mobile, which hadn't left her side. "Nothing yet but I've only got one bar." She lifted her head. "I think that's a car pulling up."

They both hurried down the hall as the front door opened and Cole rushed inside. His jacket was covered with ash and soot smeared his face.

"The wind is driving the fire towards our farm. I've got Harry and Max hooking up our fire hoses to the water tanks. Chook is rounding up the horses and donkey. He'll herd them off the property, and if it's necessary, take them over to the commune. Pop, we need a fire-break along the eastern boundary to protect the last of our crop."

Without a word, Pop grabbed his walking stick then marched out the door.

Cole looked over Sasha's shoulder. "Where're the kids?"

"In bed."

"Get them up, love, and have them ready to move when I say the word. Don't let the dogs out of the house."

"Will do."

He caught her by the shoulders. "If the house is threatened, Sasha, I want you to promise me, you'll get my kids and dogs into the Land Rover and get the hell out of here. Can you do that for me?"

Drive. She had to get in a car and drive. Surrounded by fire. Words strangled in her throat, her vision shrank to pinpoints, but she nodded; numb, sick, terrified.

"I'm sorry but there isn't anyone else. The fire has cut the road to Woodburn which means my parents can't get through. And Pop won't leave Cotton Fields Glory to burn."

"I can do it," she finally croaked, blinking Cole back into focus.

"Thank you, love." His gaze searched her face. "Stay safe. Shut all the windows and doors."

The door banged after him.

Her knees shook so badly she had to brace her body against the wall.

"Sasha, what's going on?" It was Toby.

Forcing a smile, she turned to Toby. "There's a fire. You need to get dressed."

FOR THE UMPTEENTH TIME, Sasha stared out the window at the billowing black clouds where red flames could be seen shooting upwards. The wind roared like a thwarted dragon beating its outrage upon the earth. Leaves, branches, soot and ash snapped through the air. The day had darkened into a reddish-black glow until it could have been close to sunset instead of barely ten-thirty in the morning.

Although mid-winter the air was hot; the intensity of the fire had made its own weather, super-heating the surrounding area. The grasses and cotton were bursting into conflagration seconds before the flames hit.

The rural fire brigade with Leon Rossini at the wheel had arrived an hour ago. Since then several cars had also turned up with their occupants spilling out and rushing to help save Cole and Pop's crop. They had disappeared into the swirling smoke and it had been some time since she'd seen anyone re-appear.

To Sasha's eyes, the fire appeared to be moving steadily towards the house and barns, although it was difficult to be certain with all the churning smoke obscuring her vision. She snapped her gaze down to her phone.

No messages.

No calls.

Could the fire have disrupted the signal? The reception was patchy out here at the best of times. She closed her eyes and prayed Cole was safe.

Prayed they were all safe.

After another long look, she turned away from the window. Toby was standing, his crutches wedged under his arms, gripping his little sister's hand. Although the fire in the hearth had been doused, the room was warm from the heat outside. Sweat shone on their foreheads but Sasha had refused their pleas to remove their heavy jackets and woollen beanies. If they had to make a run for safety, she wanted to ensure not a skerrick of skin could be exposed to the flames.

The two dogs were on the floor, panting and

already harnessed with their leashes tied to an armchair. She didn't want to have to go searching the house for a terrified dog if the time came to move in a hurry.

As for Cole's precious children, they wore identical solemn faces, but total trust glowed in their eyes as they gazed at her.

They reminded her of Saad who she'd been unable to save; as darkness enfolded the house, she spiralled back to that moment of agony, horror and death.

Her breathing came short and fast.

Her vision funnelled into blank nothingness.

Her heartbeats were a physical pain, twisting, clenching, squeezing tight in her chest.

What was she thinking? She couldn't save anyone!

Her mobile rang. The strident tone rang and rang and rang.

Someone was shaking her jacket. As if she floated high above the earth, she gazed down into Summer's face. Into eyes a mirror image of Cole's.

The phone.

She shook her head, focused and croaked, "Hello?"

"Sasha. Get my kids out. Take them into town." Cole's voice was harsh in her ears.

From somewhere deep inside her trembling soul, she finally found the strength to conquer her fear. "I'm on it, Cole. Stay safe. I love you."

Ending the call, she slipped her phone into her pocket, bade Summer not to move from where she stood and undid the dogs' leashes. "Toby, when we're outside, you make straight for the car. Don't stop until you get inside. Okay?"

He nodded, his face pale but resolute. "I've got water and dog biscuits in my backpack. And I've got a torch."

"Good job." Leashes in hand, Sasha pulled her satchel straps over her head, ensured she had the keys in her pocket then took Summer's hand. "Sweetheart, we have to run for the car when I say go."

Summer nodded.

"Everyone ready?" At their assents, Sasha made for the front door and opened it.

A blast of hot, smoky wind slammed into her. Gritting her teeth, she pushed open the screen door and ushered Toby through first, followed by the dogs, Summer and herself. She made certain the door closed firmly behind her. "Go!"

Through the gloom and swirling ash, she could just make out the shape of Cole's white four-wheel-drive. Toby hopped down the steps on his crutches and made for the car, leading the way.

She'd gone out earlier to unlock the doors—a just in case scenario—and now she was thankful she'd done it because there was no time to spare.

Through her thick jacket, she could feel the dragon's breath burning her back.

The noise was horrendous, snatching away Toby's words when he turned around to yell something. He gestured madly, seeming to indicate with his crutches for her to look behind.

She spun around, saw a flash of movement, jerked sideways at the last second and dodged by a centimetre the baseball bat slashing towards her head.

Using her body as a shield she bent over Summer, pushed the leads into her hands and screamed at her to run for the car.

A blow landed on her back, not far from where the piece of shrapnel had lodged. Agony splintered along her bones. Her legs buckled. She crumpled, sinking towards the ground. Her satchel tangled around her right arm, restricting movement.

A pair of legs filled her vision. And crutches. Holding her pain deep inside, she straightened just as Toby appeared beside her and lashed out at her assailant with a crutch.

Toby's eyes met Sasha's.

Sasha nodded and jerked her chin towards where Summer was crying and holding onto the barking dogs for dear life. They were straining at the leashes, teeth bared. Toby caught the keys she threw at him.

Trusting Toby would see his sister and the animals safe inside the car, she shoved her satchel out of the way, swung around, bending low and twisting at the waist. The blow that would have smashed into her head found nothing but air.

Straightening, her jaw dropped for one full second as she took in Yasmin Carter wielding the bat.

The malice shining in Yasmin's eyes as she swung again, broke through Sasha's shock. Ducking out of the way, she pivoted, then thrust the full force of her body-weight into her kick, punching the blow directly at Yasmin Carter's knee cap.

There was a satisfying crack and the woman howled. The bat appeared to slip through her fingers.

Taking advantage of her hesitation, Sasha went in close and made a play for the weapon; she had to get it away from the woman.

Yasmin struggled as if demented, her eyes wild with hate and spite. "You stupid bitch! You've ruined all my plans!"

I was right. Hiding in the shadows, Yasmin had pulled everyone's strings.

Thrusting aside her whirling thoughts, Sasha focused on winning the war over the bat. Her back throbbed and her throat burned, raw from smoke inhalation.

Terrified she'd lose and the woman would turn on the children, she rallied the last of her strength. Using her shoulders, she rammed into Yasmin's chest. The bat fell from Yasmin's fingers.

Moving fast, Sasha struck her clenched fist into the woman's windpipe.

Yasmin clutched at her throat, making gargling noises as she staggered in circles. Not far away lay a discarded petrol container with no lid. Had Yasmin lit the fire? But why?

Sasha snatched up the bat and stepped well away from the other woman. A quick glance behind revealed the kids and dogs were safely in the car. Toby held the keys up close to the window and made frantic gestures for her to get a move on.

She looked at the sky. Was it her imagination or was the ash lessening? If so, was that a good or bad sign? She hesitated another moment, her gaze going to Yasmin who was beginning to breathe more normally.

Should she take the risk of allowing that bitch in the car with Cole's kids? But before she could decide, Yasmin staggered towards the house.

There was no time to go after her; Yasmin would have to take her own chances.

Without another thought, Sasha scooped up her bag, ran to the car and yanked open the door then climbed inside. Toby handed over the car keys.

She started the engine, put the car into gear and roared down the drive towards Mindalby. She wouldn't stop until Cole's children were safe.

"You were wonderful," said Cole, hugging Sasha close.

His arms were strong, warm and wonderfully comforting. His heart beat steady and sure beneath her cheek and tears weren't far from the surface. He smelled of smoke and bushfire but underneath she discerned the scent that was all Cole.

"I can't believe you fought her off like that," he added.

"Of course she did. I trained my daughter how to get out of sticky situations," boomed her father's voice.

"Obadiah, tone your voice down. There's no need to shout. The child's exhausted," Amber admonished.

"Sorry, Cuddlepie."

Sasha roused herself sufficient to lean a little away and look into Cole's eyes. "As soon as I reached the police station, I got out of the car and vomited."

Cole grinned. "That's my girl. Nothing like a good puke to release crap out of your body."

And she knew he wasn't just talking about bile. She looked at the group gathered around them and smiled. They were standing in the bistro section of the Ace in the Hole with tankards of water and cans of cold beer on the table, courtesy of management.

Pop, Max, Chook and Harry were covered in soot and ash and were indescribably filthy. As was Amber, indicating she'd fought alongside the men and, apparently, a good number of the commune residents. Cole's parents had fought the blaze that had cut off the road to Woodburn with other members of their small village. Roger had his arm around his wife and they both looked every year their age. But their smiles were wide even if their eyes were tired and dazed.

Summer was nestled on Maisy's lap while her brother devoured a pile of hot chicken nuggets. He grinned when he caught Sasha's glance.

The firies were back at the station, completing paperwork and re-supplying the truck, having left the police to scour the blackened fields searching for any trace of Yasmin Carter.

It had been a long morning.

Sasha's father hovered behind her like a bee who couldn't find its way back to its hive. By the way he was stepping from one foot to the other in a restless manner, she knew he'd been seriously worried. She pulled out of Cole's embrace and entered her father's.

He hugged her close, whispering, "My sweet girl." He kissed the top of her head before letting her go.

With a sigh, she flopped into a chair and helped herself to water. "You were saying that Yasmin has disappeared?"

"Yes." Cole took the chair next to her. "By the time the fire was under control and we returned to the house, there was no sign of her. Rosco reckons she was the probable cause."

"I thought she'd gone to a hospital in Newcastle?"

"According to Johnson, she sneaked out of the ambulance when the blokes were attending to paper-work. God knows where she was hiding. Don Carter reckons he hasn't seen her since the day of her accident."

Sasha shook her head as her eyes met Cole's. "Unbelievable."

Cole picked up her hand played with her fingers. "That conk on the head must have sent her a little crazy."

Not knowing what to think, Sasha took another long drink of water.

"I've phoned Torianne and Delia and told them no one was hurt," Maisy said, referring to Cole's younger sisters. "They said to say how sorry they are you've lost part of your crop, Jasper."

Pop sighed. "I won't deny it was a blow but I'm thankful it wasn't worse. No one was hurt."

"Heavens, yes." Maisy shuddered, her complexion

appearing grey in the dull overhead light. "I wonder what possessed the woman."

Amber shrugged. "Who knows? Rumour has it she's about to be charged with embezzlement. Something to do with another company a few years ago."

Sasha's breath caught in her throat when she met Cole's grave eyes.

"I reckon the police will sort everything out when they find her." Cole raked a hand through his tousled, ash-covered hair and studied his children.

Summer yawned, her head drooping on his mother's chest.

He raised Sasha's knuckles to his lips and kissed her scars oh so gently before saying, "My kids are beat and to be honest, so am I. What about you, Pop? Dad?"

"I'm knackered," said Pop.

Roger struggled to hide his yawn. "Same."

"Well the house is still standing and thanks to Chook here, our livestock is safe at the commune for the moment. But the place stinks of smoke." Cole raised his brows at his parents and circled the table to pluck Summer into his arms. His little girl gave a huge sigh and nestled close. "Okay for us to crash at your place, Mum?"

"Of course, darling." Maisy hesitated then added, "You're welcome too, Sasha."

"Thank you, but I'll stay in my flat. I'm looking forward to a long shower and an even longer sleep."

Everyone began to shuffle towards the door.

Cole stayed Sasha with a hand on the small of her back. "Sasha love …" He stopped, his face a picture of uncertainty and love beneath the weariness and soot.

She knew what he wanted to ask, but she was too weary to go there right now. "We're both tired and your kids need you, Cole. Raincheck?"

His lips thinned but he nodded and turned away. "Raincheck."

AFTER THE LONGEST shower in history, Sasha fell into bed and slept the afternoon away. When she finally rolled out, night had fallen and her empty stomach reminded her how long it had been since she'd eaten.

A glance in the refrigerator revealed a covered dish which she instantly recognised as belonging to her father. Bless him. He must have come and gone while she was out for the count, leaving her with a ready-made dinner.

With her homemade vegetarian lasagne heating in the oven, she donned a warm yellow tracksuit and thick socks. Yawning, she snuggled down on the lounge and prepared to re-enter the world.

There was a lovely email waiting in her inbox from her mother, announcing the family solicitor was actively pursuing her uncle's case. Everyone sounded so hopeful about his chances that Sasha worried they'd be devastated should the new information fail to influence either the police or the courts. Her mother and uncle would need her support. It was time she went back to Sydney.

How strange it felt to think of leaving when her heart insisted her home was with Cole and his kids on Cotton Fields Glory.

His words rang in her mind—not that she could ever forget. They'd been carved in her heart. *Stay with us.*

She'd been honest.

Hadn't given him false hope but also hadn't given him a definitive answer. Both he and his children deserved to know where they stood where she was concerned.

Although she was certain she'd already made her choice, there remained that niggling voice at the back of her mind.

She needed to know it was love and not fear that held her heart captive in this outback town.

Her mobile pinged.

She was reading the lengthy text from the private investigator when a knock sounded. Without checking who it was, she opened the front door.

Yasmin stood on the porch, looking as if she'd been living wild for six months. Her clothes were filthy, her blonde hair lank. Dirt and ash smudged her face and her eyes were narrowed and filled with a hate that quaked Sasha's soul.

In her hands, Yasmin held a rifle. Squinting down

the barrel, she smirked. "You should never have come here."

HEART THUMPING HARD, Cole pulled up across the road from Sasha's flat. He took a moment to settle his shaky nerves before climbing from the Land Rover. His hand patted his pocket where a yellow sapphire ring reposed inside a velvet-lined box.

When he'd spotted the ring in the jewellers he'd known instantly, this was the ring with which he'd pledge his love for her.

The crux—whether or not she'd accept.

A man lived only one life; and as Pop always said, you'd better make it a good one.

The porch light was on, illuminating the small front yard and revealing the door stood wide open.

Strange.

He quickened his footsteps.

A gunshot cracked through the night.

In the direction of Sasha's flat!

Heart in his throat, he bounded up the path and through the open door. Then froze.

A dishevelled Yasmin stood aiming a rifle at Sasha who stood hands held in the air. The stink of cordite hung in the air and the room was hazy from gunsmoke. There was a hole in the wall opposite.

"Who …?" Yasmin swung around and Cole found the gun now aimed at his chest.

"Hey, Yasmin. What are you doing here?" He struggled to make his voice sound calm and even. No accusations, no underlying notes of fear or threat. One wrong move on either his or Sasha's part, and Yasmin could pull that bloody trigger.

Licking his dry lips, he tried again when she failed to respond. "We're glad to see you're okay. Everyone was worried about you after the fire."

The fierce expression on her face eased. A tiny frown wrinkled her forehead. "What?"

Clearly his statement had thrown her. He desperately searched his brain for a way to defuse the situation. Or distract her until the cops arrived. Someone had to have reported that gunshot.

"It's true. Dad and I went out searching for you this afternoon. We wanted to make sure that you weren't hurt."

Yasmin's mouth twisted. "What a crock. Don't come any closer." She waved the gun.

Obediently, he moved until he stood to the side of the window. Sweat pooled under his armpits. *Please don't move, Sasha love.* "Put the gun down and leave. We give our word we won't call the police for twenty-four hours. You could be well on your way to the Bahamas by then."

"Why would you say that? Oh, I see." Yasmin swung

the gun back to point at Sasha. "Been telling tales about my boat, have you?"

OMG! Her finger was tightening on the trigger. He could see the movement. She was going to fire!

"You should never have framed Uncle Isaac," Sasha said, lifting her chin and looking as cool as if she wasn't facing imminent death.

"It was too easy. But you - I warned you. But no, you had to keep pushing and pushing."

Cole moved closer.

Yasmin wavered, her gaze darting between them. The rifle dipped, the muzzle dropping away from Sasha.

Cole made his move—he lunged towards her, intending to knock the gun downwards, so it would fire towards the floor.

Yasmin snarled, began to turn, raising the weapon.

Then Sasha dived for Yasmin's legs, tackling her at the knees.

Cole kicked the rifle from Yasmin's hands, then cannoned into her. The rifle fired when it slammed onto the ground the same moment he took Yasmin down.

FIFTEEN MINUTES LATER, Sergeant Johnson and Constable Ross took Yasmin away in the patrol car. After scribbling so furiously in his notebook that he broke his pen nib, Johnson ordered Cole and Sasha to show up at the police station first thing in the morning to give their statements.

It seemed like only seconds later that Sasha's small flat was crammed full of people all talking at once. Not to mention the crowd gossiping and taking snaps on their mobiles from the front fence.

Her hands still shaking, Sasha took the sweetened tea her father pressed on her and sipped.

Cole had been busy with his phone, calling the police, her father, his parents and grandfather, his aunt; the list went on. He still had his mobile clamped to his ear, looking fatigued to the bone as he listened to one of his sisters on the other end.

"I'm very confused." Maisy sank onto the lounge beside Sasha and took hold of her free hand, patting it absently.

"Are Summer and Toby alright?" Sasha asked.

"Yes, pet. When Rog and I left them with Pop, they were sound asleep. We didn't think it right to wake them after today."

Sasha nodded. She longed for privacy. She longed to be wrapped in Cole's strong arms and feeling the steady beat of his heart beneath her cheek. She longed for his kisses to obliterate the corrosive hate that still lingered in the room even though Yasmin had departed. But she knew it was time for explanations.

She gave a brief account of Yasmin's involvement with her uncle's fraud charges, then how she, herself, had sought and obtained the position in Mindalby to suss out proof to exonerate him.

"My goodness." Maisy pressed a white handkerchief to her mouth and stared at Sasha as if she'd grown another head.

Ploughing on, Sasha then told about finding the invoice for the boat repairs which had led to finding Yasmin's offshore bank accounts. "I think Yasmin suspected the police were getting too close. Her assets had been frozen pending an investigation. She was furious and blamed me. I think she set fire to the farm to punish me because she guessed how much I care …" She broke off, her voice wobbling as she relived those terrifying moments. As long as she lived, she'd never forget the sight of a rifle aimed at Cole—the man she loved with all her heart.

He could have died. She could have lost him forever.

All she could think as she'd stood there, her entire world poised on a knife-edge, was *save him*.

How to save him.

She'd had seconds to act. And she'd done the only thing she could think of—a footy tackle, hoping her momentum would throw Yasmin's aim off. Away from Cole.

Luck or angels had been on her side.

It so easily could have gone the other way.

Deep, soul-wrenching sobs forged up from her heart and she buried her face in her hands.

"Sasha love!" Cole's deep voice penetrated her nightmare.

She felt the cushion beside her sink, then his strong arms were around her, pulling her onto his lap and giving her a taste of heaven. Fisting her hands over his shirt, she bawled into his solid chest, even as she registered his hands moving tenderly over her hair and back.

Her sobs petered out into hiccups. She pulled away and looked up into his concerned face. Deep lines bracketed his mouth and his jawline was tense. "If I'd never come here, none of this would have happened. I'm so sorry."

"It takes more than a bit of smoke and fire to keep a Mitchell down. Stone the crows, girl, none of this is your fault," stated Pop robustly.

"God no! You could have been killed, Sasha love. I came so close to losing you." Cole's voice shook.

She whispered, "As did I, with you."

They stared at each other. The frown cleared his face, replaced by a dawning grin, and his eyes sparkled like blue fire. "I'm not waiting any longer."

In response, her soul sang as bands tightened around her chest, restricting her breathing and her pulse leapt. Something in his expression made her straighten.

Ever so carefully, he eased her off his lap onto the lounge.

He slid down onto one knee in front of her.

Her pulse stuttered.

Is he ...?

His left hand slipped into his pocket then emerged with a small box cradled in his palm.

Love, pure and unbroken, welled up from her heart and she clasped her hands so hard, her nails dug into her skin. Fresh tears stung the back of her eyes.

Tears of joy.

"Finally!" shouted her father who immediately sprang to his feet and tugged a laughing Amber into his arms. They performed a crazy tango across the room.

Sasha gazed deep into Cole's eyes and read there his promise of a lifetime of passion and a life well-lived.

"Marry me, Sasha love." His deep voice cascaded over her, promising her the moon and the stars.

If only she could leave her fear behind.

EPILOGUE

The day of the Blessing of the Harvest stretched warm and balmy with a gentle wind carrying on it the sweet scents that heralded an early spring: wattle blossoms, wildflowers and eucalypt. Excitement lifting her higher than an eagle's nest, Sasha approached the outskirts of Mindalby around mid-afternoon. She was behind the wheel of a hired Pantech truck that was loaded with all her possessions.

When the main settlement of the Commune of the Golden Light came into sight, she slowed to a crawl. Her eyes widened as she took in the stalls and gaily decorated banners fluttering in the breeze. The community had embraced the spirit of the festival with a zest that had transformed the area into a bustling, lively centre.

Even more pleasing were the number of utes and

cars parked along the side of the dirt road that must belong to the townspeople who had come along as well.

In the passenger seat, her father rubbed his hands together briskly, then wound down the window to take a better look. "You wouldn't think it was the same place."

"I know. It looks fabulous."

Her father grinned at her. "Did you tell anyone you were coming back or is this supposed to be a surprise?"

"I phoned Cole last week but I asked him not to say anything to his kids or family. I wanted to surprise them." Sasha waved out the window at Warren Leadbeater who was climbing out of his battered sedan. She stifled a giggle as his jaw dropped.

"Why do I have the feeling you were keeping your options open."

"No, not this time, Dad. I've made my decision and it's one I have no intention of changing." Sasha paused to admire the sapphire glowing on her ring finger. "What about you and Amber? Does she know you've got your practice on the market and intend to go country?"

"Now that is *my* surprise."

She laughed and parked the Pantech. Her fingers tightened on the steering wheel. In a few minutes, she'd be with Cole. And for thirty horrible seconds, she wondered—what if he'd changed his mind?

Her father hopped out of the truck, rubbing his

hands. "Come on, Cuddlepie. Stop dithering. I've got an idea about that honeyshine I want to run past Amber before I broach it with those old blokes."

Linking arms, they strolled toward the meeting yurt, Sasha searching the crowd. But there was no sign of Cole.

She pulled her mobile from her satchel and checked the time. Okay, so she was sixteen minutes later than promised. She hadn't factored in the number of rest stops she'd needed to centre herself, even with her father taking over the wheel through the towns. But over the past few days, her panic attacks had lessened to such an extent she knew she'd handle driving Cole's kids to school and anywhere else.

Her fear had been vanquished by love.

Another long stare took in the jumping castle and the hordes of children, smiling parents and young teenagers jostling each other as they took selfies. Eagerness to join in the festivities rose and begin the new chapter in her life surged through her.

Cole was here somewhere and she couldn't wait to find him.

Hands trembling, she placed her phone back in her bag and tucked a strand of her loose hair behind her ears.

Her dad touched her arm. "Look, Cuddlepie. Here comes your future."

And there walking towards her was Cole, Summer and Toby. Each wore grins as big and inviting as the outback. Cream Akubras shaded their brilliant blue eyes.

She was only vaguely aware of her father moving away after a mumbled, "Love you, Sasha. Be happy."

She was too busy gobbling them up with her eyes; this small family that had, over the space of a few weeks, become her entire world.

"You were late, Sasha, so Daddy got us ice-cream," called Summer.

And then she dropped her father's hand and ran.

Sasha rushed forward to meet her, crouched down and took the force of the small body slamming into her, loving the strangling grip of thin arms around her neck.

"I missed you, Sasha." Summer began to cry.

"I missed you too, honey." Sasha squeezed her eyes shut, her happiness a powder keg of emotion.

Her neck felt sticky and wet from the little girl's fingers. She chuckled. *Welcome to motherhood.*

Another pair of arms wrapped around her and she turned to envelop Toby in a huge hug. Then he stepped back, shoving his hands in his pockets and digging his shoe into the red sand. "I knew you'd come today. Summer, stop being a baby."

"I'm not a baby." The little girl stuck out her tongue.

"See what you've missed?" Cole said in his deep voice, holding out his hands.

Sasha took them, tingles and delicious heat spreading

over her skin at his touch. Ever so carefully, he helped her rise. They stood looking at each other and Sasha could have stayed there, staring into his eyes for eternity.

"I did miss them. I missed everything about them and everything about you. I'm ready for that forever thing, Cole – for that life with you. I haven't changed my mind.'"

"So am I, Sasha love."

She gave a mock frown. "I asked you to keep my arrival a surprise."

He shrugged, his eyes glinting with laughter and a raw passion her body recognised in one breathless second. "I can't keep a secret from my kids. Not anything as big as this."

"No doubts then that I wouldn't show?" She chewed her lower lip.

"Sasha love, I have faith in you. Always." Tipping his hat further back on his head with his forefinger, he leaned closer and sealed his words with a kiss.

At last. This was what she'd hungered for these past few weeks. His lips were warm and moved over hers with the intensity that had haunted her dreams and chased away her nightmares.

With a sexy smile, he eased back and studied her flushed face. "Welcome home."

A few hours later, the sun was low in the sky and long shadows washed over the red sands. Candle-lit lanterns twinkled around stalls, amongst tree branches and from poles set about the commune, casting a gentle glow over smiling faces.

The crowd had quietened to watch the blessing, some standing, some sitting in camping chairs, on picnic rugs or strategically placed tree trunks.

Sasha snuggled close to Cole's lean body and watched with awe as his aunt led other Wiccans in an intricate dance while Tai and Ray plucked on the strings of a pair of lutes. The dancers' filmy white gowns floated and billowed with each graceful move-ment. The lilting music hung on the air with such pure notes, Sasha felt she could reach out and touch them.

Cole held Summer in his arms; on Sasha's other side, between her and Obie, Toby was devouring what must have been his fifth vegie burger.

Pop was dozing in a lounge chair, a woolly rug tucked over his knees.

The dance ended as the music faded and in the breathless hush that descended on the crowd, Amber recited an ancient Blessing of the Seeds.

The act ended to tremendous applause that died down the moment Chook and Max picked up their instruments and Harry burst into song. Several people jumped up and swung into boot-stepping.

"Come on, kids, let me show you how to dance an Irish jig." Obie caught hold of Summer's and Toby's hands, urging them to join in. They were soon joined by Amber.

Roger and Maisy sailed past in a stately waltz. A

satisfied smirk spread over Maisy's face as her gaze settled on Sasha.

Sasha nudged Cole's arm. A delicious thrill ran through her when he looked at her, his eyes sparkling with a world of love. "Any word on Yasmin?"

"She's been charged with arson and assault but is out on bail. No one knows where she's hiding though. The word is, Yasmin paid Lesley to stalk you but Lesley wanted more money so tried a blackmail attempt. She also paid Lesley to tamper with the abseiling equipment when she heard you were going on the school camp. The whole town knew I'd give a demo before I let any kids on those ropes."

Her hand pressed to her mouth, Sasha stared, horrified. "Oh my gosh. It was a deliberate attack then."

He shrugged. "Cops aren't certain whether they'll be able to get any charges to stick. Yasmin's word against Lesley's. Anyway, she's fingered Lesley as the person who pushed her at the bridge. Those precious pair had a bit of a girl spat and Yasmin fell. Knocked herself out. You know what they say about killer heels."

Despite the seriousness of the subject, Sasha laughed.

"Lesley will be charged with a bunch of stuff, too. But the important thing is, that's all over for us now." A tender smile playing about his lips, Cole reached out and fingered strands of her hair. "It's great news about your uncle."

"Yes. Our solicitor seems certain that his previous

conviction will be overturned. And ... it looks like Yasmin will be charged with taking the missing money and framing my uncle. I understand ASIC is investigating her company, Trove Financials. Who knows what else they'll find?"

"Sash love, let's hope enough to put her away for a long time. What about Don? And Mindalby Cotton Company?"

"Still investigating I believe. It may take several months to untangle the red herrings from the real trail. You have to hand it to her, Yasmin was very clever. Don may not have even known what she was up to."

"I guess time will tell." He grinned, rocking back on his heels. "You look pretty pleased with yourself. Talk about me not keeping a secret."

"You!" She play-punched his shoulder. "You were right, Cole, about plenty for me to do here. I've applied for a nursing position at the hospital while I study psychology by correspondence. Mum and Raphael are keen to help fundraise for a permanent mental health clinic to service the region. When I'm qualified, I hope to get a job there."

But that wasn't the total sum of her plans. She could only hope that a solution would be found to help the entire town. In the meantime, she'd use her savings to keep the farm afloat. Although she knew she'd have her work cut out convincing the stubborn man she loved so deeply.

Maybe a little suggestion her contribution was by

way of securing a future for their children would soften her man? The ones they had now and the ones that, God willing, they'd be blessed with in the future.

"Sounds like you're going to be busy. I hope you've factored in some time for me." He turned wounded eyes on her but she wasn't fooled.

Raising her eyebrows, she said in a lofty tone, "Oh I might be able to pencil in an hour once a week, if you're lucky."

Cole laughed, hugging her tight and lifting her off her feet. 'Sash love, one hour of me won't be enough. I guarantee you'll be wanting more: morning, mid-afternoon, cuddles here and there. And you'll be eager for my conversation too."

"You're so full of yourself." She laughed.

"Think you'll be able to handle a life well-lived?" His voice deepened, ripe with a suggestion that left her breathless and her heart pounding. "Can you handle me, Sasha love?"

Could she ever!

"With one hand tied behind my back." She smiled and placed a hand lovingly against his cheek. "And blindfolded."

"Now, that I can't wait to see." Cole raised her hand and kissed the puckered skin above her knuckles.

Hands interlocked, they walked towards the jumping castle. "Did I mention the charity horse-ride is a goer?"

"No." She narrowed her eyes. By the way his mouth

twitched at the corners she suspected he was up to something.

She wasn't wrong.

"I've put your name down as a rider. We leave next week."

The End

FROM THE AUTHOR:

I hope you enjoyed reading this romance as much as I loved writing Cole and Sasha's story and dreaming up the fictional community of Mindalby.

If you love small town / country romances that encompass engrossing characters and feel-good emotions, then keep an eye out for what's coming next in this new series titled **Outback Hearts**.

In the meantime, why not discover my other sweet, small town romances such as: the **Bindarra Creek Romance** series, and my **Edge of the Outback Romance** series.

To learn more, visit my website: www.segilchrist.com

ACKNOWLEDGMENTS

This book was originally published by Escape Publishing a digital imprint of Harlequin Australia under the title *'Cotton Field Dreams'* and was part of the Mindalby Outback Romance series which would never have reached fruition without the awesome support of: Susanne Bellamy, Linda Charles, Lee Christine, Lauren McKellar, Stacey Nash and Kerrie Paterson. May your stars continue to shine.

My sincere appreciation to Bev Rosenbaum of BKR Editing Services for a great manuscript assessment.

Huge thanks to the wonderful critiquing skills of my good friend, romantic suspense writer Erin Moira O'Hara and my lovely friend, historical romance writer, Sandie James who was such a staunch advocate of this series and helped so much with brainstorming.

I'd also like to thank the following websites for their wealth of available information: Cotton Australia; Agrifutures Australia, Australian Government Cotton

Research, and Development Corporation and Outback NSW.

Last but never least, thank you to my family for their wonderful support. And for continuing to cheer me on.

ACKNOWLEDGEMENT OF COUNTRY

In the spirit of reconciliation, the author and publisher acknowledges Aboriginal and Torres Strait Islander peoples as the First Australians and Traditional Custodians of the lands where we live, learn and work. We pay our respects to Elders past and present and all First Nations peoples and honour their unique cultural and spiritual relationships to the land, waters and seas and their rich contribution to society, and thank them for their ongoing custodianship of and care for Country.

ABOUT THE AUTHOR

An Australian author, S.E. Gilchrist, loves combining romance with adventure and suspense across different genres including science fiction, apocalyptic, and contemporary small towns. Her sweet romances are written under Suzanne Gilchrist, and several of her books have been shortlisted in writing contests.

S.E. loves walking her furbabies, travelling, and spending time with family and friends. She is the organiser behind several multi-author romance series, including the *Bindarra Creek Romance* series, the *Deadly Forces* series, and the *Mindalby Outback Romance* series.

She also participated in a multi-author collaboration under the writing name of J T Sloane in an 8-book post-apocalyptic survival thriller series called *'Swarm'* published by and with Mike Kraus.

For more information, visit her website:
www.segilchrist.com

www.ingramcontent.com/pod-product-compliance
Lightning Source LLC
Chambersburg PA
CBHW072002180726
48291CB00002BA/246